BETRAYED

Strong, handsome, and caring Kyle Trent was unlike any other man Barbara had ever known. From the moment he saved her from a brutal assault, there was magic between them. And when she at last let down the guard that another's agonizing abuse had fostered, Kyle showed her how magificent a lover a man could be, and the fiery fulfillment that love could bring.

More than that, her little boy, Matthew, was totally won over by Kyle. He could be the father Matthew never had, even as Kyle protected them both from the terrifyingly twisted pychopath who was on their trail. Even as he shielded them from the relentless lawyer who was making the child a pawn in a monstrous legal game.

Barbara, who had vowed never to give her trust and her heart to a man again, was happy to break that vow . . . until she began to learn the horrifying truth about this man who wore a lover's mask. . . .

SEE HOW THEY RUN

SEE HOW THEY RUN

Marilyn Campbell

AN ONYX BOOK

ONYX
Published by the Penguin Group
Penguin Books USA Inc., 375 Hudson Street,
New York, New York 10014, U.S.A.
Penguin Books Ltd, 27 Wrights Lane,
London W8 5TZ, England
Penguin Books Australia Ltd, Ringwood,
Victoria, Australia
Penguin Books Canada Ltd, 10 Alcorn Avenue,
Toronto, Ontario, Canada M4V 3B2
Penguin Books (N.Z.) Ltd, 182–190 Wairau Road,
Auckland 10, New Zealand

Penguin Books Ltd, Registered Offices:
Harmondsworth, Middlesex, England

First published by Onyx, an imprint of Dutton Signet,
a division of Penguin Books USA Inc.

First Printing, June, 1996
10   9   8   7   6   5   4   3   2   1

REGISTERED TRADEMARK—MARCA REGISTRADA

Printed in the United States of America

To Barbara Chevalier, the perfect friend, neighbor, surrogate mother, and fairy godmother. Thank you for always being there for us.

A special thank-you to Shannon Emmel for helping me to laugh at all the dirty jokes life played on me while this book was in progress.

Prologue

"George Washington was a wimp!"

Barbara Johnson shot a disapproving glance at her son, Matthew, then returned her attention to backing their weather-beaten Honda Civic out of the driveway. After so many years of Matt being too timid to say much of anything, she hesitated to reprimand him now that he'd begun behaving like other nine-year-old boys.

"Let me guess," she said, as if she were giving it serious thought. "Kenny gave you that bit of information."

Matt looked about ready to defend his friend, but he reconsidered. "Well, sort of. But it was in the movie we saw in class the other day."

Taking her eyes off the road for a second, she questioned his claim. "The Father of Our Country was called a *wimp* in an educational movie? What did your teacher say about that?"

Matt rolled his eyes over his mother's obvious teasing. "*Ma-a-aw*. They didn't use that word exactly. They just showed how when he was a kid, he liked to dance and write mushy poems. Junk like that."

"Oh, I see," Barbara said, nodding solemnly. "Girl junk."

Something on the side of the road distracted Matt. "Where did you say we're going today?"

His abrupt change of subject made her grin. He knew he had stumbled into sensitive territory where Mom was concerned. Rather than repeat her equality of the sexes speech, she answered his question.

"Since Washington's birthday just passed, I thought we'd go see where he was born. It sounded interesting. Besides the memorial house, there's a farm where the animals and crops are raised the same way they were in colonial days."

He perked up at the mention of farm animals. "Is it far?"

"About thirty miles. The brochure said it opens at nine. We should get there a little after that."

When she and Matt first moved into the little house in Fredericksburg, Virginia, she had vowed that they would see as much of the surrounding historic area as possible before they were forced to move again.

So far, during Matt's short life, the two of them had lived in eleven other cities, but had never really become familiar with any of them. Their stay in Fredericksburg had now stretched to nearly two years, and it definitely looked as though they finally would be able to stay some-where for as long as they wished. Nevertheless, at least one Saturday a month, Barbara still selected a famous site between Richmond and Washington, D.C., for them to visit.

The last two outings had been to the Smithsonian, where they spent the day indoors, but an unseasonable warm spell allowed Barbara a wider range of choices this weekend. And when given a choice, she knew her son's preferences well.

Just as his father had, Matt loved animals and they seemed to love him right back. An image of Howard being nuzzled by his horse popped into her mind, and she quickly erased it. She never purposely called up memories of Matt's father anymore. It was simply impossible not to think of him when every time she looked at her son's face she saw the gentle, artistic young man who had once meant the world to her. Perhaps she could have dismissed the similarities in their personalities if Matt had inherited her dark features rather than Howard's fair coloring.

Then again, perhaps not. She was a realist, and the fact was, Matt's existence, regardless of his appearance or behavior, was a constant reminder of Howard and how falling in love with him had turned her pleasant life into a roller-coaster ride through heaven and hell. But none of what had happened was Matt's fault, and she never allowed memories of the father to diminish her love for their child.

As she drove onto the bridge that would take them across the Rappahannock River, she could see the downside of the week of warm, sunny weather. Rapidly melting snow and ice had caused the river to rise higher and flow faster than she'd ever noticed before. Last night, the weather report predicted rain by the end of the weekend and warned of a possible flood.

"Hey, cool," Matt said, pointing at the railroad bridge that spanned the river a short distance from the bridge they were on. A long, sleek passenger train had started across moments ahead of them. "If you could make all the other cars on the road move out of your way, who would get to the other side first, the train or us?"

Barbara smiled as Matt began counting the railway cars. Trains came right under animals on her son's favorite things list. "Hmmm. I think that's one of those trains that carries people *and* their cars, so it's probably too heavy to go very fast." She gave the dashboard a loving pat. "I bet this old girl would win even on a cold day."

Unable to make all the other cars vanish, however, they were only halfway across the bridge when the train's engine reached the other side.

"*Ma!*" Matt shouted, and tugged on her sleeve.

Barbara shifted her gaze back to the center of the railroad bridge to see what Matt was gaping at. For a second she thought her eyes were playing tricks on her as she watched one of the concrete pillars buckle and collapse. Like a row of dominoes, the cars of the train tipped and tumbled one after another into the raging river below, while only a whisper of sound leaked inside the Honda to accompany the horrendous sight.

"Ma!" Matthew exclaimed again, and she managed to slam on the brakes a heartbeat before colliding into the car in front of them. Everyone had stopped to stare.

Eventually the line of traffic began to creep along again. By the time they were across the bridge, the initial shock had worn off sufficiently for Barbara to absorb the reality of the situation. There were people inside those train cars bobbing in the river and overturned on the banks; people who needed help.

As she turned the car toward the railroad bridge and pulled off the side of the road, she was relieved to see that she was not alone in that realization. Dozens of other cars were already parked and a crowd of men and women were heading for the crash site.

"What are we doing?" Matt asked, his bright eyes filled with curiosity.

"I'm going to see if there's anything I can do to help."

"Me, too," he declared, pushing open the passenger door.

As Barbara stepped out of the car, she considered ordering him to stay there, but with his new sense of independence, she wasn't certain he'd obey. "All right. But you hold my hand." Though he grimaced at being treated like a baby, he went to her side and offered his hand. Hurrying toward the accident, Barbara noted a number of people talking excitedly into their cellular phones and one trucker using his CB radio. Professional help would surely be arriving any moment.

For the next four hours, Barbara, Matthew, and scores of other volunteers assisted the rescue workers in any way they could. They fetched and served hot coffee, comforted terrified children, and ran errands for anyone who voiced a need. They prayed for the victims trapped inside the railway cars as they began sinking into the icy water, cheered each time someone was pulled out alive, and ached for the families of those who were not so fortunate.

When their assistance was no longer needed, Barbara and Matthew drove home feeling good about their contribution, yet too exhausted to proceed with their original plans for the day. At any rate, the experience had been worth more than a hundred trips to historical monuments.

Before Matt went to sleep that night, Barbara told him one more time, "I'm so proud of you, honey. You were as helpful as any of the grown-ups there today."

"I keep telling you I'm not a baby anymore."

Tucking the blanket under his chin, she smiled and kissed his forehead. "I know, sweetheart, but it's hard for me to remember that after so many years of taking care of you."

"Yeah, I know, but I'm going to start taking care of you now."

Barbara laughed and gave him a hug. "Don't be in such a hurry to take over. Making all the decisions isn't half as much fun as you think." She gave him one last good-night kiss and left the room, his promise echoing in her mind.

Once, before he was born, because she was too tired and sick and broken-hearted to keep going on her own, she had accepted someone's offer to "take care of her." She discovered too late that the price of that care had been her life. Although Russ Latham proved to be a man of his word, he also turned out to be brutally possessive and dangerously insane.

It took a long time, but she finally made a new life for herself and Matt, without giving up her independence. Even if she met the perfect man someday and fell in love, she would never allow him total control over her or her son.

As soon as Barbara opened the front door to bring in the newspaper the next morning, she felt the extreme drop in temperature. Wondering if it would be enough to prevent the predicted flood, she pulled the newspaper out of its plastic wrapper to see what the weather report had to say. The photo on the front page banished all thoughts of the weather, however.

It was not surprising that the headlines of the *Washington Post* focused on the train accident. What she hadn't expected to see was her face beneath those words. Shards of panic pierced her mind and froze the air in her lungs. Quickly she skimmed the caption beneath the photo: "Fredericksburg residents, Barbara and Matthew Johnson, lend a hand to drenched survivor, Louise Pilcher."

She recalled the moment pictured—Matt placing a blanket over the elderly woman's shoulders while Barbara handed her a cup of steaming coffee. She even remembered telling the woman their names and where they lived. But she had no recollection of anyone taking their photograph.

"Ma!" Matt called from the doorway. "What's taking you so long? You always yell at me if I leave the door open."

Barbara pushed aside the paralyzing fear and hurried back into the house. Forcing a smile, she said. "Looks like we're celebrities, kiddo. I guess somebody thought you were so cute yesterday, they decided to put you on the front page."

Matt's eyes opened wide with delight when he saw the photo. Then, just as suddenly, he frowned up at his mother. "Do you think *he* might see this, too?"

At times like this, she wished her baby wasn't quite so smart. Keeping her smile in place, she did her best to reassure him. "I doubt it. I'm sure they only used it in the *Post* because we're local residents, and there's no way he'd see this paper."

Matt looked at her suspiciously, but he wanted to believe her badly enough to let it go. "Good. 'Cause I like it here. I don't want to have to move again."

She gave him a quick hug. "Neither do I, honey. Neither do I."

*　　*　　*

Russ Latham squinted at the photo on the front page of the *Boston Globe*, then abruptly laughed out loud, despite the fact that he sat alone at the table in the coffee shop. The handful of other Sunday morning regulars turned toward him expecting to be let in on the joke, but he waved them off. They wouldn't see the humor in the touching picture, nor was it something he could share with them. *This* was very, very private.

The last name was different, but that didn't mean anything. She had changed that before and he'd found her anyway. But she had learned how to cover her tracks better and better over the years, until she disappeared completely, and he was forced to give up the hunt.

Apparently, fate decided it was time for him to get back to his original plan, and the photo was just the help he needed. He immediately thought of several other people who would be extremely interested if they saw it and realized who the Good Samaritans were. He would just have to move faster than they would.

He took a long drag on his cigarette and laughed again as he thought about the new angle he had come up with to gain Barbara's sympathy. He wondered if her name change might be due to a marriage, but that wouldn't matter. Any man she might have married would be a mama's boy like Howard Hamilton had been—someone she could push around. Russ didn't even consider his kind *men*, let alone obstacles to his goal.

A bitch like Barbara needed a real man to control her. He had known from the first that he was that man, but she kept running from the truth. He knew what was best for her, and this time, no matter what it took, he was going to make her accept the inevitable.

She was his, and always would be.

The boy, on the other hand, was a Hamilton, and as such, his value could be measured in dollars. But to Russ, the child represented something greater—the means to pay back the Hamilton family for what they'd done to Russ and his mother.

It took several phone calls to track down the source of the newspaper photo, but he finally reached a helpful person at the *Washington Post*. "This is the Main Street Flower Shop in Fredericksburg," he told the woman. "We have an order for Barbara Johnson, whose picture was in the paper this morning, but no address. I was hoping you could give it to me."

"I'm sorry. You're at least the twentieth call we've received about her, to say nothing for the telegrams! We're trying to locate her ourselves, but in the meantime, if you deliver it to our office, we'll see that she gets it."

Though Russ had hoped for more than that, he thanked the woman and hung up. A second later, his sense of humor returned.

All he had to do was take the flowers to the *Post* and then follow their delivery person to Barbara's door.

*   *   *

Simon Decker stopped his Mercedes sedan beside the guardhouse and waited for the security officer to emerge. Once upon a time, he had been impressed by the elaborate iron gates, the high brick wall, and the screening process required to enter the huge estate. It wasn't long, however, before the routine irritated the hell out of him and he started calling the grandiose mansion "the mausoleum."

He had been the Hamilton family's sole retainer for nineteen years, ever since his father had retired from that position, yet they still treated him like a stranger.

"Simon Decker," he told the young man, as if the guard couldn't recognize him on sight. "And *yes,* they are expecting me." He noted the time on his Rolex and pinched the bridge of his nose as the guard went back inside the compact brick building. Simon didn't need to see him to know that he was buzzing his entombed employers to announce the presence of a visitor. As required, the attorney had called his only clients for an appointment before heading there, but they still insisted on going through the whole routine before letting him drive onto the hallowed Hamilton grounds.

The gates began to open and Simon glanced at his watch again. Only thirty-two seconds had passed, barely half the usual time. Perhaps they knew what he wanted to speak to them about.

He hoped not. He was counting on his news to surprise the normally unflappable couple, while proving to them that their best interests were still of primary importance to him. Nothing specific had been said by either Howard Hamilton III or his wife, Edith, but in the last year or so, Simon had the distinct impression that they were no longer satisfied to pay him an enormous retainer for doing little more than standing by.

Between his advancing age and his taste for expensive possessions, two ex-wives, and four children, he couldn't afford to start over. In fact, ever since he'd met the woman he was hoping to make number three, he had been wracking his brain to come up with a reason to increase his fees. What he needed was a grandstand play to renew the Hamiltons' faith in him.

The touching photo in the newspaper seemed like the answer to a prayer.

He hadn't seen the woman in nearly ten years. Actually, he had completely forgotten about her until this morning. It was the boy that had captured his attention. He was a carbon copy of Howard Hamilton IV as a child.

A wild speculation had sent him rummaging through old files in search of a picture of the mother. Comparing that picture to the one in the paper, checking the dates involved, and the fact that her first name was Barbara confirmed his guess.

His foot pressed a bit harder on the accelerator. He could hardly wait to see his clients' faces when they realized they had a grandchild.

*　　*　　*

With more force than necessary, Barbara pressed the erase button on her answering machine, then unplugged the phone entirely. After the fifth call, she had quit picking it up, but the constant ringing was driving her up the wall. It was incredible how many reporters called to see if she was *the* Barbara Johnson in the photo, and even more upsetting was how easily they had obtained her unlisted number. The three she spoke to before she stopped answering the phone were told they had the wrong Barbara Johnson, but they hadn't believed her.

Two messages confirmed what she had feared the moment she'd seen the morning paper. The picture had been picked up by a wire service. After all, it was the image of compassion, a story without words. The photographer would probably win some sort of prize for it. He couldn't have any idea of what damage he had caused. He may as well have drawn a map to her home address and hand-delivered it to Russ Latham.

One of the warnings was from Shelley, a friend who had become part of a network of supporters when she'd helped Barbara and Matthew slip out of Albuquerque in the middle of the night four years ago. She was one of several acquaintances around the country who passed on messages from family and other friends to make it difficult for Russ to track her down.

Barbara had been so certain that she had finally outsmarted him and he had slithered back to where he'd come from. She desperately wanted to be able to go back home, even if it was only for a weekend visit.

Two years ago, she would have already begun packing. A part of her *was* tensed in preparation for flight, but a greater part of her resisted. She and Matt were truly happy here. He had friends and was doing well in school. She had a good job with excellent benefits. The house they were in was only rented, but they had turned it into a real home.

There had to be a way they could stay in Fredericksburg. In the past, her flights were nearly always prompted by mindless panic. Perhaps this time, knowing in advance that Russ would probably find them in the near future, she might be able to prepare better. New laws had been passed in recent years that made it easier to arrest a stalker without having to wait until the victim was hurt. If nothing else, she would hold out as long as possible without endangering Matthew.

She had been making choices based on her son's welfare for so long, it was hard to remember that she was once a young, carefree girl whose toughest decision was whether to follow her dream of being an actress to Broadway or Hollywood.

She smiled as she recalled the stunned expressions on her girlfriends' faces that long-ago day when she made her selection by plucking petals off a daisy. To her, life had been that simple then. She had identified her dream and outlined a plan to achieve it. All she had to do was go for it. Thus, she had left for New York City immediately after graduating from high school, with a two-year plan in mind. If she wasn't well on her way to becoming a Broadway star by the end of that time, she would head for Hollywood and try her luck there.

The smile that memory triggered faded as she thought about how terribly naive her plan had been.

Barbara had no idea how long it might take for Russ to find them, but she began taking protective measures the next morning. She drove Matt to and from school rather than let him take the bus. She reminded him to keep alert, stay with the crowd, and run for help if necessary. She notified the school principal and Matt's teacher, filed a watch order with the local police, and advised her employer of a potential problem. But being prepared didn't stop her from quaking inside or jumping at every sound.

She felt some relief when she picked Matt up from after-school care on Tuesday and he assured her that everything was still fine. As they approached their house, however, there was a familiar-looking van parked in the driveway, and a man wearing a parka and ski hat was at the door.

Because she had been anticipating a problem, she was able to outwardly control her fear for Matt's sake. The man turned around when she pulled the car onto the swale in front of the house and shut off the engine. Even from that distance, the dark skin on his face confirmed that he wasn't Russ, but that didn't mean they weren't in danger.

"Pop quiz, kiddo. You come home with a friend,

my car's in the driveway, but there's a strange car out front. What do you do?"

Matt rolled his eyes at her, wordlessly expressing his boredom with her constant reminders. "I look at the living room window. If the elephant is there, it's okay for me to go in. If it's not, I should go to the nearest phone and call the police."

She had originally purchased the foot-high Indian elephant because Matt was intrigued by its colorful mosaic tiles. When they moved into the house and saw the wide sill of the picture window, they decided the statue looked very impressive standing guard there. Using it as a part of their code only came to her yesterday.

She rubbed the top of his head. "Perfect. Okay, that man might not be anyone to worry about, but just in case, you stay here while I go speak to him. Watch for my hand signals." Satisfied that he was paying attention, she got out of the car and walked up to the stranger.

"May I help you?" she asked.

"If you're Barbara Johnson, you sure can," he answered with a broad smile. "I'm Otis. I deliver the newspaper."

Now she knew why the van looked familiar. "Oh, yes, of course. I'm Mrs. Johnson."

"Great. They got all kinds of stuff at the *Post* addressed to you. They asked me to deliver it, but I wasn't sure if I should just leave it—"

"What kinds of *stuff*?"

"Mostly telegrams and letters, but there were

some plants and flowers, too. It'll only take me a minute."

She waved at Matt to come help, then opened the front door. Otis made several trips to the van, bringing back a small bag of mail, four packages, three plants, and over a dozen floral arrangements.

Barbara had Matt take in the mail and packages, but inspected each plant and bouquet before handing it to him. Once she saw that there was nothing hidden in an arrangement and that the card was not from Russ, she let Matt take it inside. She was about to relax when Otis set the last two vases on the porch. They both contained beautiful sprays of roses, but one sent a shiver down her spine. She stopped Matt from carrying them inside and hurriedly dug a few dollars out of her purse to give to Otis.

Though she was fairly certain the bouquet of yellow roses was innocently sent, she read the card just to be sure, then handed the vase to Matt. As he went inside and Otis headed for his van, she carefully searched the bouquet of peach Oceanias—the same variety as the first Russ had cut for her at the Hamilton estate. There was nothing within the greenery to frighten her, not even a card to identify the sender, but that didn't mean they weren't from him.

With trembling fingers she slowly examined one rose stem after another until she found what she was looking for. Just beneath one blossom, where a person might place her fingers when sniffing the rose, was a sharp thorn. If one didn't know better, one would assume that the florist simply missed it in the process of removing all the thorns from the stems. But Barbara did know better. That single, hidden thorn had been left on intentionally. It was Russ's trademark.

She straightened and looked up and down the street. She saw no sign of him, but that meant nothing. He was nearby. She could practically smell the cigarette smoke she had come to associate with him. He might even be watching her that moment from behind a tree or bush in a neighbor's yard.

She wanted to scream loudly enough to shatter windows. She wanted to go hide under her bed and cry her fears away.

But more than anything else she wanted someone to explain how an affair that had begun so sweetly had turned into a ten-year-long nightmare. . . .

Chapter 1

"You really think you're hot shit, don't you?"

Barbara recognized the obnoxious teenager lounging against the wall outside the restaurant. She'd waited on him and his two friends a few hours before. He'd gotten fresh, and she'd sassed him right back, as she usually did with customers who thought she was on the menu. Obviously, this one hadn't thought she was very funny. Though she walked a bit faster, he quickly caught up with her, grabbed her arm, and brought her to an abrupt stop.

"I want to talk to you," he said, glaring down his nose at her.

He wasn't that much bigger than she was, but his grasp was tight enough to cut off the circulation. "Well, I don't want to talk to you. Release me this instant or I'll scream."

Instead of obeying, he laughed and yanked her against him. She took a deep breath and opened her mouth to follow through with her threat, but his hand stifled the noise she made. One couple gave them a curious glance as they walked by, but the few other people in the area paid no attention at all. She couldn't prevent the fear from showing in her eyes.

"I'm not going to hurt you," he told her with a mean smirk. "*This* time. But if you ever embarrass me in front of my friends again—"

"Excuse me," a deep voice interrupted.

Barbara's tormentor turned his head to see who had come up behind him and found he had to look up as well. The stranger was not only a head taller but considerably broader.

"I could be mistaken," the big man said in an overly polite tone. "But I don't believe the lady desires your company."

"Eat shit," the punk said, and tried to haul Barbara away, but a beefy hand clamped down on his shoulder and halted his progress. She could see by her captor's grimace that the gesture was less than friendly.

"Remove your hand from the lady's mouth and let *her* tell me what she'd like."

Obviously deciding the game wasn't worth risking more pain, the young man slowly took his hands off Barbara and backed away. "Look, I was only trying to scare her a little. You know, it was just a joke." When the big man took one menacing step toward him, he turned and ran off.

"Thank you so much," Barbara gushed as she rubbed feeling back into her arm. "I don't know if he was bluffing or not, but I sure am glad you came along."

The big man looked down at his shoes and

stuck his hands in his jeans pockets as if his confidence had fled with the bully. "Um, if you wish, I'll, uh, go to the police station with you to file a report."

"Thanks, but it would probably be a waste of time, and after putting in a ten-hour shift waiting on characters like that, I'd just as soon go home and put my feet up. If he bothers me again, I'll do something about it, but I doubt if he will. I would like to do something for you, though."

"Oh, no, uh, that's not necessary."

He looked so uncomfortable, she reached out and put her hand on his arm. "Please. I insist. At least let me buy you a cup of coffee. Or something stronger, if you'd like."

"No, um, coffee would be fine, but you said you've had a long day, and your thank-you was more than sufficient."

She smiled. His shyness was absolutely irresistible. "As long as I get off my feet, I'll be happy." In a dramatic fashion, she hooked her arm with his and headed him toward a deli she knew stayed open all night. "Come along, my knight in shining armor. Allow me to reward you for your heroism." That made him smile, and with a nod of his head, he quit protesting.

"I'm Barbara Mancuso," she said as they began walking. "And you are?"

He cleared his throat. "Howard. Howard Hamilton."

She could tell he was still feeling awkward, and she was determined to get him over it. "Well,

Howard Hamilton, it is my extreme pleasure to meet you. Are you a full-time rescuer of maidens in distress or is it just a sideline?"

She watched him smile again and was glad he had kept a straight face in front of the bully. No matter how big he was, he wasn't the least bit frightening when he smiled. In fact, she decided, he had a very gentle demeanor about him, sort of like a huge teddy bear.

"I'm a student," he said much too simply.

"Where? What year? Major? Minor?"

"Harvard. Working on my master's. Business and finance."

She tilted her head up at him and wrinkled her nose. "Really? I would never have guessed that in a zillion years."

He gave a small shrug. "What would you guess?"

She pretended to be very serious as she studied his face and body. "I don't know. A football player? Bodyguard? Professional wrestler?"

"Some people say I resemble Hulk Hogan," he murmured self-consciously.

"Well . . . you're both big and blond, but he has longer hair and a mustache, and you're much better looking." He cleared his throat again, and she wished it was daytime so she could see if he was blushing.

"What about you?" he asked.

"I'm a student also . . . sometimes. Occasionally, I'm an actress. Most of the time, though, I'm a waitress. Here's the place."

Though there were a number of customers in the deli, plenty of tables were empty. The next few minutes passed with Barbara insisting Howard should eat something with his coffee. Again, she overrode his protests with little effort.

"So tell me, Howard," she prompted as soon as the waitress took their order. "What stroke of fate caused a Harvard graduate student to be on a New York sidewalk after midnight?" She watched his mouth relax into another one of his heart-melting smiles.

"I came down for the weekend to visit a friend, but he's had a nonstop party going on in his apartment since last night. I had to get out for a while."

"Hmmm. I know how that is. I tried living with a roommate twice and finally decided to rent in a less prestigious neighborhood where I could afford it alone. Where's home?"

"Cambridge. I have an apartment off-campus."

"No, I meant *home*, as in where you go over Christmas vacation." When he didn't answer immediately, she figured she either overstepped herself or she had accidentally pushed a sensitive button. "I'm sorry. I shouldn't be so nosy. I didn't mean to be rude, honestly, but I have a habit of looking at people as if they were jigsaw puzzles. Usually I can talk to a customer for thirty seconds and feel like I have all the pieces I need to construct that character. But once in a while, I meet someone I can't figure out and my curiosity takes over."

"I'm really not terribly complicated," he said with a shake of his head.

"On the contrary, my brave knight, I think you are very complicated." Leaning forward and arching one eyebrow, she continued in a bad German accent, "But if I have to keep you here all night, I vill eventually have zee entire picture. Does that frighten you?"

He gave that a moment's consideration. "No. As a matter of fact, I rather like the sound of it."

The next instant, his sky-blue eyes met hers straight on for the first time, and she felt as though someone had vacuumed the air out of her lungs. "Oh, my," she whispered, shocked by the impact. To her relief, the waitress arrived with their food, and she was able to pull her gaze away from his. Only then did she notice how badly he was blushing and realized that he had been affected just as unexpectedly.

Her gaze dropped to his hands. They were large, like the rest of him, and showed no signs of manual labor or nicotine stains, but most important, there were no rings on his fingers or tan lines to indicate that he usually wore one.

After the response her body had to looking in his eyes, she couldn't prevent her mind from traveling to what it would feel like to have those hands on her.

She was no longer a virgin ... technically ... but she never experienced the magical sensations she'd read about. After two experiments with intimacy, she had concluded that sex wasn't worth the effort required.

She had also read thousands of paragraphs about love at first sight and heated gazes across crowded rooms, but she had reluctantly abandoned the belief that those things happened to real people. She stared at Howard's downcast eyes until he looked at her again. They weren't across a crowded room, but if that wasn't a heated gaze, her name wasn't Barbara Mancuso.

"Are you going to help me out with your puzzle or should I just assume the worst?" she asked to break the tension.

He swallowed the bite of sandwich in his mouth. "What would you like to know?"

"Okay. How about your family?"

"My parents live in Boston," he said, answering her earlier question as well. "I'm an only child."

"Oh! So am I. Wasn't it great growing up without having to compete for attention?"

He looked at her curiously. "Great? I always wished I had a dozen brothers and sisters to take away some of that attention."

She instantly analyzed that comment; there was probably a domineering or overprotective parent in the wings.

"I'm rich," he said bluntly.

"How nice," Barbara said with a laugh. "It's a little tough going to Harvard without money."

"You don't understand. I'm very, *very* rich. My father is the Hamilton of Hamilton-Greene," Howard explained in a matter-of-fact, almost embarrassed tone. "My mother was the last of the Greenes, which leaves me as the sole heir to the combined fortune."

"Good Lord," she muttered, realizing the immensity of his inheritance . . . and responsibility. "I bet half of all the products in the supermarket have a Hamilton-Greene logo."

"Half might be a bit high," he said, playing with the last french fry on his plate.

"Wait a minute. I think I have most of the puzzle now." Before she could offer her deduction, however, the waitress came back to clear the dishes and take their dessert order.

As soon as the woman walked away, she said, "Here's how it looks to me. Very simply, you had your entire life planned out before you were born. Unfortunately, you aren't terribly happy with the role you've been given to play, but being the good son, you would never rebel. So you're majoring in business, as expected, instead of . . ."

She gestured for him to complete the sentence, but he looked confused. "I'm betting there's some other career that would make you happier than taking over the leadership of Hamilton-Greene."

He began shredding his paper napkin. "I never gave it any thought."

"I don't believe that. There must be something. Tell me this: What did you want to be before they told you who you were?" His napkin was quickly becoming a small pile of strips. "Okay, we can come back to that one. Why did you tell me you were rich? I would never have asked."

He shrugged. "It's the one piece of information that explains everything about me. It seemed more expedient to get it out of the way. Now you can start telling me about *you*."

Though she felt there was still a piece missing from Howard's puzzle, she was temporarily satisfied with what she did have. Since he hadn't asked any specific questions, she told him some stories that gave him glimpses into her happy childhood, her turbulent teen years in Dayton, and how her dreams of stardom had brought her to New York two years ago.

The big city was a hell of an eye-opener for most people. For an eighteen-year-old Ohio girl, it was like being dropped on another planet inhabited by flesh-eating aliens. Reality set in swiftly and without mercy.

The talent her high school drama coach had raved about was actually mediocre. The pretty face and cute little figure she'd been complimented on back home were no more than average for a would-be actress. There simply wasn't anything exceptional or unique about her.

But Barbara had more persistence than many other hopefuls. She registered for classes at NYU to improve her acting skills and volunteered to work for free backstage at an off-off-Broadway theater.

It was at that theater that she had landed a small part in a briefly successful show six months ago, but nothing else had come through before or since. According to her plan, she should be preparing to leave for Hollywood soon.

However, the prospect of moving to the West Coast and starting from scratch no longer held any appeal. She had carved out a pleasant life for herself in New York and had even registered for some business classes at college with thoughts of upgrading her primary income source.

Though she accepted the fact that, short of a miracle, stardom was out of her reach, she still put in time at the theater and auditioned for roles she had a shot at. She loved it too much not to hold on to a piece of her dream.

Howard was much more at ease once the focus was on her, and his obvious fascination had her entertaining him much longer than she'd intended. It wasn't until she caught him stifling a yawn that she checked her watch.

"Good grief! It's after three. I was only kidding about keeping you here all night."

"Believe me, I have thoroughly enjoyed my captivity," he said with a grin that made her heart go thump again.

There was a brief tug-of-war over the check, which she won mainly because she knew the waitress, but he won the battle over accompanying her to her apartment in Queens in a cab rather than her taking the subway.

"Have you had enough time to think about it?" Barbara asked after they were on their way.

Howard narrowed his eyes in thought. "I seem to have forgotten the question."

She doubted that, but repeated it anyway. "What career would you have chosen if you were

Howard Jones instead of Howard Hamilton?" He didn't move a muscle, but she sensed his mental squirming. "Be honest, now."

"You're going to laugh."

"Only if you do first."

He turned his head away and murmured, "I draw a little."

"What kind of drawing? Like an architect, or an artist?"

"Um, I, uh, like to draw cartoon characters, and I do some caricatures. I'm pretty good."

She gently brought his face back toward her. "I bet you're better than pretty good. What would you do with your talent if you had the chance? Animation or comics?"

When he saw she was truly interested, his eyes sparkled in response. "I think animation. When I was very young, I imagined being the creator of my own cartoon series."

She could almost hear her mom warning her against what she was thinking. She and Howard were barely acquaintances, let alone close enough friends for her to meddle in his life. And yet, she couldn't stand to see someone give up his dream without even trying. When they reached her apartment she said, "Come in with me. We have work to do."

It wasn't until she closed and locked the door behind him that she realized she had better explain so that he didn't misunderstand why she'd invited him in. The words she was about to say caught in her throat as she turned around and saw him standing in the middle of her efficiency apartment, looking much too large for such a small room and looking entirely too appealing for her to be alone with him so soon.

The instant their eyes met, however, she could see that he was more nervous about the situation than she was.

"Please sit," she said, pointing to a chair instead of the trundle bed that doubled for a sofa. She located paper and a pencil; then she sat on the bed with her legs crossed Indian-style. "Draw me something. Anything. I want to decide for myself whether you're *pretty good*."

With a slow grin, he began scribbling. When she tried to watch him work, he covered the drawing with his hand. About five minutes later he tore off the sheet of paper, but he immediately started another drawing on the next sheet. She was at the edge of her patience by the time he completed a fourth drawing without letting her have as much as a peek.

"All right," he finally said. "But understand, I did these rather quickly, so they're not my best—"

He stopped talking as she snatched the sheets out of his hand and gasped with delight. "Wow! This is terrific! I *knew* you were better than pretty good. You're phenomenal."

He had drawn their initial encounter in sequence, with her portrayed as Betty Boop, the bully as a weasel, and him as a masked, caped crusader. The final scene showed the two of them walking away, arm-in-arm.

"You forgot one thing," she said, picking up the

pencil. Over Betty's head she drew a dialogue bubble, with the words "MY HERO!" inside, and held it up. She was rewarded with a smile so devastating her body temperature seemed to rise a degree. With some effort, she resisted the urge to crawl onto his lap to see if he was as comfortable as he looked.

"Now that I have no doubt about your talent, I have an important question. Is there anyone else who could take over the company if you didn't?"

He shook his head. "Not really. I have one cousin, but, my father doesn't . . ." He stopped and shook his head again. "Suffice it to say, the responsibility is mine to bear."

"Okay, you can't turn your back on your family, but that doesn't mean you can't accomplish more than one thing in your life. Look at da Vinci, Thomas Jefferson, Edison. Lots of people diversify. Why can't you?"

His eyes were sparkling again as he absorbed what she was saying. "You make it sound so simple. Of course I could do both. As CEO, most of what my father does is delegate anyway. I could easily divide up my time if I put my mind to it."

She smiled. "Sometimes a person can be so focused on what they *think* they're supposed to be doing, it takes another person to point out an alternate route."

She wished she could bottle the expression on his face so that she could bring it out to savor on sad days. His fascination with her had clearly graduated to adoration. More amazing was that she felt the same way. The phrase "love at first sight" popped into her head again, and she wondered if it could really be possible after all.

"Now, autograph every drawing for me so that when you're famous, these originals will be worth a fortune."

He shot her a skeptical glance, but did as she asked. On the first he wrote, *Only fate could have arranged a meeting this extraordinary.* The second and third read, *I'd do anything for you* and *You should have a full-time bodyguard—I'm available!* Those three tugged on her romantic heartstrings, but it was the fourth, where they were walking off together, that set her soul on fire: *Here's to love at first sight.*

"O-o-oh. These are so sweet. Thank you." Thinking only that a thank-you was inadequate for something so personal, she went over to him to give him a light peck on the cheek, but he turned his face so that her lips brushed his instead. "Oh, my," she said for the second time that night.

She knew she should back away; it was far too soon to follow through with what she was feeling. While her common sense argued in favor of restraint, however, his mouth hesitantly touched hers again, and she gave in to the need to discover whether he was truly the one she'd been waiting for—the one whose kisses would melt her bones and make the real world disappear.

Her confirmation came the instant their lips pressed together in earnest. Fortunately, he eased her onto his lap, for her legs suddenly lost the

ability to support her weight. And when he deepened the kiss, the taste of him caused a ripple of
pleasure that had her ready to discover everything
else he could make her feel. She gasped as his
one large hand slid up her arm then covered her
breast, and instinctively repositioned herself so
that she was straddling his thighs.

But when he used those incredible hands to
bring her hips closer to his and she realized he
was built big *everywhere,* it struck her that they
might not be such a perfect fit after all. Then
there was the matter of birth control. She had no
preventive supplies on hand. Though her period
had just ended and her chances of conception
should be close to nil, she knew that wasn't a very
trustworthy method.

Despite how aroused he was, he sensed her tension. "I'm sorry. I didn't mean to get carried away."

"There's no need to apologize. I got as *carried
away* as you did, but, it's just that—"

"It's too soon."

"Yes," she said, relieved that he understood.

"I guess I'd better go."

She nodded her agreement, but it took her several seconds to actually get up off his lap so he
could rise. They got as far as the door before the
desire still thrumming through their bodies fought
back. A kiss intended to say good night fanned
the flames higher instead.

"Tell me to go," he begged in a hoarse voice.

Right and wrong were suddenly all mixed up. A
powerful need, unlike anything she'd ever imag-

ined, obliterated her common sense. All that mattered was getting as close as a man and woman could get, as fast as possible, and to hell with everything else. "*Stay,*" she whispered.

Before she could reconsider, he swept her up in his arms and carried her to the bed. Barbara didn't have time to think about what had bothered her before. They each made a brief attempt to undress the other, but neither had the patience to do it properly. A few buttons were undone, his pants shoved to his knees, her uniform gathered above her waist, her panties discarded.

Then that part of him that had seemed too large plunged into her body and shot her to the next level of pleasure.

She had always felt that there was some vital piece missing to her personal puzzle, and now she knew what it was. Howard's size was irrelevant. They fit together beautifully, as if their bodies had been formed for this moment.

In mere seconds, her entire concentration was focused on the exquisite tension he was creating within her. She felt her nerves being strung higher and tighter until they exploded in one final burst of sensation. A moment later, he withdrew from her body to complete his own satisfaction.

Experiencing her first genuine climax, along with his obvious concern for her welfare, assured her that Howard was not only her knight in shining armor, but her Prince Charming as well.

Chapter 2

"Please stop worrying," Howard said for at least the tenth time, and gave her another reassuring hug. "My parents are going to love you as much as I do. I guarantee it."

She couldn't explain why she was so upset over the prospect of meeting the two people who had created the most wonderful man in all the world. Nevertheless, anxiety had set in the moment he suggested she accompany him home to announce their engagement.

As he preferred, they took the train. He even arranged for them to have a private room for the trip. It should have been another memorable, romantic experience for her. Instead, with each mile of track they left behind, her panic increased.

She knew that a large part of her worry stemmed from the fact that they'd only known each other for two weeks. Although it seemed like forever to them, it could be quite a shock to his parents.

That practical thought led to others. There were so many details about the future that they had yet to discuss. Oh, they always meant to, but *something* always got in the way.

They had been apart only five of the last four-teen days, and those five had been pure hell. Now that she had discovered the pleasures of lovemak-ing, she seemed to require it constantly. No mat-ter how often their bodies came together, it took only a glance or a touch to stir the aching need again.

When they weren't making love, Howard was giving her an education on the pleasures of being wealthy. They traveled about Manhattan in a lim-ousine, stayed in a suite in the Plaza, saw the hottest Broadway shows, and ate at the most ex-clusive restaurants. He insisted on buying her a new wardrobe, and everything else that caught her eye . . . or his.

She knew they were in love, yet she was still completely surprised when he presented her with the enormous blue marquis diamond and asked her to marry him. She hadn't hesitated a heartbeat then, but her confidence abandoned her when they boarded the train to Boston that morning. Though he kept telling her everything would be fine, she couldn't help but feel that something was very wrong.

She wasn't the least bit surprised by the long, black limo waiting for them when they arrived in Boston, but the snooty chauffeur wasn't anything like the good-humored driver they'd hired in Man-hattan. The way he looked down his nose at her, it was as if he'd judged her on sight and found her terribly lacking in suitability for the young master.

When Howard told her the man had been a full-time employee of the Hamilton-Greene Corporation for more than two decades and would probably be around for two more, the acid level in her stomach increased another notch.

Neither Howard's claim that he was very rich nor the ease with which he spent large sums of money prepared her for his family's estate. First came the great brick wall with its iron entrance gates, then the lushly landscaped lawn as sprawling as any golf course, and finally the mansion that was bigger than the average shopping mall.

As the limo pulled up to the front door, she wished she had forced Howard to talk more about his family and how and where they would live after their marriage.

An elderly butler opened the door and gave Howard a stiff nod. In a strong British accent he said, "It's good to have you home, Master Hamilton. Your parents requested that you and your guest await them in the library. They'll be down momentarily." He led them to a set of double wooden doors off the main foyer, waited for them to enter, then closed them inside a room with floor-to-ceiling bookshelves, a fireplace, and a lot of expensive furnishings. It looked precisely the way Barbara imagined a rich family's library should look.

"That was Chesterfield, the butler," Howard said in a hushed voice. "He's been with the family—"

"Let me guess," she interjected. "For centuries. But why didn't you introduce me?"

He tapped her nose and closely imitated Chesterfield's accent. "That would have been most improper, my dear." He smiled at the face she made. "Mother would have been devastated if a servant met her future daughter-in-law before she did."

"God, Howard, this really doesn't feel right. Are you sure you shouldn't have warned them about our engagement before we arrived?"

"Barbara, please. I think I know best how to deal with my parents."

There was a harsh edge to his voice that she'd never heard before, but considering the fact that she had already asked that question a dozen times, she supposed he had a right to be annoyed with her. "I'm sorry, hon. My nerves are on the outside of my skin."

He pulled her close and stroked her hair. "I know. I shouldn't have barked at you. It's this house. As long as I can remember, I've never been able to relax here."

She tipped her head back to look up at him. "We aren't going to have to live here, are we?"

He paused long enough for her to fear his answer, but before she could prod him, the library doors opened and a handsome couple entered. Barbara didn't need an introduction to guess their identity. The regal way they moved announced their status, and the man looked very much like she guessed Howard would thirty years in the future, except that he seemed to lack any softness in his features.

Howard greeted his mother with a light kiss on the cheek she offered up to him. "You look even more beautiful than the last time I was home."

Her smile failed to soften the sharpness of her response. "It's been so long since you've been home, I'm surprised you even recognized me." As the mother watched her son move on to his father, Barbara studied her.

She was more well groomed than beautiful, for her coloring was rather mousy, her features unremarkable, and her figure a bit too thin for someone so tall. Also, she was either considerably younger than her husband or had an exceptional cosmetic surgeon.

"Sweetheart," Howard said, reaching for Barbara's left hand and bringing her forward a step. "I'd like you to meet my parents, Edith and Howard Hamilton. Mother, Father, this is Barbara Mancuso, my, uh . . . my fiancée." With his final word he brought her hand up to his lips for a kiss, simultaneously showing off the engagement ring.

Barbara tried to read the expressions on their faces without blatantly staring. She had expected surprise, hoped for happiness, and dreaded anger. What she saw completely confused her. Mr. Hamilton barely acknowledged that she was in the room, and the only word she could think of to describe the look he gave his son was *bored*.

There was something odd about Mrs. Hamilton's reaction as well, but before Barbara could label it, the woman smiled, embraced her, and lightly touched their cheeks together.

"Welcome to our home, dear. This is so typical of our Howard—always springing little surprises on us to keep us on our toes." She hooked her arm through Barbara's and guided her toward the door. "Our cook has prepared a lovely tea for Howard's homecoming. Of course, she could only make *his* favorite treats since he chose to keep the identity of his guest a secret. You'll have to tell us what sort of foods you prefer so that we can have something special at dinner in your honor. *Mancuso*. That's Italian, isn't it, dear?"

Though it was phrased as a question, Barbara didn't get the impression that the woman was actually expecting an answer. All anyone had to do was look at her to guess her ancestry. "Yes, but there's no need to fix anything special for me. Howard will vouch for the fact that I eat just about anything put in front of me." She glanced over her shoulder and Howard gave her a wink, but it wasn't quite enough to settle her nerves.

Barbara had to force herself not to gape at the extravagance around her as Mrs. Hamilton led them through the center of the luxuriously furnished mansion and out to a veranda. This wasn't a home; it was the set for a movie.

Chesterfield was already on the veranda, waiting to seat them at a table set with silver and crystal. At his signal, a young woman in a black-and-white maid's uniform began the formal service.

Barbara quickly realized that conversation was put on hold as long as the servants hovered nearby. The tea and pastries were elegantly presented, and Barbara made herself swallow a little, to be polite. She felt as though a sandbag were suspended over her head and the moment the help were out of sight, someone was going to cut the rope holding the bag. She just hadn't expected the villain to be Howard.

"Barbara is an actress," he announced as soon as the table was cleared.

Barbara couldn't tell what Mr. Hamilton thought about that, but his wife's eyes widened considerably.

"How fascinating," she said. "On Broadway?"

"Not quite," Barbara replied. Encouraged by both Howard and his mother, she related her one professional stage experience, then went on to tell a few stories about people she'd met in the theater. For the next hour she wasn't certain whether she was being interviewed or interrogated, but she decided answering Mrs. Hamilton's questions honestly might help cut the tension.

Chesterfield's reappearance brought conversation to an immediate halt. He whispered into Mr. Hamilton's ear, then silently departed again.

"Please excuse me," Howard's father said as he rose from his chair. "I must take a call from overseas. Howard, I'd like to go over a few things with you later this afternoon, say, five o'clock in my office."

"I must excuse myself as well," Mrs. Hamilton

said. "I have a meeting with the Ballet Guild this afternoon that I simply must attend. But I'm sure you two lovebirds can entertain yourselves for a few hours without me. We'll visit more this evening." She gave Howard a quick peck on the forehead. "Dinner will be at eight in the dining room."

As soon as she and Howard were alone, Barbara sank back in her chair and blew out the breath she'd been holding.

Howard leaned over and kissed her tenderly. "You were wonderful, sweetheart. I think Mother was taken with you."

She made a face at him. "Maybe, but your father barely spoke to me."

"Don't worry about it. I'm sure he'll warm up to you this evening, after we have our meeting. Now I want to show you around."

He gave her a fast tour of all three floors of the mansion, occasionally pointing out an antique or painting that had an interesting history to it, and commenting on guest rooms where famous people had spent the night. She was slightly disappointed to learn that she had been assigned a room some distance from his, but he assured her it wouldn't make any difference.

He proved his point when they reached a dark corner of the wine cellar. As he lifted her and wrapped her legs around his waist, she suddenly understood why the tour had been so fast. Though she had no objection to what he had in mind, she was still lucid enough to think of protection.

"We don't have to worry about that anymore,"

he assured her. "We'll be married in a month, and we've already agreed to start a family right away. I need you too badly right now to wait."

Knowing someone could discover them at any moment added more urgency than usual, but the act was even more exciting because of it. She barely had time to straighten her clothes and catch her breath before he was pulling her back upstairs for a look at the grounds.

Riding in a golf cart, he showed her the pool, the two tennis courts, the six-car garage, the servants' bungalows, the rose gardens, and the beginning of the nine-hole golf course, but they didn't stop until they reached the stables.

He had talked about his horses, especially his favorite, D'Artagnan, often enough for her to be able to guess which was which. Watching him and the big black stallion get reacquainted was one of the most heartwarming things she had ever seen, until a man unexpectedly entered the stables. He was fair like Howard and about the same age, but his build was much more compact and he had a mischievous look about him.

"Howie, you son-of-a-bitch! Why didn't you let me know you were coming?"

Howard whirled around. "Damn! I was planning to surprise you." The two shared a manly hug and slapped each other on the back a few times.

"You know how fast the grapevine works around here," the friend said, then gave Howard a poke in the stomach. "Looks like you've lost a few pounds, pal. What I heard must be true." He turned toward Barbara and grinned. "And this must be the little gypsy who put the love spell on you!"

Since Howard laughed, Barbara did as well and held out her hand. "Hi. I'm Barbara Mancuso."

"Russ Latham," he replied, taking her hand and bringing it to his lips.

For an instant she thought she felt his tongue stroke her skin, but that was ridiculous under the circumstances.

"And now that we've met, you can forget all about this big oaf and marry me instead." He reached for her left hand and inspected her ring. "We'll hold on to this, though. Maybe trade it in for a house in Bermuda." He took a closer look at the flawless stone. "Hell, we'll get a house in Bermuda *and* a hundred-foot yacht for this thing."

Howard put his arm around Barbara and pulled her back so that Russ had to let go of her hands. "Sweetheart, you have just met my worst nightmare. Anytime I ever got in trouble, Russ was the one who instigated it. Every time I liked a girl, she fell for him."

"Don't listen to him, Barb. It was exactly the opposite. He'd pull the prank, I'd get the punishment. He'd get the pretty girl, I'd get her ugly stepsister."

It was clear that these two men had been friends for some time, but Barbara didn't recall Howard ever mentioning him. Again, she was struck by the thought that he had told her very little about the people in his life before her.

"Why don't you come back to the house for a drink, and we can catch up?" Russ asked.

Howard glanced at his watch. "If you don't mind, we'll take a rain check. I promised Barbara a ride, and I have to meet Father at five; then Mother has planned something special for dinner. How about tomorrow?"

"Sure. You know where to find me." He saluted Howard, blew a kiss to Barbara, and strode away.

Barbara waited for Howard to offer an explanation, but he simply went back to D'Artagnan and started saddling him up, so she prompted him. "I gather Russ is an old friend?"

"A very old friend," he said without stopping his task. "He's the son of the chief gardener. They've lived in one of the bungalows since before I was born. Russ, my cousin, and I used to call ourselves the three musketeers. That's how I picked D'Artagnan's name."

"You never told me that."

"There are a lot of things I haven't told you yet." He walked over and pulled her close. "It's your own fault." He gave her a kiss that erased any further questions. "When I'm around you, I can't think of anyone else. But we have the rest of our lives for me to fill you in. Let's take a ride while we still have time."

As if she were weightless, Howard lifted her up into the saddle, then mounted behind her. "Now, just relax. I'll do all the work."

She giggled as she felt his erection pressing hard against her behind. "Already?"

"Always," he said, turning her head for another soul-searing kiss.

Just when she thought he had changed his mind about which animal she would be riding, he gave D'Artagnan the order to move and they headed for the far side of the golf course. There, for the first time, they made love in the sunlight and talked about the baby they might have already created.

An hour later, she had him drop her off in the rose gardens while he went on to meet with his father. Considering the afternoon Howard had given her, she needed some time alone to gather her wits again before trying to have an intelligent conversation with anyone inside the mansion.

She meandered up and down the meticulously cultivated rows, touching velvety petals, inhaling the perfumed air, and daydreaming about the future. If a fairy godmother suddenly appeared in front of her and took full credit for everything, Barbara wouldn't have been the least bit surprised.

Snip!

The cutting sound broke into her daydream, and she sought out the source.

"Hi," Russ called from a few rows away. "Mrs. H. asked me to cut a bouquet of Oceanias for your bedroom, but if you prefer another color . . ." He held up the long-stemmed, peach-tinted rose he had just snipped.

"No, those are perfect. Thank you." She followed the path to where he was standing.

"Why don't you pick out the ones you like best?"

With only two exceptions, he cut the ones she pointed out and stuck the stems into a large bucket of ice chips at his feet. From the Oceanias he moved on to the American Beauties for the foyer.

"Did Howard ever tell you about the time he talked me into climbing on top of the roof of the main house to make a movie of him riding that crazy horse of his, and I ended up breaking my collarbone?"

Rather than admit that Howard had told her almost nothing about his childhood, she simply shook her head and smiled encouragingly. Russ was more than happy to regale her with that humorous tale and several others as he slowly filled the bucket with dozens of roses. He proved to be so entertaining that she accepted his invitation to accompany him back to his house for a cold drink and more stories, while he trimmed the thorns and arranged the bouquets in the appropriate vases.

His exceptional skill with the flowers was as interesting as his stories. Because she was watching so closely, she noticed that he missed a thorn beneath one of the blossoms and interrupted his anecdote to mention it.

With a wink, he said, "Not only beautiful, but observant. I didn't miss it, though. I always leave at least one thorn in each bouquet."

Barbara frowned. "Why would you do that?"

He stopped what he was doing and became completely serious. His eyes held hers as if challenging her to look beyond his words. "A rose is like a young, innocent girl: beautiful, soft, and fragrant, but terribly fragile. The thorns are its only protection from man's clumsy handling. By removing them, we strip it of its dignity. Some people need to be reminded that beautiful things sometimes cause pain if not handled with care."

Between his strange explanation and the intensity of his gaze, Barbara was unable to form a response. However, his humor abruptly returned with a wink and a grin, and she soon forgot the odd feeling that had come over her. All artists were a little eccentric, she supposed, and Russ's creative talent was quite evident.

She was having such a good time with Russ, she hardly minded that he smoked one cigarette after another. In fact, she wished she and Howard could have dinner there, amid the haze of friendly smoke, instead of in the formal dining room with the Hamiltons. But that was one wish her fairy godmother could not grant. At seven o'clock, when Russ had to deliver the flowers, she rode with him up to the back door of the mansion, then raced upstairs to her room.

At five to eight, correctly attired in a black Dior sheath and a single strand of perfectly matched pearls—both of which Howard had bought for her—she was congratulating herself on the fastest cleanup ever performed when Howard knocked at her door.

"You don't have to knock, silly," she teased, surprised that he'd done that. "Come in. I just have to put on my lipstick." She stopped, noted the dark brown suit he was wearing, and gave him a quick kiss. "You look extremely handsome tonight. You should wear brown more often."

He shrugged indifferently. "It's Mother's favorite. And yes, I did have to knock. For the sake of the maid in the hall. You must realize that the simplest thing you do could be observed and gossiped about from one servant to another."

She couldn't believe he was able to say that with such a straight face. "Oh, pooh. You can't tell me you really care what they think."

"No? Perhaps you'll understand better if I tell you that everyone in the house, my parents included, have heard how you and Russ spent the afternoon alone in his bungalow, that you barely made it back here in time to dress for dinner, and that he kissed you before you got out of his cart."

She gaped at him in shock. He wasn't kidding; he was seriously upset with her. "Howard! You know very well how I spent the afternoon! I shouldn't have to explain, but since you've obviously lost your mind, I will."

She took a deep breath and propped her fists on her hips. "About a half hour after you left me in the garden, Russ came by to cut roses for your mother. He told me funny stories. About *you*." Her annoyance with him increased with each sentence, and the way he kept backing away from her revealed that he was very aware of the mistake he'd made.

"I went back to his place and had a soda while he arranged the flowers. We were alone there for less than one hour, during which we continued to talk about *you*." She accented her last word by poking her finger into his chest.

"He drove me up to the house because we were both headed this way. He did kiss the back of my hand, but it was done in fun, not passion. And, as you can see, I had more than enough time to shower and dress. Did I miss anything?" She was fully prepared to punch him in the nose if he said one wrong word.

He slumped down into the rocking chair in the corner of her room and ran his hands through his hair. "I'm sorry. I don't know what came over me."

His tone and expression were so pitiful, she walked over and sat down on his lap. "I do. You were jealous. I hear that sometimes happens when you're in love."

He shook his head and kept his eyes downcast. "It's more than that. Russ and I have always had a sort of ongoing competition. When we were kids, it was all in fun. But in the last few years, I don't know, it changed somehow. He actually got aggressive over the smallest things. I guess I was really afraid he would try to seduce you away from me."

She tipped his chin up to make him look at her. "You have no reason to be jealous of Russ. Not only because he's your friend, but because I'm not the least bit attracted to him. Besides, as long as you make love to me like you did today, I'll never have any energy left for another man."

He gave her the smile she was going for. "If you keep looking at me like that, neither one of us is going to have enough energy left to go down to dinner."

He drew her head closer for a kiss, but she jumped off his lap before he could deliver it. "Oh, no, you don't. I refuse to arrive downstairs late or mindless. There's already been enough talk about me for my first visit."

On the way to the dining room, he assured her he would clear up any misunderstanding with his parents, though he was certain they hadn't taken the gossip seriously anyway. Only he was foolish enough to be upset by it.

"Ah, here they are now," Mrs. Hamilton announced from the foot of the stairs. "We were just about to go into the dining room without you."

Mr. Hamilton pulled back his jacket sleeve, checked the time, and gave Howard a warning look that punctuated his wife's statement.

Barbara was positive it was no more than a minute or two after eight, but apparently being late in this house was a hanging offense. She was about to apologize when Chesterfield announced the arrival of a visitor.

"Simon Decker."

A medium-built, late-middle-aged man with salt-and-pepper hair hurried toward the group. He looked hot and flustered as he bobbed his head to each of the family members. "Mr. and Mrs. Hamilton, Howard. Sorry I'm late. Crosstown traffic was murder. Had you called a little earlier—"

Mr. Hamilton loudly cleared his throat to cut off his guest's rambling. "Howard, present your guest so that we can go inside."

Barbara noted the flush on Howard's cheeks and squeezed his hand. He appeared to be more nervous than she was.

"Barbara, this is Simon Decker, my parents' attorney. His father was the Hamilton family retainer before him. Mr. Decker, it is my pleasure to present my future bride, Barbara Mancuso."

Decker's surprised gaze darted to each of Howard's parents before settling on Barbara. He slowly extended his hand to greet her as if he wasn't quite certain that was the proper thing to do. When she briefly touched her hand to his, his palm was damp.

"How do you do, Miss Mancuso. This is quite a surprise."

Mr. Hamilton made a show of looking at his watch and clearing his throat again.

"We can all get acquainted over dinner," Mrs. Hamilton declared with a bright smile, and smoothly took Barbara by the arm to lead her to the dining room ahead of the men.

As with brunch, dinner conversation was limited to impersonal, nonbusiness topics. Still unsure of herself, Barbara spoke only when directly addressed, and then kept her responses as brief and uncontroversial as possible. By the time coffee and dessert were served, Barbara had formed her character analyses for each person at the table.

Howard became the invisible man in his parents' presence.

Mr. Hamilton was stiffly formal, cold, egotistical, and probably ruthless in both his business and family affairs. She had the feeling that the only way he would have acknowledged her was if Howard had brought her home as part of a business deal.

Mrs. Hamilton seemed to care deeply for her husband and son, but her social position had equal importance. She was basically a good woman, yet spoiled by wealth and power and probably used it to get what she wanted in life.

Optimist that she was, Barbara had no doubt she could straighten them all out in time.

Simon Decker was as close to a bad stereotype as she had ever seen. He was blatantly ingratiating, and there was something untrustworthy about the way he kept his eyelids partially lowered all the time while he sneaked peeks at everyone in the room, particularly the one young female servant. Did he really believe no one else noticed what he was doing? Barbara couldn't help but wonder if he was a competent attorney or if the Hamiltons retained him because it had become a family tradition.

The moment Mr. Hamilton swallowed the last spoonful of his mocha mousse, he excused himself and Decker, saying only that they had business to discuss and didn't want to be disturbed.

"It was a pleasure to meet you, Miss Mancuso," the attorney said as he hurriedly left the table to follow his client. "Congratulations, Howard."

"How nice," Mrs. Hamilton said, sitting back in her chair and folding her hands on her lap. "Now the three of us can get down to business as well. It takes a lot of work to plan a big wedding, so we need to begin immediately."

Barbara gave Howard a second to speak up, but he just sat there, stirring his coffee, so she took the initiative. "Howard and I have discussed it, and we decided against a big wedding. I always imagined my wedding taking place in my parents' backyard and—" The look of horror on Mrs. Hamilton's face cut off the rest of what she would have said.

"That . . . that's simply not possible," the woman stammered in a higher-pitched voice than normal. "A wedding for someone of Howard's status requires certain . . . I mean, it would be expected . . . What *would* people say?" Her widened eyes took on a glazed appearance and her pale complexion suddenly turned a bright shade of pink.

Howard bolted out of his chair, knelt beside her, and grasped her hands. "Mother, please, don't be upset. It was just an idea we had to save you from having to work so hard. You already do much more than the doctor wants you to. But if

it's that important to you, we can be married however you want."

Barbara was shocked by Howard's instant capit-
ulation to his mother's wishes and dismissal of
hers. Her shock turned to resentment when she
noted how quickly the woman recuperated from
her "spell" once she had her way.

As if there were no question of the bride's ob-
jecting, Mrs. Hamilton asked, "Which would you
prefer, dear, May or June?"

Barbara narrowed her brows in confusion. "*May
or June?* You mean a year from now? Oh, but
Howard and I had planned—"

"Of course a year from now. It takes at least
that long to plan for an event of this magnitude,
and those *are* the only acceptable months for a
wedding."

Howard sat down beside Barbara again, but
when he reached for her hand, she pulled it away.
His mother continued to make pronouncements
about who "absolutely must be included in the
wedding party" and who should design the
dresses, but Barbara quit listening. It was either
that or explode. The pleading look Howard gave
her only made her angrier with him for being so
easily manipulated.

Before thinking it through, she said something
that she knew would upset both mother and son.
"I can see that it would be best to leave all the
plans in your hands, Mrs. Hamilton. You just tell
me when and where to show up, and I'll do my

best to be accommodating. For now, though, I wonder if you'd help us work something else out."

Howard looked worried, as he should have, but his mother was glowing. "But of course, dear," she said, clearly pleased. "I want you both to always feel comfortable coming to me for advice."

"That's so kind of you," Barbara said putting on her most grateful expression. "You see, once I saw how much artistic talent Howard had, I knew it would be a sin for him to throw it all away on a business career. I'm sure you agree that his idea for a cartoon series is absolutely brilliant and definitely worth a readjustment of his priorities."

Another rush of blood flowed to Mrs. Hamilton's face, immediately followed by some serious hyperventilating, but not a word came out of her mouth.

Howard's loyalties were clearly torn, but he made his choice. "Barbara! This was hardly the time— Calm down, Mother. *Please*. She didn't mean it the way it sounded."

Barbara clucked her tongue and got up from the table. "I'm going to my room, Howard. I'd like to speak with you alone, but I'll understand if you don't join me. After all, it's very difficult climbing stairs without a backbone."

Chapter 3

As Barbara stormed into her room, she was positive she was justified. By the time a half hour passed and Howard hadn't shown up, she was contemplating how to save a little face while she begged for another chance to prove that she wasn't an ill-mannered brat.

Because he didn't knock first, Howard caught her with tears streaking down her face.

"I'm sorry," they both said at once, then clung to each other while exchanging lengthier apologies. Howard confessed that he was so accustomed to catering to his mother's desires, he hadn't even realized what he was doing to Barbara. He promised it wouldn't happen again.

She admitted that she had behaved spitefully, and that she understood his mother's attitude about the wedding, but she wanted a say in the planning also. He agreed, but suggested they not push the issue on this visit.

"Shouldn't you go to your room now?" Barbara whispered, though it was the last thing she wanted him to do.

"Don't you want me to sleep with you?"

That made her laugh. "You know I do. But you said the servants would talk and—"

"I don't give a fuck about the servants."

"*Howard*! Such language! Your mother would have a seizure if she heard you."

"Fuck my mother, too."

She ran her hand down his abdomen. "No, thanks. I'll stick with the Hamilton I've already got."

Barbara's intention to improve the Hamiltons' opinion of her was thwarted by time and circumstances. Both parents had left for church before she and Howard went down to breakfast, and weren't expected back until midday.

She and Howard took advantage of the unexpected free time by visiting Russ. As soon as Russ realized how possessive Howard was about his bride-to-be, he went out of his way to torment him. No matter how funny Russ was, however, Barbara was careful not to give Howard anything to be jealous over. As it was, he kept his hands on her the entire time, which only gave Russ something else to tease him about.

Midday passed without Mr. and Mrs. Hamilton returning to the house, and soon the time came for Barbara to leave for the train station. She had promised her boss she would continue working for a few more weeks and he was counting on her to be there the next day. It was left to Howard to make amends for her with his parents, but after their talk last night, she was certain he would handle it just fine.

The next weekend, Howard came down to New York and treated her to a delightful stay at the Waldorf. He assured her he was making progress with his mother about the date and size of the wedding, but it was probably best to give her another week before they both confronted her.

This was hardly going the way Barbara had hoped, but she remained positive that the relationship with her future in-laws would settle into something they could all live with.

Howard returned to Cambridge that Sunday night and called her as usual when he got in. But he didn't call at the regular time on Monday or Tuesday, so she phoned his apartment and left a message on his answering machine. She was somewhat worried when she got home and he hadn't left a return message on her machine, but she didn't want to call and wake him at such a late hour.

By the time she had to leave for work on Thursday afternoon and still hadn't heard from him, she placed a call to his home in Boston. Chesterfield stiffly informed her that no one was available to speak to her, that he was unable to give her any further information, but that he would take her name and number ... as though she were a total stranger.

At two in the morning, she tried Howard's apartment again and left another message on his machine. Bewildered and on the verge of panic, she got Russ Latham's number from information and kept dialing it the next day until she reached him.

"I'm sorry to bother you, Russ, but I'm really worried about Howard. Have you seen or heard from him in the last few days?"

The acid in her stomach churned as several seconds passed before he spoke. "I . . . I heard he was up here Monday."

"You heard? You mean, like the servant grapevine?"

"Yeah."

"Russ, please help me. I don't know what's going on. He hasn't called, and Chesterfield wouldn't tell me anything. Has something happened to Howard?" She heard him sigh and held her own breath as she waited for him to speak again.

"Look, it's really not my place—"

"Dammit, Russ! Tell me what you know or I'm going to fly through this telephone line and choke it out of you!"

"Easy, babe. I just didn't want to pass on gossip that I'm not sure about. I heard the limo was loaded with luggage Tuesday morning, and Howard and his mother left together."

"Left? I don't understand. What could possibly be going on that he wouldn't let me know where he was?"

"I have no idea, but why don't you give me your number, and I'll call if I can find anything out for you."

The next day, she was debating whether to call him again when someone knocked at her door. Through the peephole she recognized the attorney, Simon Decker, and only her desperation to hear news of Howard made her invite the unlikable man into her apartment. It didn't compel her to be gracious, however.

"I won't take up much of your time, Miss Mancuso," he said in a bored tone as soon as he came in. "I believe this will explain everything." He took a sheet of paper out of his briefcase and handed it to her.

One glance told her it was an agreement of some kind. Howard had already signed it and there was a line for her signature below his. Her first thought was that it was a prenuptial agreement, which would have been annoying enough under the circumstances, but as she began to read the typed words, she realized it was much worse than that.

The brief document officially terminated the engagement to be married between Barbara Mancuso and Howard Hamilton IV and absolved them each from any and all promises made or implied. As recompense for her cooperation in this matter, she was to retain possession of all gifts, including the diamond ring.

She had never seen anything so insane in her life. Furious, she tore the paper in half, balled up the pieces, and threw them at the trash basket across the room. "You didn't actually expect me to sign that, did you? Where is he? Why hasn't he contacted me himself?"

"There wasn't time. It was necessary for him to escort his mother to a clinic in Switzerland for emergency treatment of her heart condition. I assumed you would recognize his signature, but I brought along some other documents he signed in the past, if you wish to make a comparison."

He pulled an envelope out of his briefcase and held it out to her. "Inside are copies of correspondence to his parents and credit card receipts which bear his signature. I also took the precaution of including another signed copy of the agreement just in case something should happen to the first one I showed you."

Barbara had the strongest urge to take the envelope and use it to slap the snide expression off his face, but she forced herself to behave in a civilized manner. "Get out, Mr. Decker. I will not believe the engagement is broken until I hear it from Howard directly."

Decker shook his head in disgust and set the envelope on the table. "I'll give you two weeks to think about it. Then you will either sign the agreement or legal action will be taken to repossess the items mentioned."

Barbara's only response was to slam the apartment door behind him. For some time she paced back and forth, venting her anger into the empty room. What colossal nerve! Who was responsible? Howard's father? His mother? Or both? Did Howard even know what they were up to?

She wanted badly to believe this was all a dirty trick to get rid of her. Howard could have been in an accident, lying in a coma in a hospital somewhere, unaware that his parents were taking advantage of his inability to defy them. Surely only unconsciousness would prevent him from calling her. His signature could have been forged.

She picked the crumpled paper up off the floor and smoothed out both halves on the table. It sure looked like Howard's signature. Was it possible that he actually, *willingly* agreed to this absurdity? Could he really be so spineless that his parents could have convinced him to go along with it in spite of everything they meant to each other?

An image of Howard crouched beside his "stricken" mother flashed into her mind. But then she erased it by recalling his promise not to allow the woman to manipulate him like that ever again.

Her eye latched on to the phrase in the agreement about his being absolved from any and all promises, and her doubts resurfaced. She made sure the torn agreement made it into the trash can this time and was about to do the same with the envelope, but something held her back. Without knowing why, she stuck it in a dresser drawer, where she wouldn't have to look at it, but could if she wanted to.

She managed to get to work, but nothing seemed real. The hours she and Howard had spent together kept replaying in her head. Sleep refused to come that night, or the next, or the next. She called the mansion twice and begged to speak to Mr. Hamilton, but was only referred to Simon Decker's office. She tried to reach Russ several times, but he was never in.

Three days after Decker's visit, she called him and promised to sign the agreement if he would give her a number in Switzerland where she could contact Howard. She just wanted a few minutes of his time, to hear him tell her in his own words that it was over. But Decker insisted there were no phones where Howard and Mrs. Hamilton were staying. She should sign the agreement and get on with her life.

The problem with that recommendation was that in the blink of an eye, a life with Howard had become the only life she wanted to get on with. None of the things that had been important up to a month ago made her feel the way he did. That's what true love was supposed to be like, and now that she had discovered it, "getting on with her life" without that love seemed impossible.

She had never experienced a severe heartbreak before and had no idea how to fight it. Each day she felt herself sinking lower and caring less about everything—her appearance, her apartment, her job all suffered from her indifference. She couldn't even scrape up the energy to go to the theater to work on the new set as she had promised she would. It simply didn't interest her anymore.

Depression and fatigue had clouded her mind

so thoroughly, she didn't immediately recognize Russ when he showed up at her door.

"You look like hell," he told her bluntly, then opened his arms to offer a hug if she needed one.

And, bóy, did she ever. Even the smell of cigarette smoke on his shirt somehow comforted her, as it took her back to the pleasant hours she and Howard had spent with him in his bungalow. Before she could stop herself, she was sobbing uncontrollably.

"It's okay, babe," Russ murmured soothingly. "Let it out. I understand." He held her and stroked her back until only a few sniffles were left. "I'll get you a tissue." He gently eased her down onto a chair and went to the bathroom. He was back in an instant with the whole box and, without discussing it, pulled her up from the chair long enough to seat himself, then brought her back down on his lap.

Though Russ was only trying to comfort her, all Barbara could think of was how she and Howard had sat cuddled in this same chair, and she burst into tears again. "I'm s-s-sorry. I c-c-can't help it."

He wiped her cheek with a tissue, then held it to her nose. "Blow. C'mon, take a big breath and blow your nose for Uncle Russ."

For the first time in a week, her mouth turned up at the corners. "*Uncle* Russ? Does my mother know about you?"

"You mean she never mentioned me? Hmmph.

I'll have to have a talk with her at the next family reunion."

Barbara took the tissue from him, blew her nose, then got another one to wipe her face. "Gawd, I needed that." She got off his lap and threw away the used tissues. "How did you—" Her unfinished question hung in the air as she caught sight of the colorful bruise surrounding his left eye. "Wow. What's the other guy look like?"

When he realized what she was talking about, his fingers carefully touched his cheekbone and he snorted. "It was even dumber than getting in a fight. I stepped on a rake and the handle flew up and practically knocked me out."

Barbara clucked her tongue and frowned sympathetically, but there was something odd in his voice and the way he examined his knuckles instead of looking at her that made her think he was lying about what had actually happened. Since it really wasn't her business, however, she went back to her earlier thought.

"How did you know where I lived?"

"I told you I'd see what I could find out for you. Apparently the Hamiltons' attorney, Simon Decker, heard I was asking questions, and he came to see me."

The mere mention of that man's name made Barbara's stomach queasy. She sat down on the bed to hear what Russ had come to tell her. "Go on. Whatever it is, I want to hear it. I'll be okay now."

He hesitated, then leaned forward with his elbows on his knees to deliver the final blow. "Howie signed that agreement Decker showed you. I didn't actually see him put his name on it, but from everything I found out, I have no doubt he signed it, then left the country with the queen mother. I also have no doubt he's feeling guilty as sin about it. But, hey, nobody in the world has a bigger guilt complex than old Howie. Mummy did one hell of a number on him."

By taking a slow breath, Barbara was able to hold down the nausea that had been plaguing her since the day Howard dropped out of her life. "How did she do it, Russ? What could she possibly have said to turn him against me?"

"From what I heard, it was the old man who did the convincing. And what he said was loud enough for several of the servants to hear. Stuff about responsibilities and duty and the importance of choosing a wife who would be a help rather than a ... what did he call you? ... a hindrance—someone more like Edith Hamilton. I understand he referred to you as— Never mind. You don't need to hear that."

"Yes, I do," she said in a flat tone. "I need to hear everything."

Russ grimaced, but went on. "He said you were suitable mistress material, and that Howard could keep you as a diversion as long as he wished, but under no circumstances would you be welcomed back into their home as if you were their equal. I gather the lecture took him most of the way, but a convenient heart attack on his mother's part pushed their precious prince back into his usual position as royal wimp. Apparently, Mrs. H. only pretended to make wedding plans to avoid an *unpleasant scene*.

He let that sink in for a moment while he went to sit beside her and patted her hand. "I'm really sorry, babe. I can't tell you how many fights we had over that kind of shit when we were kids, but he was always too big for me to beat any sense into him." He winced and touched his cheekbone again, as though referring to a beating made his bruise ache.

Having seen an exhibition of Howard's weakness with her own eyes, she couldn't help but believe what Russ was telling her. She felt the knife sink a little deeper in her heart. "You said Decker went to see you. Why?"

"Yeah. What an asshole. He heard about how you and I had hit it off—he winked when he said that—and told me I should come talk to you to convince you that you should forget Howard. He even offered to pay me my Christmas bonus early if I could and, I quote, redirect your attentions to me and get you to sign that agreement. He's the one who gave me your address. As soon as I could this morning, I borrowed Pop's truck and drove down here to talk to you in person."

"Well, whatever got you here, I am glad you came. I guess I knew the truth, deep down inside, but I needed someone else, someone I could trust, to say it out loud." She straightened her spine and took another deep cleansing breath. "I'll be okay. Maybe not today or tomorrow, but soon. Just out of curiosity, how did Decker figure you could convince me to sign the agreement?"

Russ laughed. "I asked him the same thing. He said he'd heard that women find me rather charming. He suggested I come here on the pretense of being sympathetic, then while I'm consoling you over your loss of Howard, I get into your pants. How am I doing so far?"

She rubbed her chin thoughtfully. "Hmmm. You did the sympathy and consoling parts very well. But I think you're going to look kind of silly in my pants. Most of them are nothing more than little scraps of lace and satin."

It took him a second to get her joke, but when he did, he rewarded her with a tight hug. "God, I wish I'd met you before Howard." He released her, stood up, and straightened the creases down the front of his jeans. "Okay, since I can't get into your pants, how about if we go see a movie or something?"

She pretended not to notice the bulge his actions failed to hide. "I'd like that very much." Just before they left, she did the one thing she'd been putting off for days. She removed the diamond ring from her finger and put it in her dresser drawer with Decker's envelope.

They went to a romantic comedy and followed it up with an Italian dinner, during which Russ did his best to keep a smile on Barbara's face. Unfortunately, one of his methods was to encourage her to drink more Chianti than she normally would. At first it gave her a good case of the giggles, but then it backfired. Depression set in before they left the restaurant, and she cried most of the way home. Then the minute they entered her apartment, she got horribly sick.

Claiming full responsibility for her condition, Russ stayed and took care of her most of the night, helping her in and out of the bathroom, placing cold compresses on her head, and assuring her that the walls weren't really moving. At some point she did fall asleep, only to awaken with a wretched headache and an excess of embarrassment.

As she dragged herself out of bed, she noted that Russ was asleep on the trundle bed normally hidden beneath hers. A sheet covered the lower part of his body, but his chest was bare. Glancing down at herself, she saw a cotton nightshirt with nothing underneath and was disturbed that she had no memory of changing her clothes.

She scolded herself for jumping to the worst conclusion possible after Russ had been so nice to her. Nothing sexual had happened. She would have remembered that, even if she couldn't explain how she got her nightshirt on.

She desperately needed aspirin and coffee, and though she tried to be quiet, she awakened Russ.

He sat up and stretched. "Hey, babe, how do you feel?"

"Like I fell out of an airplane onto my head.

What would you like first, the embarrassed apology or the vow of undying gratitude?"

"I'll settle for a cup of whatever you're having, but make it to go, okay? I promised Pop I'd have his truck back last night. I'm not sure how much help I'll be today, but I have to make an appearance."

"Now I feel even worse. At least promise that if you ever need somebody to keep you from drowning in a toilet bowl, you'll call me."

"I promise," he said, crossing his heart.

She turned her back as he stood up, but she was able to confirm that he had slept in his briefs.

Before he headed out, he gave her a brotherly hug and a kiss on the forehead. "Try to get some sleep today. You look even worse now than you did when I got here."

She did make an effort to rest, but she awoke with the dry heaves the next morning as well. She couldn't remember ever having a two-day hangover, but chalked it up to the previous week's lack of food and sleep.

Or perhaps it was something else. Something that would affect her a lot longer than a bad hangover.

With her mind totally occupied with Howard's vanishing act, she hadn't given any thought to her menstrual cycle. Her period was eleven days late, and it was never, ever late. But everyone knows stress causes all sorts of physical problems, and she had *definitely* been under a tremendous amount of stress lately.

It was probably too soon to worry about it. Once she let the thought in, however, it wouldn't go away. What would she do if she was pregnant? An abortion? Out of the question. Regardless of how she felt about the father, she believed abortion was a form of murder. She also couldn't imagine giving away a child she'd created.

So she would have the baby and keep it. Could she do that on her own? She rejected the idea of going home to her parents. Not only were they too old for her to dump her problems in their lap, it was a matter of pride. When she'd left home, she was so sure of herself, her talent, her success. It was bad enough to admit she'd failed, but to crawl home, broke and pregnant . . .

No! She would do this on her own, or she would die trying. Lots of women stay active throughout their pregnancy and go right back to work after they've delivered. She was young and healthy. She could do it if she had to.

But until she was certain, she decided to pray very hard that it wouldn't be necessary.

Her worry was temporarily put on hold shortly after she got home that night, when Russ reappeared with a large suitcase in his hand and a sheepish expression on his face. "I'm not drowning in a toilet bowl, but I could use a favor if you still feel you owe me one."

She opened the door wider and stood aside for him to enter, but he continued to stand in the hallway looking embarrassed. "What's the matter?"

"I got kicked off the estate. I was kind of hoping you'd let me camp out here for a few days ... just until I figure out what I'm going to do."

The idea of him staying in the one-room apartment for even a few days gave her a very uncomfortable feeling, but she couldn't think of a credible excuse to turn him down under the circumstances. "Of course," she replied with a forced smile. "Come on in."

Chapter 4

"Do you want to talk about it?"

Russ set his suitcase down and let out a frustrated groan. "I doubt if it would help. But I could sure use a hug if you've got one to spare."

How could she refuse to return the same comfort he'd given her when she had needed it so badly? As he stepped into her open arms, she could actually feel the tension in his body. He relaxed against her; then, all too quickly, she sensed a change in the way his hands were moving over her back. She was about to ease away when he made a very unmanly confession.

"I'm scared, babe. I have no idea what I'm going to do." He released her and turned away.

Her concern that he was looking for something more than sympathy from her was overridden by her natural inclination to answer a cry for help. She touched his arm to get him to face her again. "Why don't I make us some tea while you tell me what happened? It may not help, but it can't hurt."

Rather than sitting down, he stayed by her side

as she filled the kettle with water and got out two cups and tea bags. She found it a bit unnerving that he was barely giving her enough space to move, but she didn't want to say anything that might make him feel worse than he already did.

"I've lived on the estate my whole life," he said, more to himself than her. "Everyone always figured I'd take over Pop's position one of these days."

"Maybe they'll ask you to come back."

Russ snorted. "Not after everything I said to Mr. Hamilton." In a frighteningly swift mood change, he slammed his fist down on the counter so hard the cups rattled. "Damn, but that son-of-a-bitch had it coming. He never cared how many people he stepped on to get what he wanted. You wouldn't believe how many times I almost told him off, but I always managed to keep my mouth shut. But breaking up you and Howard the way he did—I thought that was the lowest. Then I heard him talking filthy about you with that creep lawyer of his, and, well, I guess I went a little nuts."

Barbara felt the queasiness in her stomach again. "Oh, Russ, please don't tell me you lost your job and your home because of me."

He ran his hand over her hair and grinned. "Don't worry about it, babe. With my temper, it was bound to happen sooner or later."

The teakettle whistled as she was about to question him further. When he reached around her to take it off the burner and their hands bumped, she said, "Why don't you go sit down and I'll bring you a cup?"

"That's okay. I'd rather help. I don't want you treating me like a guest while I'm here."

Despite her gentle hint, he remained close to her until the tea was brewed. She couldn't put her finger on it, but something about him seemed different. Or was it the change in her own circumstances that made the difference? When he sat down on the bed, she purposely chose the chair farthest from him to give herself some breathing room. He had only been staying with her for fifteen minutes, but she was already feeling crowded. Though she didn't want to be rude, she suddenly needed to know exactly how long he planned to stay. "So, what are your options?"

He shrugged and made a face. "Gardening is the only work I've ever done, and I sure can't expect to get a recommendation from Mr. Hamilton to go work for one of his rich friends." He pulled a cigarette out of the pack in his shirt pocket, then remembered his manners. "Do you mind?"

She remembered how long the smoke had lingered after his last visit and decided honesty would be better than choking to death. "Actually, I do," she said in an apologetic tone. "It's just that this is such a small apartment—"

"Hey, that's cool," he said, tucking the cigarette away. "I should cut down anyway."

"Good idea. Now to decide what you could do for work." Recalling the beautiful floral arrangements he had effortlessly put together for the mansion, she suggested, "You could open a flower shop."

A flash of interest showed in his eyes before he killed it. "I've only got two thousand dollars. It would take a lot more than that just to get started. Anyway, I don't know anything about running a business."

"Okay. But you could learn. How about if you went to work for a florist to learn the ropes, and in the meantime you'd keep saving up for your own shop?"

The interest came alive again. "Maybe I could even have a little street vendor business on the side . . . when the weather's good."

"Or you could move to a place with a warmer climate and do the street vendor thing year-round." She was thinking of Los Angeles or Miami, somewhere far from New York.

He shook his head. "Nah. I wouldn't want to move that far from Pop. He's getting up there, you know. But I think you've got me on the right track."

"Good," she said, and drank the last of her tea. "Now, since you don't want to be treated like a guest, I won't bother being polite. I'm beat, and you're sitting on my bed."

As he had the other night, he pulled the lower trundle mattress out, but didn't raise it to be level with hers. She would have preferred to disconnect the framework completely and put some space between them, but there was no place for it to be moved without rearranging the entire room. As exhausted as she'd been lately, the effort didn't seem worth it for just a few nights.

She expected to have trouble falling asleep with him so close. The moment her head touched the pillow, however, she was out and remained in a deep, dreamless sleep until her stomach performed its new wake-up ritual.

The worst of it was over, and she was splashing her face with cool water when Russ knocked on the bathroom door.

"Babe? Are you okay?"

"I'm fine," she lied. "I'll be out in a few minutes." Fighting her quivering muscles, she quickly brushed the foul taste out of her mouth and took a hot shower to wash away the cold sweat. By the time she opened the bathroom door, she was more or less back to normal, but Russ stepped in front of her so unexpectedly, she nearly dropped to her knees again.

His hands caught and supported her as she headed back to the bed. "You're not fine," he scolded. "What's the matter?"

"You just frightened me, that's all." Her words were contradicted by the way her body gave in to the need to lie down.

"Uh-uh. You can't lie to Uncle Russ. In case you've forgotten, I'm very familiar with the sound of you heaving up your guts in the toilet. But that wasn't from drinking too much Chianti, was it?"

She closed her eyes. If she could just rest for

a few minutes, she might make it through another day.

"*Barbara*. Answer me."

"It's probably the flu," she murmured. "There's a lot of it going around."

"Do you want me to call the restaurant for you and tell them you won't be in?"

The need to return to sleep was rapidly seducing her. "No, I'll be fine in an hour."

When she awoke again, her stomach was only slightly queasy . . . until she blinked the sleep out of her eyes and saw Russ sitting in a chair right next to her. He was staring at her so intently she wondered if she'd grown horns while she was asleep. "Why are you looking at me like that?" she asked as she got up and wrapped the robe more tightly around her.

"How do you feel?"

She felt his eyes following her to the kitchenette. "Fine."

"No kidding. I never heard of a one-hour flu bug," he said, coming up behind her. His hands closed over her shoulders and turned her to face him. "Is there something you'd like to tell me?"

She stepped away from him and opened the cupboard door. "What I'd like is a cup of tea and some toast without conversation. We'll get along much better when you realize I'm not very sociable when I first wake up."

He shrugged and went back to the chair he'd vacated, but his gaze remained glued to her while she prepared and ate her light breakfast.

"All right!" she finally said. "What do you want me to tell you?"

"Did Howard knock you up?"

Her objection to the way he phrased it made her want to defend Howard despite the fact that he didn't deserve her support. "I don't know." She sighed, realizing that the lie wasn't fooling either one of them. "Probably. I'm two weeks late and have every other symptom in the book, but I haven't been to a doctor."

"Not seeing a doctor won't make the baby disappear."

"Don't you think I know that?" she shot back at him in an exasperated voice. "I'm sorry. This isn't your problem."

He walked over and sat down at the kitchen table with her. "How can you think that?" He grasped her hand and squeezed it. "Howard is the best friend I ever had, and you're already more of a friend than he was. Did you turn me away yesterday when I came to you for help? Of course not. And I'm not going to turn away from you now. In fact this could work out great. We could help each other."

She tried to retrieve her hand, but he held fast. "That's very sweet of you, Russ, but I'd rather not rely on anyone else to get through this."

He frowned, but didn't argue the point. He gave her hand another squeeze, then let it go. "Sure, babe. I understand. Just know that I'm here if you do need someone."

Now that her fear had been spoken aloud, she

had no choice but to do something about it. On the recommendation of one of the waitresses she worked with, she called a woman obstetrician, Dr. Roselli, and was able to get an appointment the next afternoon.

About an hour before her shift ended that night, Russ showed up at the restaurant. "I went to see a movie," he explained, "and figured we could go home together."

Barbara was pleased to have the company, especially since he kept her laughing for most of the trip. She also decided it wasn't so bad having someone around the next day to help her get through the bout of sickness, and was actually relieved to have him accompany her to the doctor for moral support.

Dr. Roselli was the perfect obstetrician for Barbara. Her examination revealed that Barbara should have no problems with a natural delivery and that the baby was due in mid-February. There was only one problem. The doctor required payment of half of her standard fee by the next appointment and the balance by the end of the second trimester. Since Barbara had no health insurance, she either had to come up with the cash or go to a public clinic.

"How much do you need?" Russ asked before he left Barbara at the restaurant.

"Three thousand dollars, but it might as well be a million. I only have about seven hundred in the bank and it took me two years to save that much."

"Can you borrow it from someone? Your parents? Friends?"

Barbara didn't need to give that much thought. "No. I've decided not to tell my parents until after the baby is born. And most of my friends have less money than I do."

"You could probably get it from the Hamiltons."

Her eyes widened in panic. "You wouldn't tell them, would you? I'd rather die than have any of them find out."

"Even Howard?" Russ prodded.

"Especially Howard. If he didn't love me enough to choose me over his mother, I certainly don't want him to feel obligated to come to me because of a baby. Please, Russ, promise, no, *swear* on your life that you won't tell a soul about this. Heaven knows what twisted plans they'd have for my child. As much as I hate the idea of going to a clinic, I'll do that before I take one penny from the Hamiltons."

Russ gave her a hug and a kiss on the forehead. "You won't have to do either. I swear. Something will come up."

She was surprised to see him back at the restaurant a few hours later.

"I have something for you that just couldn't wait until you got home." He handed her a folded white piece of paper.

It took Barbara a moment to comprehend that it was a receipt from Dr. Roselli's office for fifteen hundred dollars.

"I need the other five hundred for an investment that should bring in the rest in plenty of time."

Instead of being overjoyed as he expected her to be, she was extremely annoyed with him. "*Russ!* That was all the money you had. I don't know when I'd ever be able to repay you. You've got to get your money back."

"Now, babe. I know you wanted to do this on your own, but you have a little one to consider. I'm going to help one way or the other, so you may as well stop being so stubborn about it. And you don't have to repay me; consider it my portion of the rent. Anyway, I owe you for giving me the idea about the florist. The owner of the third shop I went to this afternoon jumped at the idea of my operating a sidewalk franchise of his store. The money I have left should be plenty to get started, and in exchange for his help with the business end, I'll work for him for free a few hours each week."

"That's wonderful." She was elated that her suggestion had helped him, but his offhand remark that he had just prepaid his share of the rent for an indefinite number of months nullified her pleasure.

She was determined to get his money back and have a straightforward conversation with him about her preference to live alone, but another issue took precedence that night. Russ hung around for the remainder of her shift, exchanging jokes with the waitresses when they had a minute and talking at length about sports with her boss.

Barbara was repeatedly told what a great guy Russ was and how cute he was.

"You be nice to this boy, Barbara," her boss told her as they were leaving. "You make him wait too long and some other girl will steal him away!"

"What was that all about?" she asked Russ after they were outside. Russ winked at her. "Just laying the groundwork for your cover story."

"I beg your pardon?"

"In a few months everyone's going to know you're pregnant and wonder what happened to the father. I told them how I want to marry you, but you keep putting me off."

"You *what*? Why would you make up such a crazy story?" He looked so crushed, she regretted her choice of words, but it made no sense to her.

With much more force than necessary, he kicked a crushed can out of his way. "I only thought it would be easier on you if your friends thought the baby's father actually wanted to marry you."

She knew he didn't mean to be hurtful, but his words cut through her chest like a razor.

"I would, you know," he said quietly.

"Would, what?"

"Marry you." He stopped and took her hands in his. "If you'd have me, I'd be your husband and claim the baby as my own."

She was too stunned to respond. Apparently he misunderstood her silence, for he got down on one knee and made his offer more formally.

"Will you marry me, Barbara? Become Mrs.

Russell Latham, to have and to hold, till death do us part. If we did it right away, no one would ever need to know that the baby wasn't mine."

"My God, Russ," she whispered. "You're serious, aren't you?"

He stood up and kissed both her hands. "Completely."

"But we hardly know each other."

"How long did you and Howard know each other when you said yes to him?" His voice revealed more than a little jealousy.

"Obviously it wasn't long enough. I won't make that mistake twice."

He gave that a moment's consideration, then gave each of her hands another kiss. "Good enough. I'll accept that as a maybe for now. There's just one more thing."

Without further warning, he embraced her and pressed his lips to hers. This was no tender caress to seduce her into submission. This was a raw assault on her mouth, meant to conquer and dominate. When she moaned and tried to push him away, he held her tighter, slid one hand down to brace her backside, and pressed his lower body hard against hers.

"I didn't want you to misunderstand," he murmured in her ear. "My offer wasn't made because I feel sorry for you, or because I'm such a nice guy. I want you bad, babe. I have since the first day I saw you in the barn with Howard." He shifted his hips from side to side so that she couldn't be mistaken about the extent of his desire for her. "I've been in this condition almost constantly since then. But the timing hasn't exactly been right for me to show you how I feel."

Instead of his words and actions exciting her, she felt threatened, and it must have shown.

"Don't worry about it now, babe. I know you don't feel good and you've had a lot of shocks lately. Nothing will happen between us unless you tell me you're ready. Until then we're just friends."

She hadn't realized how hard her heart was pounding until he released her.

"Of course, I may have to take a lot of cold showers in the meantime."

He said that with such a comical expression, she was put at ease again. She had to give Russ credit for keeping her spirits up most of the time. Perhaps, after her heart completely healed from the damage Howard did, she might be able to care for Russ the way he was hoping she would. But at the moment, she just wasn't ready for another relationship.

His proposal made her even more determined to convince him to move out, but her body thwarted those plans. The next day, the nausea and vomiting didn't alleviate after an hour. Though she managed to drag herself to the restaurant, her reaction to the smell of food was so bad, she had to go home again.

When it didn't subside after another day, Dr. Roselli prescribed some medicine that controlled it most of the time, but made Barbara so sleepy she couldn't pull herself out of bed. The doctor assured her that she would feel better by the end of the twelfth week, but Barbara wasn't sure she would live that long.

Russ was a saint through it all—the sickness, the fatigue, the depression and crying jags. He went out to work for a while each day, but he was always back in time to coax her to eat something, take her vitamins, and make sure she bathed and brushed her teeth no matter how awful she felt. After a week of being nearly helpless, she gave up all pretenses of modesty, yet he continued to behave like the perfect gentleman, or more precisely, the perfect male nursemaid.

The only complaint she had—and it seemed too petty to voice—was the musty odor of cigarette smoke that now hung throughout the small apartment. Though he didn't smoke inside, his clothes and hair reeked of his bad habit, and it seemed to slide off him onto the furniture.

It was during one of Russ's brief absences that Simon Decker called Barbara and informed her that the two-week grace period had passed. He would be at her apartment the following day to pick up either the signed agreement or the gifts, particularly the jewelry.

"I suppose I should just give him everything," she told Russ when he returned. "But I have the feeling that what they're trying to do isn't even legal, and that bugs the hell out of me."

"But you haven't got the money or the energy to fight them. Would you mind if I looked at the agreement?"

Thinking that an unbiased opinion could help, she got the envelope out of the drawer and handed it to him. As he pulled the papers out the ring fell to the floor.

"Jesus Christ," he muttered, and picked the diamond up to look at it more closely. "I wonder what this thing is worth?"

Barbara shrugged. "I never asked. After I saw how much he paid for a pair of simple gold earrings, I didn't want to know the cost of anything else he bought me."

"Do you still have it all?" he asked as his eyes scanned the agreement.

"Of course. It's mainly clothes and jewelry, and the VCR, but there were a few other things that don't have any real value to anyone but me." Like the autographed cartoons, she thought. She would keep those for her child.

"Show me. Show me everything he ever gave you. I might have an idea."

She couldn't imagine what he had in mind, but she had no objection to giving him a quick tour of her newest possessions. He encouraged her to talk about the circumstances surrounding the various gifts, and she discovered that it was somewhat cathartic to be able to talk to someone about those times.

"I think you should sign the agreement," he said after she finished.

She frowned at him. "Why?"

"You said you don't want the Hamiltons' help or interference. Well, reread that sentence." He pointed at the line he was referring to: *Barbara Mancuso and Howard Hamilton IV shall be henceforth absolved from any and all promises made or implied to one or the other.* "I don't know a lot about legal stuff or business, but if I'm reading this right, it works both ways. You would have no claim on Howard, but he would have no claim on you, either, which would also mean the baby growing inside you."

She combed her fingers through her hair as she considered his interpretation of the legal words. "I'm not so sure. That might be stretching it a bit, but it could give me some power if it ever came down to a battle."

"Besides that," he continued, "I've been thinking. It isn't right that your child should suffer because his father's an asshole. What if you can't go back to work right away? I mean, I wouldn't mind supporting you both . . . if I could. But there's no telling how long it'll take me to get on my feet. And then there's still the rest of the doctor's bill and the hospital, and let's not forget rent, utilities—"

"Okay! I get the point. I need money. Dr. Roselli said I should be feeling better in a few more weeks, then I can get back to work—"

"And what if you can't? Some women *can't* do it all, you know."

She wanted to argue that statement, but her stomach chose that moment to rebel again, and she rushed to the bathroom.

"See what I mean?" Russ said, following close

behind. "You need to consider the worst possible situation." He automatically made a cool compress for her forehead and poured her a cup of water with mouthwash to rinse with. "What I'm getting at is this: You sign the agreement and demand receipts for everything. That way, whenever you need money you can sell something."

The fact that he could continue to carry on an important discussion on top of her gagging said a lot for their peculiar relationship. By the time she was relatively composed again, he had convinced her that she should sign the agreement.

"By the way," he said once that was decided, "I stopped by the restaurant today. Everybody asked about you."

"Oh, *gawd*. I really need to call in again."

"No, you don't. I told your boss the truth, and he understands. He said to tell you he's got to hire another girl, but whenever you're ready to get back to work, he'll try to find room for you."

Barbara couldn't believe her ears. She didn't know which angered her more, his taking on another responsibility that she hadn't asked him to, or that her illegitimate pregnancy was no longer a secret. "You told *my* boss that I'm pregnant and too sick to return to work? How could you do that? I've worked for him for almost two years. It was up to me to tell him what my problem was, not you!"

Her angry tone caused him to respond in kind. "Oh, yeah? And just when were you going to tell him? While you were vomiting or sleeping?" With each word he closed in on her until he was shouting in her face. "I was only trying to take care of something that was long overdue and save you some embarrassment. But could you just say 'Thank you, Russ,' and shut your mouth? No way! Not the high and mighty 'I can do it all myself' bitch goddess! If you weren't so busy feeling sorry for yourself, you might have noticed that you haven't done one goddamned thing by yourself lately. Well, I'll tell you what you can do now. You can go fuck yourself."

He raised his fist as if to strike her, then abruptly turned and strode out the door.

For several seconds, Barbara simply stood there, staring at the open door in utter confusion. Had she been wrong to be upset? Would he come back? Did she want him to?

Yes. No. Maybe. It was all mixed up in her head. She didn't want to need him, yet she did. She had clearly come to rely on him, even though she'd never asked for his help.

Between being sick and the argument, she barely had the strength to walk to the door and close it. What she needed was a short nap; then she could think about it more clearly when she awoke. Before lying down, she took one of the pills the doctor had prescribed to settle her stomach. As her eyes drifted shut, she tried to remember when she had last thanked Russ for his kindness. In her determination to do it alone, had she failed to be the least bit appreciative, as he had accused? She would also think about that . . . after her nap.

She felt something touch her cheek and heard her name being whispered, but it wasn't enough to make her want to surface from the murky darkness.

"Barbara. I'm sorry."

She felt her body being shifted to make room for his alongside her. Howard was such a big man. They really needed to get a larger bed. She sighed and nestled into him as his hands stroked her back. He was sorry. Everything was going to be just fine again.

"I shouldn't have gotten angry. It's just that I've been trying so hard to be the man you want me to be and not push you into anything before you're ready."

That wasn't Howard's voice. Nor was it a dream. The smell of cigarette smoke drifted into her nostrils and she forced herself to concentrate on waking up.

"I can't keep pretending. I can't keep lying here beside you without touching you night after night. It's making me nuts. All I think about is fucking you and sucking on your tits. They're so much bigger than they used to be."

Through her cotton nightgown, Barbara felt his hand molding her breast as his mouth closed over the peak, and she found the energy to open her eyes. "Oh, Russ. No. I don't—" A spear of pleasure shot through her, stealing away her breath and her words.

"Don't say no. Say yes. You need this as much as I do." His fingers ran down her abdomen and cupped the soft flesh between her thighs while his mouth captured hers in a searing kiss.

Her body responded before her mind could form an argument. He was right. She may not want Russ the way he wanted her, but she did need this—the fundamental proof that she was still a desirable woman. She suddenly, desperately needed to lose herself in physical pleasure, to be assured that she could still feel something good.

Without waiting for her verbal answer, Russ pushed up her nightgown and pulled her panties off. Only then did she realize he had come to her bed already undressed and fully aroused. A second later his teeth clamped down on one of her nipples and he sucked her into his mouth so hard she gasped.

"*Ouch!* Remember, I'm tender."

He released her breast only to assault an even more sensitive area with the same aggressive manner.

"Please, slow down," she complained. "You're hurting me."

Drawing himself up, he practically growled at her. "I can't slow down. You made me wait too long." And with barely a pause, he pushed her thighs apart and rammed his penis into her body.

Thankfully, it only took him a matter of seconds to finish and roll off.

"Oh, babe, I knew it was going to be great between us. Next time, though, we'll get you started before me. That way you'll want it as hard and fast as I like it."

Barbara was stunned. It was incredible to her that the man who had given her such gentle care while she was sick could be so thoughtless when it came to lovemaking. *Next time?* She shouldn't have given in once, let alone repeat the animalistic act again.

As she got up to go to the bathroom, she saw the satisfied smile on his face as he lay sprawled on her bed. He actually thought what had just happened between them was great! She cleaned herself up and bolstered her courage in preparation for the talk they needed to have. She appreciated his help, but she was not willing to thank him with physical favors. He had caught her at a weak moment. Had she been thinking clearly, it wouldn't have happened. The best thing for both of them would be for him to move out as soon as possible.

Her firm resolve disintegrated when she returned to the main room and heard him peacefully snoring. He had been pushing himself so hard lately, trying to get his business started and taking care of her around the clock. He certainly deserved one good night's sleep before she rejected him again.

Damn! She was so confused. She knew she hadn't requested his help and shouldn't feel obligated because of it. Yet she had allowed it to go on. Every time she thought of ordering him to leave, she felt guilty because she knew how hurt he was going to be.

The more she thought about it, she even became confused about what had happened that night. She could have said no, up front, but she didn't. Was it his fault that he wasn't able to make her feel the way Howard had? She thought of Russ's words: *hard and fast*. With Howard, hard and fast had been exactly how she had wanted him. It was always perfect with him.

She wiped away the tears that instantly built up when she thought of Howard. Surely this grieving would stop someday, but obviously that time hadn't come yet. With a sigh of resignation, she took another pill and put on a clean nightshirt and underpants.

Not wanting to disturb Russ, she pulled out the lower mattress for herself. The effort strained her lower back a little, but she figured it was from lack of exercise.

The next morning she knew differently. Her lower abdomen was cramping as if she were having a very bad period, and when she went to the bathroom, there was a dark stain on her underwear.

As always, Russ was hovering close enough to hear her groan. The next instant he was at her side. "What's the matter?" He saw the blood before she could answer and rushed to the phone. Within minutes, he'd arranged for Dr. Roselli to meet them at the hospital emergency room, had called for a taxi, and was helping Barbara dress.

"I can't afford a taxi *or* the emergency room," she protested, but he wouldn't discuss it, and Barbara didn't have the fortitude to fight with him.

Once again, it was simply easier to let Russ take care of everything.

Chapter 5

Dr. Roselli's orders were quite explicit. Since Barbara could not afford to stay in the hospital for observation, she was to take a cab home and go directly to bed. She was not even to get up to go to the bathroom for the next forty-eight hours. After that, she could be on her feet a few minutes each day, but otherwise, was to remain in bed for at least four weeks. The only exception was for her doctor's appointments. Sex was absolutely forbidden. She was given a shot, a supply of pills, a bedpan, and the warning that if she did not do as she was told, she would be risking a miscarriage.

All the way home, Barbara thought about that warning. Had she miscarried naturally, it could have solved a lot of problems. But if she purposely ignored the doctor's instructions and lost the baby, in her mind that would be the same as getting an abortion.

Russ held her hand and repeatedly told her not to worry. He would take the very best care of her.

She reconsidered her only alternative: going home to her parents. Now that she was practically an invalid, it was more unthinkable than it was in the beginning. She rationalized that she had a way of paying Russ back for his help. If she sold the jewelry Howard had given her, the money could support both Russ and her and help him get his new business started. And since the doctor had warned them not to engage in intercourse or any other strenuous sexual activities, she no longer had to deal with that problem.

When they arrived home, Russ insisted on carrying her up the stairs. Since she had already decided to heed the doctor's warning, she didn't bother to dissuade him.

"Have you ever considered making a career out of being an angel of mercy?" she asked as he lifted her off the ground. "You have a real knack for it."

He grinned and winked at her. "I just like having *you* at my mercy." Briefly tightening his hold on her, he made a growling sound and pretended to bite her neck.

"Miss Mancuso!" a man's voice called from a short distance down the sidewalk.

Russ turned and Barbara recognized Simon Decker hurrying toward them, ever-present briefcase in hand. In the midst of everything else that had happened, she had forgotten that he was coming that afternoon. "Put me down," she whispered to Russ. "I don't want him to know anything's wrong."

"No. You are not climbing those stairs. I'll cover for you."

Decker was slightly out of breath by the time

he reached them. "You weren't here when I arrived, so I thought I'd take a walk. Hello, Russ. I didn't expect to see you today. I was sorry to hear about the, uh, confrontation you had with Mr. Hamilton." His gaze narrowed as he took in the couple's intimate embrace. "But I see that you're not suffering overmuch."

Russ laughed. "She promised to play Scarlett for me if I showed her my Rhett Butler imitation." Decker either didn't get it or didn't want to.

"Could we go inside?" he said impatiently. "It's rather warm out here."

Russ led the way into the apartment, then set Barbara down on the bed with a kiss on the forehead and a look that warned her to stay put.

Decker eyed the unmade bed and the clothes strewn about the room, and loudly cleared his throat. "If we could get to the business at hand, the two of you could get on with your, uh, performance."

His obvious insinuation brought a blush to Barbara's cheeks, but denying what he assumed was going on required an explanation that she wasn't prepared to give. "I've decided to sign the agreement, after I receive bills of sale for the gifts."

"I assumed that would be your decision and prepared this in advance." He pulled a sheaf of papers out of his briefcase. "Howard provided us with an inventory of the items concerned, and I have managed to obtain receipts for everything except those things purchased from street vendors. I believe you'll find it in order."

Barbara's hand trembled as she took the papers from him and read over the typed words. It was so cold, an unemotional list of *things*. How could Howard have done this? Each of his presents had held a special meaning to her. They continued to bring back warm memories that his abandonment had failed to chill. Yet, no one but Howard could have compiled this list. Only one thing was missing—the set of cartoons. Then again, he probably never put any value on them to begin with.

Up until that moment, she had accepted the fact that Howard had been manipulated into leaving her, but she had kept herself sane by believing that, wherever he was, he still loved her. As she reviewed the inventory, her last spark of hope burned out. "Russ, will you get me the agreement, please?"

Seconds later, she had signed, Russ had witnessed, and Decker departed before she could change her mind.

During the course of her month of confinement, she slowly began to feel a little better, and as the nausea and cramping decreased, her boredom increased. Russ took on the additional responsibility of personally keeping her entertained when he was home, which was most of the time, and provided her with a variety of paperback books to read when he had to go out. He was so constant in his attentions to her that she occasionally suggested that he not hurry back. Though she truly appreciated his help, there were times when she thought she'd scream if she didn't soon get a day all to herself.

With her consent, he had taken a few pieces of jewelry back to Tiffany's and received sufficient cash to reimburse himself, pay off the doctor, set aside money for the hospital bill, and cover their living expenses for the next few months. For the moment, she gave up the idea of independence, but as soon as she was on her feet, she intended to sell the engagement ring and give Russ enough money to set out on his own.

Though she was aware that he was hoping for something more personal, she was certain he would start looking at other women again when her pregnancy mutated her into a blimp.

At first an acquaintance from the restaurant or theater would call to say hello, but that stopped very quickly. She supposed their lives were too busy to give much time to her, and she didn't want to impose. Other than Russ, her parents were the only contacts she had outside of the apartment. She made a point of keeping those conversations brief and vague, rather than tell a lot of lies she'd have to apologize for later.

She had told her parents about Howard's entrance and exit and they were concerned about her suffering from a broken heart, until she had Russ say hello to them one day and implied that she had a new man in her life. She kept promising to come home soon.

Toward the end of her stay in bed, an unexpected call broke their routine.

As he usually did, Russ answered the phone. "May I ask who's calling?" Placing his hand over the mouthpiece, he whispered to Barbara. "Some guy wants to talk to you. Says he's *Mister* Teasdale."

Barbara brightened instantly. She couldn't have been more surprised or delighted. She held out her hand for Russ to give her the phone, but he held on to it.

"Who is he?" he asked in a low voice.

She didn't care for the suspicious look on his face, or the fact that he was keeping the phone out of her reach, but she figured it would be faster to simply answer his question. "That's Dusty. The boy I grew up with. I told you about him." He reluctantly handed her the phone, then sat down in the chair across from her.

"Hi, sweetie! I've been thinking of calling you for weeks, but I was afraid you were up to your ears in finals."

"All finished. I'm home now." He paused for an audible breath. "It sure is good to hear your voice, Bobbi. The truth is, I'm calling because your mom told me what's been going on in your life. She said you probably weren't coming home to visit for a while."

She'd forgotten all about her promise to spend time with Dusty while he was on vacation. "I'm sorry. I was really looking forward to seeing you, but it's just impossible right now. See, there's this, um, audition coming up that I have a really good shot at. It could be the break I've been waiting for. I'd have you come here, but between that and work and school . . ."

"Sure, I understand. Maybe later this summer something will open up. I guess that means your two-year plan has been amended."

She made herself laugh as if it were no big deal. "Hey, even the Constitution has amendments. So tell me, did you ace all your finals or what?"

While Dusty filled her in, she had to work at ignoring Russ. He just sat there, scowling at her as if she'd committed some terrible offense. The instant she said good-bye, Russ grabbed the phone from her and slammed it into its cradle.

"What is your problem?" she asked incredulously.

"*My* problem?" he shouted. His hands balled into fists as he loomed over her. "The only problem I've got here is *you*." He turned and marched over to the kitchenette. One after another he opened and slammed cupboard doors.

"What are you looking for?"

"Something to drink. There's not one god-damned thing a man can drink in this fucking place."

"Russ, I've asked you not to use that language—"

"Fuck you, Miss Bitch. I'll use any goddamned language I want to." His glare challenged her to reprimand him again. "I'm going out."

She flinched as the front door slammed behind

him. Russ had shown her small glimpses of his bad temper before. This time, however, he had seemed truly enraged, and she hadn't the slightest idea what had set him off.

He had been relaxed and pleasant during dinner. The abrupt mood swing seemed to hit him while she was talking to Dusty. Had she said something that upset him? She replayed her end of the conversation in her mind and was positive she hadn't mentioned Russ at all.

Was that it? Could he be angry because she didn't tell Dusty about him? That line of thinking took her straight to the only possible answer. Russ was jealous.

Though she'd been careful not to lead him on, she knew he was still hoping she'd have a change of heart. Perhaps he really was in love with her and doing his best to hide it.

There were times when she wished she could fall in love with him. It would certainly solve all her problems. But that deep, intense feeling was absent, and she wasn't certain she ever wanted to feel that way again. She never wanted to give another man the kind of power over her that she had so freely given to Howard. It wasn't worth the pain.

Recalling what had happened the last time he'd yelled at her and stormed out, she wanted to stay awake until he was back and calmed down. But after three hours crept by and he hadn't returned, she switched off the light.

She had barely drifted off when she heard a key

being turned in the lock. The night-light in the bathroom allowed her to see Russ's clumsy entrance without his knowing she was awake. She could also see him take a long swallow out of a bottle before he placed it on the table. As he headed toward the bathroom, he bumped into the end table and almost knocked over the lamp.

Catching it, he whispered. "Sh-sh-sh. You'll wake Sleeping Beauty."

He was obviously too drunk for her to question his temper tantrum tonight. While he was in the bathroom, she turned on her side, facing the wall, and determined to feign sleep and avoid dealing with him entirely.

A few minutes later she heard him open the door. Even without the stench of cigarette smoke and whiskey, he was breathing heavily enough for her to know when he was standing next to her, and she prayed he would just pull out his bed and go right to sleep. As seconds ticked by and he didn't move, she wondered what he was doing, but if she turned to see, he might realize she was awake.

Because she was already tense, she managed not to react when he stroked her back. But when his hand covered her breast and kneaded it, she gave a sleepy groan and turned onto her stomach.

"Tha's right," he mumbled. "Look, but don't touch. But ol' Howie touched you, didn't he, *sweetie*? Girls always wanted Howie. You know what the funny part is? He didn't want any of that free pussy, so guess who he'd pass 'em on to?" He hiccoughed and laughed aloud. "Poor little Russ, the gardener's boy, finally got one Howie *did* want and couldn't keep. So what if I can't fuck her? I got her. An' there's always my friend Mary. Hello, Mary. Say hi to Peter."

Barbara had heard of people who hallucinated when they drank too much and assumed that's what was happening to Russ. She realized her mistake moments later as she heard his breathing become more labored along with another sound that had a steady, recognizable rhythm.

Not seeing him didn't make it all right. She wanted to cover her ears to shut out what he was doing, but then he'd know she was awake. She couldn't help but wonder how many other times he'd watched her and done this while she slept. Suddenly the beat quickened, he groaned, and something wet hit her bare arm. Russ let out a relieved sigh and laughed again.

She heard him pull out his bed and collapse onto it, but she waited several long minutes more, until he began snoring, before she wiped his leavings from her arm. She was both embarrassed and repulsed by his act, but it was his words that started her stomach churning. Was he infatuated with her only because Howard had wanted to marry her? It seemed unlikely that any man would turn himself into a nursemaid for a woman for such a flimsy reason. Surely he would have to have deep, personal feelings for her. His jealousy seemed to confirm those feelings.

And yet, there was something about the way he

had spoken of her, as though she were his possession, that made her terribly uncomfortable.

The next day, Russ was nursing himself for a change, and she understood well enough to leave him alone. The day after that was her doctor's appointment, and he was being so solicitous that she thought it would have been horrid of her to start picking at him over something that was already two days old. As to what happened after he'd come home . . . well, he was drunk, and it was best forgotten.

Dr. Roselli gave Barbara permission to be a little more active, but warned her that she wasn't completely in the clear. She should continue to get plenty of rest. Working at a job where she stood on her feet, strenuous physical activity, and intercourse were still out.

Exactly as Dr. Roselli had predicted, after Barbara passed the twelfth week of her pregnancy, she regained her strength and high energy level. Her weight was finally on target and the fog that had clouded her brain for the last three months miraculously lifted.

Although Russ hadn't displayed any more temper tantrums or tried to push their relationship beyond companionship, Barbara knew the time had come for them to go their separate ways. She was guilty of taking advantage of his attraction to her. He was guilty of taking advantage of her physical weakness. In reality they were doing each other more harm than good.

There were no alternatives. She had to sell the

ring and get it over with. Russ had told her how simple it had been to return the smaller pieces to Tiffany's. Of course, the Hamilton name on the receipt helped a lot.

Rather than give him warning of what was coming, she waited for him to leave for the florist shop before taking her first steps toward independence. Her confidence was shaken, however, when she opened her jewelry box and discovered that the diamond was the only valuable piece inside. She had thought there were a number of items left, such as the blue topaz earrings. Had Russ returned those and she'd forgotten?

She pulled out the envelope where she'd left all the receipts from Decker. The agreement and inventory list was there as well as the VCR and clothing receipts, but the only Tiffany's receipt left was for the ring. Her brain had been fuzzy for so long, she could have forgotten, yet she clearly recalled when Russ had taken other pieces.

There was one way to double-check. After Russ returned the jewelry, he'd deposited the money in her checking account for her. She remembered his telling her that he'd put the deposit slips in her accounting box with her other financial records. However, after going through every piece of paper in the box, she hadn't found evidence of any recent deposit.

To make things easier on her, he had been writing out the checks for the various bills. All she had to do was sign her name a few times and her financial responsibilities had been taken care of.

According to the check stubs, she had paid out thousands of dollars, so the money must have been there, even though no deposits were recorded and no running balance had been kept.

She also thought he told her he'd balanced her account a few weeks ago when the bank statement had arrived, yet there was no bank statement in the box. It wasn't that she distrusted Russ. He was a saint. The deposit slips and statement were probably in another drawer somewhere. But a quick search of the apartment didn't uncover them, and she didn't want to waste any more of her free time.

The manager of Tiffany's was courteous and seemed sympathetic to Barbara's plight, but they would only refund seventy-five percent of the original cost of the ring: $45,000. She had known it had been expensive, but had never imagined an amount that high. The discounted refund was more than acceptable.

Her next stop was the bank, where she deposited the Tiffany's check and met with a bookkeeper to review her account. She was shocked to hear that her current balance was under a hundred dollars rather than the three thousand something Russ had told her she had after he'd balanced her account. There was only one moderate deposit, made last month, and that had been expended.

She was relieved to see that the checks she'd signed had all cleared, but that didn't explain where the rest of the money from the returned jewelry had gone. She was no longer positive Russ was such a saint.

He was pacing the apartment when she returned late in the day.

"Where have you been?" he demanded. "I've been worried sick!"

"I went out for a while. I'm allowed now, remember?" She calmly set down her purse and went to the refrigerator for some orange juice.

"You could have at least left a note! Don't you have any idea what I've been going through for the last two hours? I called the hospital thinking you had another emergency and I wasn't here to help!"

Guilt pierced the protective shell she'd built around herself on the way home. No matter what he may have done with her money, she knew his concern for her was genuine. "Geez, I'm really sorry. I didn't expect to be gone longer than you. It was very inconsiderate of me."

Her apology placated him enough to lower his voice. "How do you feel?"

She walked over to her favorite chair and curled up in it. "Tired. The doctor was right about overdoing it too soon, but I'm okay."

Russ sat down on the bed and studied her face. "But something's wrong. What? Where did you go for so long?"

"I re-registered at school. I'm going to take computer, typing, and bookkeeping this term."

His shoulders relaxed and he took a breath. "Are you sure you can handle that much?"

"What's to handle? I just have to sit and use my hands and eyes. Since I can afford not to work for a few months, I want to make the most of my time before the baby comes. Anyway, I purposely picked three courses that run together on Monday, Wednesday, and Friday, so that I'd still have four whole days to rest. Classes start next week."

Russ nodded, but his expression remained skeptical. "I guess it was real crowded at registration, huh?"

"Not really. I had two other stops to make." She said it as casually as possible.

"Oh?"

"I returned the ring. Then I went to the bank." She watched his eyes narrow and had the feeling she should take great care with her next words. "There seems to be a discrepancy. I know I've been out of it lately, but I thought you said I had about three thousand dollars."

Russ ran his hands through his hair and bowed his head. "I should have known you'd find out before I could explain. I only meant to borrow it." When he met her gaze again, his eyes were moist. "I was sure I'd be able to pay you back before you found out."

A tear slipped out of the corner of his eye and Barbara's heart wrenched. She went over to him, wiped the tear away, and took his hand. "I knew there had to be an explanation. Tell me what happened."

"I feel like such a stupid ass. I thought I could take a few shortcuts, you know, get rich quick.

I'm too embarrassed to even tell you about it. I lost all the money. There's nothing left and I didn't know how to tell you."

He was guilty, but clearly remorseful. "So you sold the other pieces, too?"

He looked away. "Yes. If you want to call the police, I won't stop you."

"The police? Good God, Russ, I can't have you arrested. What you did was wrong, but you're not a criminal. With everything you've done for me, you've proven what a good man you are. But this brings me to what else we have to talk about."

She rose, got her purse, and sat down next to him. Russ watched her take out her checkbook and write a check for five thousand dollars, payable to him. "This is my way of saying thank you for getting me through these last two months. I couldn't have done it without you. This should be enough to get your own place and start over with your career plans."

He frowned at the check in her hand. "I don't understand. What do you mean, get my own place?"

She took a slow breath, knowing this was going to be the hardest part. "Russ, I know you were hoping something more . . . personal was going to happen between us. I care for you, but as a friend. I wish I felt differently, but—"

"You haven't even given me a chance. You've been sick and depressed. Nobody could fall in love while they feel like that. But you'll see, it'll be different now that you're feeling better."

She was about to contradict him, but he grasped her shoulders and looked as though he might start crying again. "Barbara, please. I've shown you what a good friend I can be. You owe me the chance to show you what a good husband I could be. I swear I won't push you into anything you're not ready for.

"Just let me stay with you until after the baby's born. After everything we've been through together, I couldn't care more about this child if it were my own. I don't want anything to happen to you or the baby now. You need someone in the delivery room with you. Let it be me. *Please*. If you still don't want to marry me by then, I'll walk away without another word. In the meantime, I'll work twice as hard and ten times smarter, so I can pay you back every penny I took."

Her plan had seemed much stronger when he hadn't been able to present his arguments. She wanted her privacy back, but she also acknowledged the fact that she might need someone in the coming months. She reasoned that with her classes and him working more, they wouldn't have to spend so much time together in the cramped apartment. That could make a big difference. Perhaps she did owe him another chance. "All right. You can stay. But I can't make any promises."

His face relaxed into a smile; then he gave her a soft kiss on the mouth and tore up the check. "You won't be sorry."

*   *   *

Barbara recalled those words again and again in the months that followed. He'd been wrong. She was sorrier than she'd thought possible and trapped by her own reasoning.

For three months, she held to her agreement to give him a chance. He was helpful. He was romantic. He was entertaining. He was contributing for his share of the expenses.

And he was driving her crazy.

He got a night job so that they would only be separated while she was sleeping. He registered for the same classes she did so he could learn some business skills and study with her. If she needed to go to the store, he went with her, for assistance and protection. She had no idea when he slept, if he did at all.

He never forced himself on her, but he touched her constantly. His kisses and hugs were undemanding, but there was no mistaking the fact that he was only waiting for her to give the slightest encouragement.

By the time she approached the seventh-month mark, she knew her feelings toward him were lessening rather than growing as he'd hoped, yet she didn't want to hurt him, either. How could he be expected to understand that his worst fault was the constant, devoted attention he showered on her? It might have given her great pleasure if she'd been wildly in love with him, but as it was, it was driving her **up** the wall.

"This isn't working, Russ," she finally said one night before he left for work. "I swear to God,

I've tried to make it work, but I need some time to myself. We can still see each other occasionally, as friends, but I think it would be best if you moved out."

He promised to give her more space, to stop making even the slightest advance, be whatever she wanted him to be. He pleaded. He cried. Christmas was only three weeks away.

And in the end, she gave in again, rationalizing that she'd probably be glad to have his help now that her body had begun the final, unwieldy stage of pregnancy.

On the first day of the new year, her reasoning was proven faulty again.

They were watching the six o'clock news as they usually did during dinner when a picture of Howard appeared behind the commentator's head.

"Some sad news this evening," he said with an appropriately sincere expression. "Howard Hamilton the IV, sole heir to the Hamilton-Greene fortune, died today from injuries sustained in a car accident early this morning. . . ."

Barbara didn't hear another word. Her fork dropped onto her plate as she stared at the television screen. There was Howard, playing polo astride D'Artagnan, laughing and chatting with celebrities. There were glimpses of his parents trying to evade reporters, and Simon Decker giving a statement.

"Stop that!" Russ ordered.

She shut out his words as well. *Howard, dead? That was impossible. If he had died, she would have felt it. Somehow she would have known and felt his pain.*

"I said stop crying! He was a bastard! He deserted you. He isn't worth your tears."

If Howard is dead, he'll never realize what a mistake he made. He'll never find out he has a child.

Russ slapped her across the face, but she barely felt it.

"Snap out of it, you lousy two-faced cunt!"

He hit her again, and the metallic taste of blood in her mouth jolted her back to reality.

"You're still in love with him, aren't you? All this time, pretending to care about me, leading me on. You were only using me until he came back!"

Barbara pushed herself up from the chair and tried to back away, but the kitchen counter was behind her. "Russ, please. You're wrong. Don't—" The back of his hand crashed into the side of her head and she stumbled to the floor.

"You're the one who's wrong, bitch. He's never coming back now. It's way past time for you to realize who you belong to!"

Desperate to escape his mad assault, she scrambled across the floor on her knees, trying to reach the door, but he delivered a vicious kick to her hip that knocked her onto her back. The next instant he straddled her at the base of her swollen stomach with her maternity dress pushed up to her breasts. As she squirmed upward to get away, he tightened his knees and grabbed both her wrists.

"He should see you now, with your fat belly and cow tits. I bet you'd comb your hair and put on makeup for him, wouldn't you, *bitch*?"

He was twisting one of her wrists at such a painful angle, tears ran down her face. "Russ, please stop. You're really hurting me."

"I bet you'd have taken care of his needs even if you couldn't fuck. But then maybe you've been lying all the time about not being able to do it. Maybe you were just holding out, hoping he'd come back and fuck you with his big dick again. Well, too late, baby. All you got now is me. And I've waited as long as I'm gonna wait."

She heard the crack before she felt the pain in her wrist. It shot up her arm and stole her breath, so that her scream was nothing more than a high-pitched whimper. Incapacitated by the searing pain and disbelief, she couldn't stop him from ripping her underpants. A moment later he invaded her unprepared body with a savage force that burned and tore her flesh as if he were using a knife on her.

She tried to scream again, but his fingers wrapped around her throat and choked off the sound. As she struggled for breath, she begged for mercy with her eyes, but he didn't seem to see her.

"Bitch. Fucking bitch cunt. You're mine. And I'll never let you forget it again." He grunted and pushed and strained, and Barbara felt herself slip out of consciousness.

*　　*　　*

With the return of awareness came an intense pain that enveloped her entire body. The horror of what had happened nearly paralyzed her, but the fear that it wasn't over countered it. Russ was gone, but he could come back any moment. Fighting against the excruciating pain, she dragged herself to the table, pulled the phone down to her level, and dialed 911.

Chapter 6

Barbara dropped the peach-colored roses, vase and all, into the garbage can at the side of the house. If Russ was watching for her reaction, he couldn't possibly misunderstand that one.

The local police had told her to call immediately if her stalker made contact and to hold on to any messages or tokens that might be used as evidence. She figured the big rubber receptacle was an appropriate place to store one of Russ's gifts until she called the authorities.

As she came around the front of the house again, a new-looking burgundy Cadillac pulled into the driveway. The make of the car was a solid clue that Russ was not the driver, so she curbed the impulse to dash inside the house, but she kept her guard up while a man in a trenchcoat and hat stepped out of the car.

Before she got close enough to see his face, she heard the front door open behind her.

"Mom?"

She gave a look over her shoulder and tapped her nose with her index finger. *Stay alert.* "Go back inside, honey. I'll be right in." As he obeyed, she turned back to greet the man, but stopped cold as recognition hit. He'd aged considerably more than the ten years it had been since she'd last seen him, but she could never forget the man who disposed of the Hamiltons' dirty laundry. "Simon Decker. I'm afraid I can't say that it's a pleasure to see you again."

He raised his gray eyebrows. "Still holding a grudge after all these years, Miss Mancuso? How very Italian of you."

"My name is Mrs. Johnson, and I—"

"Legally, your name may be Johnson, but it never has been *Mrs.* anything. I already checked."

"We have nothing to say to each other, Mr. Decker, and my son is waiting for dinner." She turned and walked toward the door.

"Your son is a very handsome young man," he said, raising his voice to make sure she heard him. "The image of his father at that age."

Barbara felt the blood rush from her head and ordered herself to stay calm. She waved Matthew away from the window and slowly faced the attorney. "Yes. Mr. Johnson was a very handsome man."

"You may as well stop wasting both our time, Miss Mancuso. My investigation uncovered the fact that you gave birth to your son, Matthew *Howard* Mancuso, on January first, nine years ago, about nine months after you and *Howard* Hamilton, *ahem,* spent time together."

Needing time to think of a response, she forced

a friendly smile and asked him a question for which she could guess the answer. "Since you've already admitted to having me investigated, perhaps you wouldn't mind telling me how you found me here." As she hoped, his overblown ego urged him to boast of his accomplishment.

"Once your photo appeared in the newspaper with your names and city of residence, it was a simple matter of hiring an investigator. I understand he tracked you down through Virginia's Department of Motor Vehicles, but he could have done it through your telephone number as easily."

"But it's unlisted."

He sneered at her naïveté. "Unlisted numbers only prevent the general public from accessing you. Any law enforcement agency, licensed investigator, or talented computer hack could get your number and cross-reference your address with very little effort."

"I see," she said, shaking her head. "Thank you for the information. Now, regarding my son—I was already impregnated by Matt's father when I met Howard. He was born seven and a half months after that. I gave Matt his middle name because I learned of Howard's death only hours before I went into labor. It was a gesture, nothing else."

"You've prepared your defense well, but it will only take another day or so for me to verify what you've said. I can't help but wonder why you are now so certain of who the father was, and yet, on the birth certificate it states that Matthew's father is *Unknown*. Most women wouldn't admit to such blatant promiscuity."

She managed not to look away from his challenging stare, but she felt a telltale line of perspiration rise on her upper lip. "What do you want, Mr. Decker?"

He cupped his hands over his mouth and blew a breath to warm them. "Perhaps we could go inside—"

"I don't want you in my home. Either say why you're here or go away."

"Very well. I'm here on behalf of Howard and Edith Hamilton. As you can imagine, the loss of their only child nine years ago completely devastated them. They never fully recovered from the tragedy. Discovering that Howard fathered a son has given them new hope, though they find your keeping his existence a secret from them cruel in the extreme."

"They find *me* cruel!" Barbara threw up her hands and strode toward the house again.

"They're willing to pay you," Decker said quickly.

Still walking, she glared back at him and shook her head is disbelief.

"One hundred thousand dollars, with all taxes paid, for you to grant them custody of their grandson."

Barbara stopped and marched back to him. "That is the most disgusting thing I've ever heard. Now, I want you off my property by the time I count to ten, or I'll call the police and have you arrested for trespassing."

He held up his hands as if to ward her off. "No need for that. I'll give you some time to consider the offer."

"One."

"You could never provide for him the way they could."

"Two."

He raised his voice again as he started backing down the driveway. "He's the heir to a corporate empire."

"Three."

He sped up his retreat. "You can't keep him from his birthright!"

"Four. Five. Six."

"I'm in room 220 at the Sheraton, when you're ready to discuss this rationally." He was in his car before she finished her countdown.

Of all the nerve! How could they suggest such a thing? The Hamiltons gave up any rights they had to their grandson ten years ago! It had never occurred to her that the photo in the paper could dredge up even worse scum than Russ.

"Matthew!" she called as soon as she got in the house.

He was beside her in a flash. "Did you see what I did? The funny way you waved your hand, I knew you wanted me to hide, so I went into your bedroom and watched you from behind your drapes. Wasn't that good?"

She hated the fact that he spoke of hiding and

watching as if it were a normal activity, but it was a necessary evil in their lives. She playfully chucked him under the chin. "That was great. And what would you have done if I'd scratched my head?"

"Call 911."

"Ten points, kiddo. Another perfect score. Did you get a good look at him?"

Matt made a face. "It was kind of hard with his hat and all, but I think I saw him okay. Is he a bad guy, too?"

She sighed. Bad guys. Good guys. Black and white. Little boys had no concept of gray. "As far as you're concerned, yes. You mustn't let him get near you, either. Even if you just see him hanging around, you tell me. Come here, sweetie."

He stepped into her open arms, and she gave him a hug that she needed more than he did. At nine years old, he already came up to her chin. He was going to be a big man, like his father, but for now, he was still a little, frightened boy. "Nothing bad is going to happen, and we're not moving this time. You got that, kiddo?"

He looked up at her and smiled. "Got it, Mommyo."

"You're not a helpless little baby anymore. If somebody tries to mess with you now, you can use some of that karate stuff you're getting so good at."

He whirled out of her arms and performed a kick-and-punch exercise he'd learned. "Maybe I'll ask Sensei to show me some new moves, just in case."

She mussed his blond hair. "I was only kidding. If anybody bothers you, the rules are still the same. You run for help as fast as you can."

"Aw, Maw!"

"I mean it. Now, how about burgers and fries tonight? If you do your homework before I'm done cooking, we can watch the video we rented while we eat." And while he was occupied with homework, she would make her call to the police and hope this time they might actually be able to help.

Russ Latham tossed the binoculars onto the floor of his Volkswagen and started the engine as the Cadillac passed where he was parked. He had been so turned on at the sight of Barbara after such a long separation, he had thought he might have to jerk off before approaching her, but Simon Decker's unexpected appearance was as good as a cold shower.

Now that he knew where to find the bitch and her kid, he could come back anytime. His number-one priority had just switched to finding out what the attorney's plans were, and how he could either take advantage of them or disrupt them.

He grinned as he recalled the last time he "helped" Decker along with his plans for Barbara. Not only had he gotten some fun out of it, the little jobs he was given had a personal bonus that the attorney knew nothing about. In fact, only two other people on earth knew the secret behind everything he'd done for the last twelve years.

Decker had no idea that when he paid Russ to help the Hamiltons get rid of Howard's Italian whore, he also handed him the weapon he'd needed to see justice done. Thanks to the attorney's dirty dealing, Russ was able to learn of Barbara's pregnancy and a plan came to him that should have evened the score. All he had to do was marry Barbara and adopt Howard's bastard.

But the bitch hadn't fallen in line like she should have. He courted her, played nursemaid for her, bullied and threatened her; none of it worked. To make matters worse, the more she resisted him, the hotter he got for her, until he wanted her as badly as he wanted vengeance.

Russ noted the Cadillac's turn signal flashing and followed Decker into the Sheraton parking lot. The ass-licking lawyer had always figured Russ was stupid and Russ never let on otherwise. For now, he would continue to pretend idiocy, but one of these days they would all be in for a very big surprise.

Barbara hung up the phone on the kitchen wall and got started on dinner. Over the years she had talked to a lot of police officers in a number of cities, yet it never failed to make her nervous.

The first time, before she discovered how useless the system was, was probably the easiest. When Dr. Roselli had brought the police officer to her in the hospital while she lay bruised and broken, she had been confident that he would protect her and hadn't hesitated to press charges against Russ. She wanted to see him punished for what he had done to her. Before Russ was arrested, however, he managed to get into her hospital room . . . to beg forgiveness and proclaim his love and devotion to her and *their* son.

That first officer had done the only thing he could; he arrested Russ and helped her get a restraining order against him, but warned that her attacker would probably be out on bail within a few days and the trial wouldn't be held for months. He suggested she find a safe place to hide until then. If she had been alone, she might have stayed in New York, but she had a baby to think of first, so she followed his advice.

The sound of the doorbell pulled her thoughts back to the present. Glancing out the front window, she was quite surprised to see a uniformed policewoman on the front porch.

"I didn't expect such a fast response," Barbara said after inviting her in.

The woman gave her a friendly smile that went a long way toward relaxing her. "I was only a few blocks away when I heard the call and recognized your name from the report you filed the other day. I'd been planning on stopping by to talk to you tonight anyway."

"Oh?" Before Barbara could ask why, Matt came into the room. "As you've already guessed, I'm Barbara Johnson, and this is my son, Matthew."

The officer offered her hand to Barbara, then Matt. "Sergeant Danielle Pfeiffer. Call me Dani."

Matt shook her hand politely, then complained to his mother. "Is dinner ready yet? I'm starved."

"Not quite. Is your homework done?"

"Not quite," he said, mimicking her.

"Then get back to it. I'll call you when food's on the table." He made a face, but returned to his bedroom. Turning to Dani, Barbara asked, "Will you have something to eat with us? It's just hamburgers, fries, and salad, but I have plenty."

"That would be terrific, thank you. I just have to let dispatch know where I am, and hopefully, it will stay quiet long enough for me to eat."

The officer radioed in, then removed her hat and heavy jacket. Barbara found it interesting that the woman wasn't much bigger than herself and had similar coloring, though her uniform and gun belt made her appear bulkier and her hair was twisted into a knot on top of her head. Although it was unreasonable, she had always assumed that women who went into police work were big and rather masculine.

"What can I do to help?" Dani asked as she followed Barbara into the kitchen. Although Barbara assured her she had everything under control, Dani took over the task of cutting up the salad vegetables.

"Is your stalker Matthew's father?" Dani asked casually, as if she were personally rather than officially interested.

Barbara shook her head no and, as she formed

a trayful of hamburger patties, briefly explained how Russ became a part of their life. She had told other officers the basic facts before, but Dani made her feel as though she were sharing her story with a friend, and she soon found herself telling more than the basic facts. "After Russ was arrested, I took Matt to my parents' home in Dayton. I was naive enough to think that he wouldn't jump bail to come after me. Two weeks later, he showed up on their doorstep, determined to convince me to go back with him and drop the assault charges."

"Did you?"

"No. I refused to be one of those women who let men get away with rape because they're intimidated by them. I went to the local police, but there wasn't much they could do, except notify New York as to his whereabouts. That only got Russ angrier. He began harassing me, my family, my friends. He'd leave little gifts or notes in places I was bound to find them. My parents changed the locks on the house and got a new phone number, but nothing stopped him from getting to me whenever he felt like it."

"Did he threaten you?"

"Oh, yes. Verbally and in writing. But the police just kept saying that as long as he didn't act on the threats, they couldn't do anything to help. Eventually, the bondsman arrived and hauled him back to New York for the trial. In spite of everyone's warnings, I testified against him. I thought I'd be safer if he was behind bars."

"How did the trial go?"

Barbara huffed. "It was a nightmare, but I thought it was worth it when he was found guilty . . . until the judge sentenced him to only one year with the possibility of parole in three months. Russ's last words as he left the courtroom were a promise to kill both my son and me when he got out."

She put the burgers into the oven to grill them, turned the gas on under the oil for the french fries, and started setting the table for three. "I was terrified for my son and my parents more than myself. I stayed with them for a while, but before Russ was released, I took off with Matt. I thought if we hid somewhere for a while, Russ would forget about me."

"Obviously, he didn't." Dani carried the bowl of salad to the table, then sat down.

Barbara took the chair opposite her. "I never figured out all the tricks he used to find me wherever we went. I got better at sneaking out of town, using disguises, making up phony names and histories. I stuck to larger cities, thinking we could blend in unnoticed. I only worked for temporary office services, so I couldn't be found in the same place for any length of time. None of it was ever good enough to lose him, and he never got tired of the chase."

"Did he ever try to get hold of your son?"

Barbara nodded. "Three times, that I know of. The night after Russ first got to Dayton, I woke up and saw him in the rocking chair in the corner of my room, holding Matt. It was the first time in my life I ever thought of killing someone with my bare hands. That was one of the reasons I felt I had to testify against him. The second time was three years later in Chicago. He followed us to a park and attempted to lure Matt away from me, but I stopped him.

"The third was the scariest. He actually kidnapped Matt off the school playground in Denver and forced him to spend an afternoon with him, during which he tried to convince him that he was his father and I was an evil witch for keeping them apart. He dropped Matt off at our apartment building, frightened, but unhurt. After that, I had to explain the ugly facts of our life to Matt for his own protection." She got up to finish cooking.

"How long has it been since you saw him last?"

As Barbara flipped over the hamburgers, she said, "About two years. Before I moved to Fredericksburg, I hired an expert to help me disappear. I legally changed our last name to Johnson, one of the most common names in America. I closed out my bank accounts and started dealing only in cash to eliminate any possible paper trail. I sold the car I had and bought one that looked like a lot of other vehicles on the road; then I got a new license tag registered in my new name."

Satisfied that the meat would be done in a few minutes, she lowered the wire basket of fries into the hot oil. "That man showed me how to set up a communication system with a network of contacts so that Russ couldn't track me through my parents' mail or phone bills. He even helped me leave a false trail for Russ to follow to the West Coast, while I headed east."

Dani shook her head and clucked her tongue sympathetically. "And then your photo appeared on the front page."

"Exactly."

"Have you had any indication that he's on his way here?"

"Yes. That's why I called. I think he's already in the area." She told Dani about the roses and where they could be found. "Despite the floral display in the living room tonight, I don't usually have flowers or plants in the house. They remind us too much of him."

"I'll take them with me and see if we can pick up any prints. Other than that, it sounds like you've done everything you're supposed to do to protect yourselves. The more people you tell and the more eyes you have working for you, the less chance the stalker has of surprising you, which is how he gains part of his satisfaction."

"Yes, and the less fear I show, the less pleasure he gets, too. I'm going to stick it out this time. It's pretty obvious that running never accomplished anything."

"Don't put yourself down for running from Russ. It may have been the smartest thing to do under the circumstances."

That was the first time she'd heard a law enforcement figure voice that opinion. "Why do you say that?"

Dani's gaze drifted to the calendar on the wall. "My older sister was the target of a stalker. No matter how frustrated she got or how frightened he made her, she never believed he was really capable of hurting her. She didn't ask the police for help because he hadn't broken any laws. To an outsider, he just sounded like a very devoted admirer, so she told very few people about the strange things he was doing. She didn't run away even when he began threatening her life."

Barbara saw the end of the story in Dani's eyes, but she asked anyway. "What happened?"

"He broke into her apartment one night. For six hours, he tortured her, cut, burned, raped, and sodomized her, then left her, gagged and tied to her bed. She survived, but her mind left her body that night and never completely returned. He turned himself in, pleaded temporary insanity, and served less than a year in a state institution. I was still in high school at the time, without any idea of what I wanted to do for a living. After that, I knew it had to be something where I could help women like my sister.

"The laws have been improved since then and the public is more aware of the problem, but it's no guarantee. That's why I wanted to talk to you, to let you know that there's someone in a position of authority who understands and cares what happens to you."

"Thank you," Barbara said sincerely. "That means a lot to me."

Dani got up and moved to Barbara's side. "Just out of curiosity, did you ever marry?"

"No. Being engaged to Matt's father was the closest I ever got." She dumped the cooked fries onto a paper-towel-covered platter and pulled the tray of hamburgers out of the oven. "The way I've moved around the last nine years, I barely had the opportunity to make friends, let alone fall in love."

Dani's radio squawked at her before she could say more. Barbara couldn't understand what the dispatcher was saying, but from Dani's end of the conversation, she knew the officer would soon be on her way.

"I have to take this call," she said after signing off. "I appreciate the offer of dinner, though. Hopefully we can make it another time when I'm off duty. Would you mind if I spoke to Matt before I left?"

"Of course not. Just follow the hall out of the living room." As Dani walked away, Barbara quickly wrapped up a hamburger and some fries and put them in a paper bag with a drink box of juice and some napkins. The three of them met a few minutes later in the living room.

Dani handed Barbara her card on the way out the door. "This has several numbers where you can reach me, including my home. I expect you to call me for the smallest problem."

"And this is for you," Barbara replied, handing her the bag. "I wasn't sure if you'd be able to manage any salad, but I could put some in a container if you'd like."

Dani sniffed the food and laughed. "No, this is great. Thank you. Hey, maybe I should marry you and solve both our problems. You'd have a live-in protector, and I'd have a cook who understands the phrase *eating on the run*."

Barbara and Matt both watched the police car drive away; then they headed for the kitchen. "What did Sergeant Pfeiffer want to talk to you about?" Barbara asked.

Matt gave a little shrug. "Same old stuff. You know, don't talk to strangers, run for help or scream if I have to, tell my mother everything that happens to me, and call her if you or I need help. She even gave me her beeper number, for crying out loud. Don't worry, I was polite."

She touched his cheek. "Of course you were. You're my little angel." The way he raised his eyes to the ceiling made her laugh. "Okay. Okay. I forgot again. Come on, the burgers are getting cold."

Since they no longer had company for dinner and Matt had finished his homework, they ate in front of the television as promised. The video they had rented was a slapstick comedy that had Matt howling and failed to distract Barbara in the slightest.

She kept thinking about how comfortable she had been talking with Dani. Over the years, experience had taught her to use her intuition to judge new acquaintances, and her readings on Dani were all positive. Even though Dani hadn't had the opportunity to talk about herself, Barbara could easily imagine their becoming close friends, if time and circumstances permitted.

While she tucked Matt in that night, she did her best to reassure him one more time that they were going to stay in Fredericksburg no matter what. But as she got ready for bed herself, her positive attitude disintegrated. Because of the past, she couldn't help but dread what lay ahead: going through the motions of a normal life while constantly looking over her shoulder, scanning strangers' faces in every crowd, fearing that one would be familiar; waiting for the phone to ring or a knock at the door, only to hold her breath until the caller hung up or the visitor left.

Knowing she had a police officer personally interested in her case gave her confidence a slight boost, however. She wondered if she should have told Dani about Simon Decker's visit, but she didn't consider the lawyer a danger—only a major annoyance. Besides, she never told *anyone* who Matt's father was.

The memory of the day she named her son came back to her. What she had told Decker was partially true. Giving Matt the middle name Howard had been a gesture. She had looked at the tiny, blond-haired baby in the nursery incubator and had felt sad that he would grow up without his father's last name, but no one could stop her from giving him his first.

She had also felt horribly unprepared for the responsibility that had been handed her, but after some encouraging words from Dr. Roselli, she made her child several promises. From that moment on, nothing in the world would ever be as important to her as the welfare of Matthew Howard Mancuso.

Whatever maternal skills didn't come naturally, she'd learn. Whatever he needed, she'd find a way to give it to him. She would encourage him to be gentle and loving like his father, and outgoing and independent like her. She would teach him all the lessons she'd learned and remember to listen when he had something to teach her. And, above all, she would do everything in her power to make sure no one ever caused him any pain.

Every night since, when she tucked her baby in bed, she reminded herself of those promises and prayed that keeping them would get easier with time.

Chapter 7

Barbara slept very little that night, which used to be normal. In the last year, however, she had rediscovered the pleasure of deep sleep and resented giving it up again.

With concentrated effort, she was able to stop thinking about Russ and Decker by the time she pulled into the parking garage of the high-rise building in Richmond where she worked.

She really enjoyed her job as customer service rep for a bank that owned the building and filled the first three floors. Her supervisor and co-workers were easy to get along with, the pay and benefits were excellent, she was able to work hours that coincided with Matt's school day, and best of all, she was able to help people with their problems.

One of the benefits was a very affordable cafeteria on the fourth floor, where most of the employees in the building had lunch. Each morning, she had a cup of coffee and a doughnut with the same group of women, but occasionally, as happened that day, someone new sat down with them.

"Hi. Mind if I join you? I hate sitting alone."

Barbara looked up and smiled at the young woman. "Not at all." She pushed aside a twinge of envy as the newcomer set down her low-fat yogurt and apple juice. Not only was the girl barely out of her teens, she had long, silky blond hair, high cheekbones, vivid green eyes with an exotic slant to them, a figure to die for, and the height to carry it. Barbara hated her on sight, and from the expressions on her friends' faces, so did they.

"I'm Barbara. This is Nellie, Ann Marie, and Karen. We work downstairs."

The much-too-pretty woman gave each of their hands a brief, firm shake before sitting down. "I'm Tammy Garrett and I work *up*stairs, for the insurance company. I really hope you don't mind my joining you. People hardly ever come up and talk to me, so I make it a practice to go to them. I try to meet someone new every day."

Good grief, Barbara thought listening to her perky, slightly accented tone. She didn't know they had valley girls in Virginia. "I don't think we've seen you before. Are you new?"

"Oh, no," she said, flipping her hair back over her shoulder with a sexy toss of her head. "I've been there for almost a year, but they just changed me from the evening to the day shift. I'm willing to give it a try, but I'm not too crazy about getting up before noon."

"None of us are, honey," Nellie said, and everyone laughed.

At lunch, Barbara saw Tammy eating alone and recalled her comment about people not walking up to her. She supposed being that beautiful could be a curse when it came to making female friends. When Tammy waved a greeting, Barbara felt obliged to sit with her.

"I was hoping this was your lunchtime," Tammy gushed with a big smile. "You were so nice this morning. Really made me feel welcome. I know you're not going to believe this, but some women just seem to hate me on sight. They don't even try to get to know me."

Barbara opted for the honest route. "I'm not all that surprised. A woman would have to have tremendous self-confidence to be your friend."

Tammy's cheerful expression faded. "You mean because of what I look like, don't you?" She gave that less than three seconds of thought. "Oh, well. If a person can't see past what's on my outside, I don't think I want them as a friend anyway."

Barbara smiled. "Good attitude."

"So, I guess that means you must have a lot of self-confidence, huh?"

"Nah. I'm just a masochist."

Laughing, Tammy said, "Then I'll be sure to look my most drop-dead gorgeous every day so you'll become the best friend I ever had!"

With the largest obstacle between them reduced to a joke, the two women spent the rest of their lunch hour getting to know each other. Barbara told her the story she had used since arriving in Virginia: that she and her son had moved there from Seattle after her divorce to be close to her aging parents, who live in Richmond.

Tammy was intrigued by the idea of moving across the country. She had been born in Richmond twenty-two years ago and the only place she'd ever gone was to Washington, D.C. Her boyfriend, Michael, kept promising to take her to Disney World in Florida, but something always came up to postpone it. Sometimes she suspected that he didn't like taking her out in public at all.

"What about you?" Tammy asked. "Have you got a man that drives you nuts most of the time?"

Barbara smiled and gave another standard answer. "No way. After my ex, I swore off men entirely. Except for Matthew, of course, and the most annoying thing about him is that he's growing up too fast."

An hour later, Barbara was back at her desk talking on the phone, when she got a funny feeling that she was being stared at. She tried to maintain a casual appearance as she raised her eyes, then slowly swiveled her chair around. One or two customers caught her gaze, but the sensation wasn't being caused by them, nor anyone else in view.

Continuing to scan the lobby area, she quickly completed her call, then let the receptionist know she was taking a break. She went the longest possible route to the ladies' room, peering down hallways, out into the parking lot, even inside the janitor's closet. As a last resort, she asked the security guard to go into the men's room for her, but no one fitting Russ's description was anywhere around.

She had more or less dispelled the uneasiness when, while driving home, it came back again. Her intuition told her someone was following her, but in the midst of rush-hour traffic on the expressway, it was impossible to confirm. As she exited, she kept an eye on her rearview mirror and made note of which cars were behind her. She purposely made several unnecessary turns and stopped for milk at a convenience store to see if she could single out one car that stayed with her. Again, her intuition seemed to have failed. Though she remained cautious, she gave up looking for a shadow and went on to Matt's school.

The next morning on the way out the door, the feeling returned and stayed with her all the way to work, but as before, there seemed to be no reason for it.

Was it paranoia causing her to imagine things, or could Russ have changed his methods from direct assault to hide-and-seek? Either way, her nerves were being strung tighter by the hour.

Though she and Tammy had very little in common, the girl was funny and helped keep her mind off Russ, so Barbara welcomed the company at lunch again. By the end of the week their noon meeting had become part of her workday routine.

"We ought to go out together tonight," Tammy suggested before they went back to work Friday afternoon. "There's a super club I go to whenever

I get mad at Michael. The music's mostly alternative, and the men aren't too young."

"I'm sorry. I really don't like to go out at night. That's the time I spend with my son."

"Well, maybe I could drive up to your place sometime this weekend, and we could just, sort of, you know, hang out. I'd like to meet Matthew after all the great things you've said about him."

Barbara hedged. "I honestly don't know what I'll be doing this weekend. Between catching up on the housework and laundry, my son and my parents . . ."

"Oh," Tammy murmured, rejection clouding her eyes.

"I'll tell you what. Give me your phone number and I'll call if I've got some free time."

Tammy brightened instantly and wrote her number on a paper napkin. "And yours?" she asked with her pen poised over another napkin.

Barbara didn't like giving her unlisted number out, but it would have been terribly rude not to after she'd asked for Tammy's first. She told her the number, then had to rush back to her desk.

She felt somewhat guilty for having lied to Tammy about that night. The truth was, Matthew would be happy to spend the night at his best friend Kenny's house, as he sometimes did on Fridays. She could have gone out if she'd wanted to. She simply had no interest in the singles scene. Had Tammy suggested dinner and a movie, her answer might have been different.

Then again, she couldn't dismiss the probability

that Russ was about to make an appearance, and she didn't want to be parted from Matt any more than necessary. Three full days and nights had passed since the delivery of the roses, yet he hadn't shown up, nor had he called or sent anything else. The absence of a follow-up was making her more nervous than his usual methods of harassment. *What in God's name was he up to this time?*

As she cleared her desk at the end of the day, she couldn't help but think of what a strange week she'd had. All things considered, meeting Tammy was probably the high point. Perhaps she should call and invite her up to Fredericksburg tomorrow.

Still contemplating that idea as she entered the parking garage, she didn't notice the boy running toward her in the hooded sweatshirt until he was practically on top of her. Then it was too late.

In a flurry of movement, he slammed into her, knocking them both to the concrete floor. Then he grabbed her purse and was running off again in the blink of an eye.

There were a number of people in the garage, but it happened too fast for anyone to react— except for one man who had been getting out of his car a good distance down the row when the mugging occurred. He shouted at the boy as he flew by; then he took off after the thief on foot.

Within seconds, a dozen people hovered around Barbara, helping her up, asking if she wanted the police or an ambulance. She insisted she was only stunned and was debating if it was worth spending several hours to report the incident.

After the initial shock, she thought of what was in that purse. She wondered if Russ could have paid someone to mug her just so he could get the keys to her house. Though that wasn't his usual way of doing things, she wouldn't put anything past him.

She was thinking of the problems she was going to have replacing all the items in her purse when it was suddenly handed to her.

Immediately the crowd's attention turned to the heroic man who had chased down the purse snatcher, recovered the loot, and was now bent over at the waist, gasping for air.

"He . . . dropped the purse . . . when . . . he realized I was right behind him. He got away, though." He straightened up, took one long deep breath which seemed to help, then addressed Barbara. "The parking attendant called the police. Are you all right?"

She was completely overwhelmed by his bravery. Looking up at him with open admiration, she said, "Yes. I'm fine. I can't believe you did that. How can I thank you?"

He smiled and showed off the most perfect white teeth she'd ever seen. "No thanks needed. If I had stopped to think what I was doing, I probably would have chickened out." He combed his fingers through his dark, wavy hair to push it away from his face. Though it appeared to be professionally styled, his hair was thoroughly mussed from the run, too long for a man over thirty wearing a business suit, and looked unbelievably good anyway.

Since it was impossible to guess how long it would take for the police to arrive, she needed to make arrangements for Matt. She told one of the witnesses who'd agreed to stay that she had to make a phone call, but would be right back. As she walked into the building, she felt as though she was being followed and glanced back to see her hero coming up behind her.

"I need to make a call also," he explained. "There's no way I'll make my five o'clock appointment. Would you mind guiding me to a telephone I can use?"

"I'm just going to use the pay phone in the lobby. It will be faster than going to my office and explaining why I'm back before Monday morning."

He waited a polite distance away while she called Laura French, Kenny's mother, and asked her to pick Matthew up and keep him at her house until she could get there, then called the school to let them know that Matt could go home with Mrs. French.

Her hero asked her to wait for him while he made his brief call telling someone he had to postpone their appointment until Monday. Now that Matthew was taken care of, she was in no hurry to go anywhere. Under the bright fluorescent lights the man in front of her was even more striking than he had appeared in the dimly lit garage. His suit looked expensive, but then he had the kind of tall, lean build that wore a suit well. She guessed he was between thirty and thirty-five and probably jogged for exercise. He hung up and offered her his hand.

"We haven't actually met. I'm Kyle Trent."

Taking his hand, she was unexpectedly stricken by the sensuality of his touch. She met his gaze and felt another stab of awareness. Good Lord, she hadn't been able to see his eyes in the garage. They were faded denim blue, and they were saying outrageously sexy things to her. "Barbara Ma— Johnson." How could she forget her name? She felt his hand slide away from hers and the tingling left behind gave her the answer. It had been a very long time, but having experienced a severe chemical reaction once before in her life was enough to recognize the symptoms. "We should go back."

He let her lead, but she sensed him behind her the whole time, just as she had on the way in. Chemistry was a very interesting thing. Unfortunately, for her it was also a very dangerous thing.

While the statements were being taken by the police, Barbara had to consciously work at keeping her gaze from drifting back to him. She knew she should steer clear, yet she felt there had to be some way to properly show her appreciation. "Mr. Trent? I can't thank you enough for what you did. I've been standing here thinking of how I would have had to get a locksmith to get into my car, all my identification would have had to be replaced, to say nothing of my paycheck. I wonder if you'd allow me to buy you a drink, or a cup of coffee . . . something to let me feel like I repaid you in some way."

His mouth curved into a slow grin and his eyes made a naughty suggestion. "A drink would be very nice. I just moved here from St. Louis. Is there someplace nearby?"

She hadn't thought beyond her invitation. The only place she knew of was a restaurant a few blocks away where her friends had taken her for her thirtieth birthday. She remembered it having a bar. "Do you mind walking a little?"

He laughed. "Walking's fine. These shoes just weren't made for running."

She looked down at his loafers. They looked as expensive as his suit and haircut. She hoped he was rich. That would turn off her hormones in a heartbeat. As he got his trench coat out of his late-model sedan, she said, "I'm a customer service rep in the bank. What do you do, Mr. Trent?"

"Please call me Kyle. I work for IBM. Actually, I was a service rep, too, before I got into sales. I was just promoted to regional sales manager."

"Does a car come with that kind of job?"

"That's one of the benefits. Save's me the cost of owning one."

Okay, so he's not rich like Howard. He wears good clothes because he's in sales. What else?

"The other good thing about the job is I can pretty much make my own hours."

Aha, another bum like Russ. Doesn't like to work.

"The problem with that is I always end up putting in more than forty hours a week because no one tells me when to start and stop."

There's got to be something wrong with this guy. "That must drive your wife up a wall."

He gave her another one of those slow grins. "No wife. No ex-wives. No fiancées or steady companions. No children, legitimate or otherwise. And yes, I am one hundred percent heterosexual."

She felt her cheeks flush. "I'm sorry. I was being nosy."

"Actually, I was trying to figure out how to bring it up. Your interview method is quite impressive. Now it's your turn."

Relief that he wasn't annoyed made her giggle. "All of the above, except one ex-husband and a nine-year-old son."

"Good. Then let's have dinner with our drinks."

She was tempted. "I'm sorry. I can't. Not that I wouldn't be pleased to buy you dinner after what you did for me. But I promised to pick up my son by . . ." she looked at her watch, "by seven, in Fredericksburg. That's about a forty-five-minute drive, and—"

"It's all right. I got the point. Let's see if we can stand each other through a drink first. We can work up to an entire meal later."

His tone was teasing, not angry, over her clumsy rejection. He had to have some fault she could focus on to stop this train before it picked up more steam. If she had learned one important lesson in life, it was that she could never trust her feelings when it came to men.

"I swear to God, man, this crazy dude tackled me and stole the purse back! Look at my fuckin' cheek, man. You think I threw myself down on the sidewalk for the hell of it?"

Russ relaxed his grip on the kid's skinny throat, then shoved him against the concrete wall. "Get the fuck away from me."

"What about my pay, man? You said—"

Russ delivered a hard punch to the kid's diaphragm. "There's your pay, asshole. You're lucky I don't make you give back what you got up front. Now get lost."

The kid wasted no time following his order as Russ headed in the opposite direction. After a moment, Russ allowed himself a chuckle over the screw-up. He could hardly wait to throw in his partner's I've-got-every-detail-perfectly-planned face.

She shouldn't have remained celibate for so many years. Long-neglected physical need was obviously catching up with a vengeance. She was actually perspiring despite the freezing temperature. One drink," she reminded herself. Surely she wouldn't do or say anything she'd regret in the time it took to have one drink.

As it turned out, she wasn't required to do or say much of anything while they were at the bar. He did most of the talking. All she had to do was ask an occasional question and pay attention.

Unfortunately, that required looking directly into his incredible eyes. She wondered what he'd say if she asked him to put on sunglasses.

To make things worse, he was bright and, depending on the topic, he could be funny or very serious. Like her, he came from a middle-class background, was an only child with happy childhood memories, took some college classes without working toward a degree, and loved the theater.

She didn't understand why she felt such a strong attraction to him. He wasn't needy or looking for a caretaker. He knew what he wanted and was working toward it. He didn't seem to be weak or indecisive like the men who had drawn her before. Kyle seemed genuinely pleased with his life without any assistance or advice from her.

By the time he walked her to her car, she knew she was in deep trouble and hoped he had found something terribly undesirable about her, so she wouldn't have to drum up any resistance on her own.

"Thank you again, Kyle. Not only are you a hero, but you are delightful company." She held out her hand to shake his, but he brought it to his lips for a kiss.

"It was my pleasure. Now, about dinner, how about tomorrow night?"

Resist, you weak-kneed, horny twit. You can't afford the complication or distraction of a man in your life. She swallowed hard. "I can't."

He moved an inch closer, turned her hand around, and kissed her palm. "You could if you wanted to. And I think you want to. What are you afraid of?"

He pulled back her coat sleeve and kissed the inside of her wrist. She felt it all the way to her toes. "I'm not afraid of anything. I just have a lot of things going on in my life right now, and dating would only make it more difficult."

"If things are that difficult, a night out could be just what you need."

His eyes promised her a night that would make her forget the rest of the world existed, which was exactly what she was afraid of.

"All right," he said with a look of exasperation. "I'm going to pull out all the stops now and destroy my macho image. I've always wanted to believe in love at first sight and happily ever after, but it never happened for me. That's why I never got married. This afternoon, the first time our eyes met, I felt like I'd been gut-punched. Of course, it could be the flu, but unless my instincts have taken a vacation, I'd say you felt the same thing." His hands moved up her arms and into her hair.

She couldn't move. She could barely breathe. "It's only because of what you did," she murmured. "It was romantic, like a knight in shining armor and the maiden in distress. It doesn't mean anything."

"Oh, I see. Well, if you're right about that, this probably won't make any difference." He tilted her head back and lowered his.

His lips on hers were as light and velvety as a

butterfly's wing. Barely touching, he brushed his mouth from side to side over hers, then gently caressed each corner until she began to follow the rhythm he set. Only then did he kiss her in earnest, drawing her into his heat, making her want to ease her body closer, wrap her arms around him, give him anything he wanted to take.

His seduction worked. She felt as though they were having sex, despite half a dozen layers of clothing between them. When he freed her lips, she wasn't much more than a puddle at his feet.

"Am I still standing?" she whispered.

"Barely. I'm pretty sure we're holding each other up. And I'm definitely sure this isn't the flu or a fairy tale. I'll pick you up at seven tomorrow. Dinner, a movie, or dancing, your choice. I'll have you home by midnight, and I swear on my Boy Scout oath that I won't try for more than some heavy necking in your driveway before you go inside."

"I won't promise more than one date."

"Understood."

"And that's only if I can make arrangements for someone to sit with my son."

"Also understood. And to prove that I know when to back off, I won't even ask for your number. I'll wait for you to call me. I'm temporarily staying at the Hilton here in Richmond. I'll be in and out, apartment hunting, but leave a message, and I'll call you back. You can give me directions then." He took a step away from her and shoved his hands in his coat pockets. "If I don't leave now, I'm going to lose my good behavior badge."

Fearing she had even less willpower than he did, she got in her car and escaped while she had the chance.

There was no way in hell she was keeping that date.

Kyle let out a low whistle as he watched Barbara's taillights disappear around the corner of the garage. His "accidental" meeting with her had turned out so much better than he'd planned that he decided it was a sure sign that he was doing the right thing. He thought he'd figured every possible angle, but never in his most far-fetched ponderings had he imagined a mugger in the scene. Nor had he ever considered the possibility that he'd be attracted to her in such an elemental way.

The totally unexpected effect they had on each other convinced him that his original plan was no longer adequate, but he wasn't quite sure how to revise it.

As he folded his body into the driver's seat of his car and had to adjust the crotch of his slacks, he grinned. It looked like his body was way ahead of his mind on this one.

Despite her obvious interest in him, however, she hadn't jumped at the idea of seeing him again. In fact, now that he thought about it, he got the impression that she was afraid of what he made her feel. That didn't sound at all like the woman he'd heard about. *That* woman was passionate, strong, and independent, and not afraid of anything or anyone. *That* woman would want to follow through with what they'd started, but the woman who had just driven away probably intended to stand him up tomorrow night.

Fortunately, his accountant's friend at the IRS had supplied him with her home address as well as where she was employed.

There was no way in hell he was going to let her out of his grasp now that he'd finally found her.

Chapter 8

By noon on Saturday, Barbara had scratched off every chore on her list and was looking for some other way to burn off her surplus physical energy. She knew precisely what her problem was: Kyle Trent and his amazing chemistry. Her body was screaming for her to call and give him directions to her house, and the sooner he could get there, the better.

On the other hand, her mind kept sifting through choices of how best to get out of it. She could tell him she couldn't get a sitter or say she forgot about promising her parents to see them. But then he might push for anther time. The best plan seemed to be not to call at all, to let him think she was rude and thoughtless.

When the phone rang, she worried that it might be him, then reminded herself that she hadn't given him her number. On the second ring, she fretted that it could be Russ or Decker. Though she hadn't given them her number, either, Decker had confirmed what she already knew from past experience—that they could get it if they were determined enough. On the third ring, the answering machine picked up the call.

"Barbara? This is Tammy, I was hoping . . ."

Desperate for a distraction, Barbara picked up the receiver. "Hi. I was just thinking of calling you."

"Cool. I'm bored out of my tree today. I had a terrible fight with Michael last night, and I'd even come help you with your housework just to have somebody to talk to."

Barbara laughed. Listening to Tammy's problems would at least keep her mind off her own. "Then by all means, get yourself up here and we can spend the whole afternoon male-bashing." She gave her directions and told her to plan on having lunch there.

By the time Tammy arrived an hour later, Barbara had prepared chef's salads for the two of them and franks and beans for Matt. In spite of her initial reaction to Tammy's ultraglamorous appearance, Barbara had gotten past that. The girl was endowed with all the attributes that turn men's brains into mush. It hadn't occurred to Barbara, however, that those attributes would have the same effect on a nine-year-old boy.

Matt came into the kitchen with food on his mind, took one look at Tammy in her tight little shorts and scoop-necked body suit, and instantaneously lost his mental virginity. He spent the next hour playing with his food in order to stay at the table as long as possible. With enormous eyes he watched her every move and hung on every word she uttered. His mouth only closed when he absolutely had to swallow.

To Tammy's credit, she included him in her conversation and asked him questions about his friends and school.

"Do you have one of those video game systems, like Nintendo?" she asked.

His eyes sparkled a bit more. "Yeah. My gramma and grampap just got it for me for my birthday. Kenny's been letting me borrow some of his games till I get more of my own. He's a real expert, but I'm getting pretty good, too."

"Would you teach me one later on? I've always wanted to try it."

Barbara hid her smile as her son practically exploded with his first case of puppy love. "Matt, why don't you give Kenny a call and see if he wants to come over." When he hesitated, she gave him the look that told him it was time to leave the grown-ups alone.

After Matt left the kitchen, Barbara said, "I didn't want him to hear this, but since you'll probably find out about it on Monday, I wanted to tell you first. I had my purse snatched in the parking garage yesterday afternoon."

Tammy gasped. "You're kidding! What happened?"

Barbara gave her a recap of the incident.

"Do you mean to tell me that the man actually chased the little creep and didn't even know you? Wow. Was he cute?"

Barbara laughed. "As a matter of fact, he was almost as gorgeous as you are."

"So, did you ask him out?"

Barbara made a face at her. "Not the way you mean. I bought him a drink. To show my appreciation. That's all."

"Then why are you blushing?"

Barbara's hands touched her cheeks, then confessed. "He had a very strange effect on me."

"Strange good or strange bad?"

"Both. He was one of the sexiest men I've ever met, but I told you I swore off men after my ex-husband. *He* had a strange effect on me at first, too."

"You can't judge every man by one bad one. And nobody's saying you have to marry this guy. Just have some fun with him. Did he ask you for your phone number?"

"No." She paused, then decided to tell her the rest of it. "He gave me his. He thinks we're going out tonight."

Tammy was delighted. "Why didn't you say so to begin with?"

"Because I'm not going. Now tell me what happened between you and Michael."

"No way, girl. We solve your hang-up first. Why aren't you going?"

"I'm not interested."

"Liar. The man has you sweating just talking about him!"

Barbara recalled her list of excuses. "I can't leave Matt alone for a whole evening."

"I'll stay with him," Tammy offered without hesitation.

"Oh, no. I couldn't impose on you like—"

"*Matt!*" Tammy called, and he appeared in a flash. "Your mom has a chance to go out and have a good time tonight. Would you mind terribly if I stayed and kept you company? Maybe we could even rent a new video game and learn it together."

Barbara knew she'd lost before Matt opened his mouth.

"I wouldn't mind at all," he told Tammy in a voice as mature as he could manage. He looked at his mother with eyes that begged her to go away and leave him alone with the supermodel of his dreams. "You know, Mom, you really should go out and have fun with someone your own age once in a while."

That profound statement coming out of her baby's mouth was more than she could resist. To make things even easier for Barbara to get ready, Tammy offered to take Matt and Kenny out for fast food and an action movie at five o'clock.

As a last resort, she told Tammy the bare-bones facts about Russ stalking them for years and warned that he could show up anytime. But Tammy wasn't even slightly disturbed by that information. There was nothing Barbara could do to protect Matt that Tammy couldn't do. In fact, Matt would probably be safer in public with her and Kenny because Russ would be looking for Barbara and one little blond boy, not Tammy and two young men.

Before she knew it, the two of them had sided with her carnal urges and talked her into calling Kyle to confirm their date in spite of all her reasons why she shouldn't go.

Barbara made Tammy swear she wouldn't let the boys out of her sight for a second, that she'd keep her guard up for strangers approaching them, and she'd be back by ten. Under no circumstances did Barbara want Kyle bringing her home to an empty house. Much to Matt's amusement, Tammy called her a big chicken, but she gave her word to return early.

That left only one problem, and it wasn't really that big a deal. In order for Tammy to be back before Barbara, she needed a key to get in. Because of Russ, Barbara was always overly careful about her keys, but if she didn't give her extra set of keys to Tammy, the boys would be very disappointed and Tammy would think she wasn't trusted.

At five o'clock, the threesome took off with the keys, and Barbara headed for the bathroom to get ready for her first real date in a decade.

She changed outfits three times; painted her nails, then took it off because her hands had been shaking too badly to do a neat job; snagged her stockings after she was all dressed; and was still ready twenty minutes too early. She was a nervous wreck, and her antiperspirant had chosen that night to stop working. Having been certain this was a bad idea from the start, she called Kyle's hotel to cancel, but he'd already left.

It helped a little that Kyle showed up fifteen minutes early armed with flattery and a long-stemmed red rose.

"I hope I'm not too early," he said as he stepped inside. "I couldn't wait any longer to see you." His gaze slid from her hair to her shoes. "You look even more beautiful than you did yesterday. I love your hair like that."

She self-consciously touched her hair. All she'd done differently was brush it up and back on the sides and put clips in to hold it there. But it felt good that he noticed. Of course, she was also wearing eye makeup, which she never bothered with for work. The fact that she'd taken the extra effort to look nice for him reconfirmed how much trouble she was in.

"Where's your son?"

She had thought about having people in the house when they returned, but not about his arrival. "Um, Matt's with a friend. He'll be back any second."

He smiled and drew her close. "Then we're alone?"

She quickly pressed her hands against his chest and tilted her head back. "Not for long."

"Long enough for one kiss? To say hello. No more than that. I gave you my Boy Scout word of honor, remember?"

Barbara told herself she could say no. All she had to do was gather enough breath to say the word.

His head dipped down and she closed her eyes.

It occurred to her that he didn't actually *kiss,* as most people defined the word. He played with her mouth, nipped and tickled her lips, tasted and smelled her.

"You're much too good at this," she said, desperately struggling to retain her senses.

He winked and set her away from him. "Get your coat while you still can, milady. The carriage awaits."

The Hilton manager had recommended a restaurant in Richmond that also had a live band and a dance floor. Barbara had no preference as to where they went, so their date began with a long drive.

On the way, Kyle made her do most of the talking, since he felt he had monopolized their first conversation. As she usually did with new people, she avoided specific details about the last ten years and focused on her life before Howard or talked about Matthew.

Sometime during dinner she told him about how she and her son had been at the scene of last week's train wreck and ended up with their picture in the paper.

"I must have seen it," he said with a laugh. "But I didn't pay any attention to the names. Did you keep a copy?"

She nodded. "Matt wouldn't let me throw it away."

"I'll bet you heard from a few long-lost friends after it appeared."

The simple comment made her spine stiffen.

"What do you mean?" His expression told her he noticed her reaction, and she quickly relaxed her posture.

"You know, like when someone wins the lottery, relatives show up who the winner never even heard of before."

"Oh. Yes, I did get quite a few calls afterward. Some reporters tried to get interviews with us, too, but I didn't want the publicity."

His surprise showed. "Really? I would have thought that someone who once had acting ambitions would enjoy the attention."

"That was a long time ago. Real life has a way of changing one's attitude."

He reached across the table and covered her hand with his. "I'm sorry."

"What for?"

"You were laughing, having a good time, and I made you think of something that upset you."

She looked away, but he gave her hand a squeeze and she brought her eyes back to his.

"I wish we had met when you still had your dreams of stardom. I would have prevented whatever it was that happened to change your attitude."

His thumb stroked the back of her hand as his eyes apologized for not being there.

"That's one of the sweetest things I've ever heard," she said sincerely.

"You've told me a lot about the good things in your life. Will you tell me about *him* now?"

She tensed again. "Him?"

"I'm assuming your ex-husband was the monster who destroyed your dreams. I'd like to understand."

The urge to tell him everything was terribly strong, but she hadn't confided in any man in nine years. Besides, sharing confidences was something friends did, and in spite of the chemistry between them, Kyle was still a virtual stranger. "I'd rather do something less depressing. I believe you promised to dance with me."

That had sounded like a good idea when she said it. But the moment they were on the dance floor and he took her in his arms, she realized how much safer sharing a confidence would have been.

Like his kisses, dancing with Kyle was no simple act. It wasn't that he performed any fancy footwork; it was what the rest of his body parts were doing while the music played. He had a way of stroking her back as though she were one of the instruments in the band. With each breath she took, he brought their bodies closer and closer, until there was no mystery left between them. He kissed her temple, her ear, her neck, inhaled her perfume, then sighed with unmistakable pleasure.

The band played three slow songs without a break, and by the time they changed the pace, Barbara's common sense had retired for the night.

To her delight, Kyle was good at fast dancing as well, something she had always enjoyed but hadn't done since she was a teenager. The music was too loud to carry on a conversation, but there really was no need for more words. He was determined to seduce her, and she was ready to be seduced.

He held her hand during the drive back to Fredericksburg, occasionally bringing it to his lips for a kiss. They talked a little, about things far removed from what they were thinking.

The sensual haze lifted when he pulled into her driveway and she saw Tammy's car. Her son was home, probably waiting up for her, might even be peeking out a window.

Kyle shifted his car into park, then turned to her. With an easy smile, he ran his finger over her lips. "You don't have to invite me in. I understand."

She wondered if he was telepathic on top of all his other outstanding qualities. "I'm confused," she murmured.

"I can tell," he returned, then gave her a soft, slow kiss on her mouth. "And that's reason enough for me to leave you without doing a single one of the things I'm dying to do."

She leaned toward him and gave him a hug. "Thank you. I had a lovely evening." Then, despite his promise to do nothing, he gave her a kiss good night that crossed the circuits in her brain.

He waited until she had her front door open, then blew her a kiss and backed out of the driveway.

"Ma-aw! You're letting the cold air in again."

Matthew's voice yanked her back to earth. She swiftly stepped inside and closed the door. Expecting to be inundated with questions, she didn't know how to react when they completely ignored her. Matt and Tammy were sitting side by side on the floor in front of the television, frantically pressing buttons on their individual controllers while animated wrestlers on the screen acted out their orders. It was hardly the sort of activity she would have pictured Tammy doing, let alone enjoying. "Hey, guys, how was the movie?"

"Wait a minute," Matt said without looking at her. "The match is almost over."

It occurred to Barbara that she could have stayed in Kyle's car indefinitely and these two might not have noticed.

A few minutes later, Matt let out a victorious "*Yes!*" and Tammy tweaked his nose. "I'll get you next time, Hammerhead," she threatened in an imitation of a professional wrestler. As Matt turned off the game, she asked Barbara, "How'd it go?"

"Very nice," she answered honestly. "Better than I expected."

"When are you going out with him again?"

"Yeah, Ma, when? Tammy said she'd come back and keep me company anytime you wanted to go out. Maybe this guy would like to take you away for a whole weekend sometime."

"Matthew! Where would you get such an idea?" She looked at Tammy, but the girl shook her head in denial. Contact with Tammy seemed to have aged him considerably since that morning. "I gather you had a good time tonight."

"The best!" he exclaimed, then launched into a minute-by-minute account of what he did, what Kenny said, what Tammy didn't do, and moved on to give a review of the movie.

After an hour, he was finally calming down, so she announced that it was well past bedtime. He started to whine, but a pout from Tammy put a stop to that. She promised to come back again and gave him a hug.

When Matt went to his room, Barbara thanked Tammy profusely for befriending her son. "I've never seen him attach himself to anyone as quickly as he did you."

Tammy laughed. "I'm glad he did, because I think he's adorable. I really ought to thank you, though. I was really missing my kid brother before today. We used to be very close, but it was never the same after I moved out of the house. He probably thought I deserted him."

"I'm sure he'll come around when he gets a little older. In the meantime, I'm sure Matt would be happy to step in once in a while."

It took Matt another half hour after Tammy left to calm down enough to sleep, and by that time Barbara was more than ready for bed herself.

For some reason, she had always imagined that Matt would be jealous if she ever dated. The fact that he wasn't even curious about what the man was like gave her a sense of relief, but left her feeling a little jealous of Tammy.

The next day the green-eyed monster rose again when Matt couldn't seem to talk about anything else. It was silly, she knew. Having to share Matt's affection with another woman was something she had to get used to sooner or later. One day in the not-too-distant future, he would be a handsome young man who would fall in love for real and might forget his mother even existed. She hoped that was an exaggeration, but the reality was, someday he would make his own life and she would no longer be the center of it.

When that time came, she would simply have to adjust to being alone . . . for the rest of her life.

That depressing line of thought was interrupted by a knock at the door. Matt was checking out the visitor through the window before she could get up from her chair.

"It's a man," he told her as she came up behind him. "A stranger."

Barbara was more than a bit surprised to see that it was Kyle. "That's the man I went out with last night," she explained quickly. She hesitated a second and considered letting Matt greet him so that she could go brush her hair and put on lipstick. The hell with it, she decided, and opened the door. "Hello. This is a surprise."

Kyle came inside looking slightly embarrassed. "I'm sorry for dropping in like this, but you never did give me your phone number, and I wanted to invite you and your son to the Ringling Brothers Circus this afternoon. It's the last day they're in town."

Matt's face lit up. "The circus! Wow! Can we go, Ma, *please*?"

Barbara wondered if Kyle was always this spontaneous. Didn't she used to be like that, once upon a time? "Wouldn't you like an introduction first?" she asked Matt with a look meant to remind him about the stranger rule.

He let out a loud sigh, then showed off how smart he was. "His name is Kyle. You went out with him last night. And if he was a bad guy, you wouldn't have smiled when you saw him through the window." He held out his small hand to Kyle for a brief shake. "Hi. In case you didn't already figure it out, I'm Matt." Necessities out of the way, he turned back to his mother. "So, can we go, huh?"

Laughing, she asked Kyle, "Do we have time to get cleaned up a little?"

"If we leave here within the hour, we should still get to the arena before the show starts. If it's all right with you, we can eat there."

"Okay. Matt, take a fast shower while I clear away the breakfast dishes, then put on something without holes in it." He rolled his eyes at her in exasperation. She supposed she was going to have to start letting him do things on his own.

"One other thing," Kyle said before Matt left the room. "I remember when I was a boy it was always more fun to go somewhere with my parents if I could take a friend, so I got four tickets in case you'd like to invite someone."

"Can I, Ma?"

"Sure. Now hurry. I need to use the shower, too."

As Matt rushed to the telephone in the kitchen, Barb took Kyle's coat and hung it up. "Coffee?"

"If it's no trouble," he said, following her into the kitchen.

Matt held the phone out to her as they entered. "Tammy said she could meet us there, but she wants to talk to you first."

Barbara blinked at him. *Tammy?* Covering the mouthpiece with her hand, she whispered, "I thought you'd invite Kenny."

He grinned up at her. "I like Tammy better."

"How did you know her number?"

"She wrote it here on the message board for me. See?"

Barbara's mind jumped from her son's unexpected choice to how Kyle would react to the stunning, *younger* woman. Would he be as easily infatuated as Matt? She certainly couldn't compete with Tammy on a physical level. With a shake of her head, she thought this could be a blessing in disguise. She told Tammy that she was most welcome, and with Kyle's prompting, told her where to meet them.

After Matt said good-bye to Tammy and headed for the shower, Kyle said, "I hope that girl's parents aren't just going to drop her off."

Barbara smiled. "That *girl* is twenty-two. She works in the building where I do. Matt just met her yesterday, but apparently it was love at first sight for him—his first crush. She's the one who sat with him last night. If I'd known he was calling her instead of his buddy down the street, I would have tried to discourage him."

"Maybe you'd better talk to the lady and make sure she takes special care with his heart. A boy's first attack of true love is nothing to make fun of."

She angled her head at him. "Do you remember your first?"

He grinned. "As if it were yesterday." Stepping close to her, he ran his fingers through her hair. "Actually, it was the day before." He tried to embrace her for a kiss, but she glanced at the doorway and backed away from him.

"Your son's in the shower," he said in a low voice, and drew her against him. "Be nice to me now, and I promise to be a perfect gentleman in front of Matt for the rest of the day."

Thinking that once he saw Tammy, he may never want to kiss her again, she decided to take advantage of his offer. With a smile, she rose up on tiptoes and brought his head down to hers for a kiss that he wouldn't easily forget.

A few seconds later, he broke it off and took a deep breath. "For future reference, that is *not* the way to convince me to be a perfect gentleman."

She smothered a giggle and finished fixing his coffee. "Make yourself at home. I'll be as quick as I can."

As she walked away from him, she felt something else she hadn't known in many years—confidence in her femininity. And damned if it didn't feel great for a change.

Tammy was waiting for them when they arrived

at the arena. She looked fabulous as usual. Men and women both openly stared at the beauty as they passed, and Barbara held her breath as she introduced her to Kyle. They smiled at each other and said the appropriate polite phrases, but neither appeared to be terribly impressed with the other.

The circus was an awesome display of daring feats and eye-popping costumes. At first Matt was clearly having the time of his life, but about half-way through the show his mood changed. Considering how much junk food Kyle had bought him, Barbara chalked up his sour expression to an upset tummy, and his response to Kyle's dinner invitation on the way home confirmed that.

"I just want to go home," he snapped. "I don't feel good."

Recalling her spontaneous days of long ago, she said to Kyle, "We could order something to be delivered. Chinese or Italian."

Her suggestion brought a groan of complaint from Matt, so she tried to get his mind on something besides his stomach. "I was telling Kyle about your collection of baseball and football cards, and he said he used to collect them, too."

"*So?*" he replied in such an uncharacteristically rude tone, Barbara raised her eyebrows at him.

Kyle touched her hand to stop her from scolding the boy. "So-o-o," he said, "I was hoping you'd show me your collection."

Barbara gave Matt a look meant to remind him

of his manners no matter how queasy his stomach was.

"Fine," Matt murmured with absolutely zero enthusiasm.

After they arrived home, and Kyle proved to Matt that he did, in fact, know something about card collecting, Matt perked up a bit. Watching them together as they discussed the two sports, Barbara was struck by the realization that her fears had prevented Matt from experiencing a normal relationship with an adult male. She had always thought she could be both mother and father for her son. Was she wrong? As he approached puberty, would he need a real father figure to talk to?

Two days of excitement caught up with Matt after dinner and he fell asleep while they were watching a movie on television. Though he roused enough to be guided to bed, Barbara knew he was out for the night.

As she pulled the covers up to his chin and kissed him on the forehead, she got nervous about returning alone to Kyle. He had only promised to be a gentleman in front of Matt, and she wasn't sure she could trust herself if he was intent on seducing her.

Knowing there was even the tiniest possibility that Matt could wake up was deterrent enough to give her the courage to resist anything Kyle could do to her.

That courage faltered, however, when she walked into the living room and saw the way Kyle was looking at her. He wanted her, now, and knew she was his for the taking. She stopped a few feet away from him and crossed her arms. "Matt said to thank you for giving him such a fun day."

Kyle crooked his finger at her. "Come here."

Chapter 9

"Kyle, it was a wonderful day for me, too, but—"

"Stop. I know what you're about to say, and it's not necessary. I'm not a teenage boy who can't control his hormones. Please come here."

She sighed, uncrossed her arms, and sat down on the couch beside him. "I'm still confused."

He smiled and eased her into his arms. "It's a temporary condition that I'm sure I can remedy if you'll give me the chance." He gave her a peck on the forehead. "Now, as I was saying, I'm not going to lose control of my sex drive just because your son went to sleep. I haven't made any secret of how you make me feel, but I'm in no hurry to act on it."

He stopped to laugh at himself. "That's not entirely true. I *am* in a hurry, but I can wait, because I'm absolutely certain that this is only the beginning. We're going to have a lifetime of opportunities to make love, when circumstances are more favorable. For tonight, I'll be happy just to hold you for a while, then I'll leave. All right?"

She relaxed against him and showed her appreciation for his understanding with a shy smile.

For a long comfortable time, while the movie ran to its conclusion, he merely held her close and caressed her with his hands. But when the credits began rolling, he clicked off the television and focused his complete attention on kissing her senseless.

"I can't get over how good you taste to me," he whispered in her ear, then nibbled the lobe. "I haven't stopped thinking about that since I first kissed you in the parking garage. I'll keep my promise to wait, but you should know how badly I want you. At completely inappropriate times, I imagine feeling your bare skin sliding against mine, and get harder than I've ever been in my life."

His words were even more unnerving than his caresses. He must have sensed her tension, for he stopped talking and kissed her for another long time until the reason for her tension changed from uncertainty to needing more. The chemistry was much too strong, and her body had been deprived of pleasure for much too long for her to control its response to him.

"Do you have any idea how much I want to taste the rest of you?" His one hand moved from her back to her breast. "I'd give anything right now to taste you here." His hand loved that flesh, then slid down her stomach, over her hip, her bottom, and pressed between her thighs. "And here."

His mouth recaptured hers as she sharply inhaled, and she took his tongue as a substitute for what he made her want.

"Touch me," he pleaded. "And I won't ask for more tonight."

His request echoed her need to feel his desire for her in the most primitive way. Without hesitation, she stroked him through his slacks, wanting to inflame his senses as he was doing to her.

Abruptly he grasped her hand and brought it to his chest. With his heart pounding heavily against her fingertips, he hugged her tightly for several seconds, then murmured, "I'm sorry. That's not the way our first time is going to be."

She would have told him she felt the same way, but speech was beyond her capabilities at the moment.

"When we make love for the first time, we'll be completely alone, without any chance of being interrupted, and we'll have all night because that's how long it's going to take for me to know every inch of your body."

His bold promise sent another shiver of pleasure through her, making it harder for her to remember why tonight couldn't be that night.

"I'd better go," he said, though he didn't attempt to move.

"I have to get up early in the morning," she added, but stayed where she was.

"Me, too. I have to be on the road before the sun comes up." He groaned and created some space between them. Lifting her chin with his finger, he gave her a light kiss and said, "For the first time in my life, I'm not looking forward to a business trip, but I can't change it at this late hour. As the new regional manager, I promised to pay personal visits to all my salespeople this week. I won't be back in Richmond until Friday afternoon. Can I see you that night?"

Rather than being disappointed that he'd be away all week, she was relieved. A physical separation from him was probably exactly what she needed to decide whether she really wanted to get involved as deeply as he did.

"Can I let you know later in the week?" She called up her standard excuses. "I have to make sure Matt's taken care of and that my parents don't need me."

He wasn't happy with her answer, but he didn't push further, except to ask for her home and work numbers so that he could call her. Since he would be traveling from place to place, he gave her his beeper number, which he explained was always the fastest way to reach him even when he was in town.

It was a little easier to think after he left, and she spent the rest of the night dong that instead of sleeping. There was nothing wrong with Kyle; as far as she could tell so far, he was perfect. It was just too much, too fast. Like with Howard. Or was it just the déjà vu way they met that had alarms going off in her head?

Even if she dismissed the eery coincidence and allowed for the possibility that her hormones might not get her in trouble this time, there was something else to be considered before seeing Kyle again. Russ could show up any minute and throw her life into turmoil again, in which case, wouldn't it be less heartbreaking if she broke things off with Kyle before they got more involved?

Or should she grab a chance for momentary happiness and not worry how soon it must end?

No answers came during the night and a conversation with Matt over breakfast only added to her confusion.

"Are you going to go out with him again?" Matt asked in a tone that said he was hoping for a negative response.

"I . . . I'm not sure. Why?"

" 'Cause he's a creep."

Barbara stopped herself from reacting thoughtlessly. She had been afraid this might happen. He was jealous. "If he's such a creep, why didn't you turn down his invitation to the circus?"

Matt shrugged and pushed his scrambled eggs around on his plate. "I didn't know what a creep he was then."

"But you do now? I'm a little confused. Friday night you were suggesting I go away for a weekend with him. You jumped at the chance to go to the circus with him yesterday and you were having a great time until you got an upset stomach. Then after we got home—"

"I didn't have an upset stomach. I was mad."

"Over what?"

He sighed, practically out of patience with her. "Sorry, kiddo, you're going to have to give me a few more clues. I mean, if he's really a creep I wouldn't want to go out with him again, but since I didn't see him do anything creepy—"

"That's 'cause you didn't go to the men's room with us."

Every hair on Barbara's body stood on end. She leaned forward and spoke very slowly so as not to frighten him into silence. "What did he do, Matthew? Tell me everything." As unbelievable as the prospect of Kyle being a child molester seemed, she braced herself for the worst.

Matt played with his eggs for a few more seconds, then decided to tell her. "He waited outside the men's room while I went in. When I came out, I saw them, standing real close together, and he was whispering something in her ear that made her laugh. And when she saw me she pushed him away, but it was too late. I already saw."

Though he sat there looking very smug, his explanation didn't clear up anything for Barbara. "*She,* who?" He rolled his eyes in exasperation. She quickly thought back to their trip to the men's room together. Tammy had excused herself seconds later, so Barbara had stayed behind to guard their seats. "Are you talking about Kyle and Tammy?"

She was so relieved that it wasn't the conclusion she'd jumped to, she almost laughed out loud, but his sad little pout held her in check. He wasn't jealous of his mother having a boyfriend; this was about Tammy.

"Oh, sweetie. You know how noisy it was there. He was probably only leaning close so she could hear him."

"You think so?"

"Yes, but I think you ought to know, Tammy has a boyfriend."

He made a face. "You mean Michael. They had a fight. She told me she had more fun with me."

Barbara decided she and Tammy would have to have a talk about Matt's feelings, but for now, it was time to get moving.

On the way to school, he talked about his and Kenny's plans for the week, but before he got out of the car, he got back to his first comment of the day. "I've been thinking. I guess it would be okay if you wanted to go out with Kyle again."

"You don't think he's a creep anymore?"

"I don't know. I just figured I'd invite Kenny next time instead of Tammy."

She sent him off with a hug and a smile, but as she drove to work, she kept thinking back to their time at the circus. Could Matt have been right? Had there been a few sparks between Kyle and Tammy and she'd missed it entirely? She was just so very, very bad at analyzing men. In this case, she would actually be relieved if Kyle decided to turn his attentions elsewhere. It would save her the trouble of making any decisions about him.

*   *   *

Russ slowly exhaled the pungent smoke, then offered the joint to the woman lying beside him.

"No more. I have to go to work. I don't know how I'm going to get through the day as it is." Rather than get up, she snuggled closer and stroked his stomach.

He took another deep drag, then snuffed out the burning tip with his fingertips. He wondered if he needed to do her one more time before she left. God, he hoped not. It was bad enough in the dark. Her fat fingers drifted down between his legs, and he had his answer. Since he couldn't shut out the morning sun, he closed his eyes and pictured Barbara.

When Decker offered him a chunk of money to run a little errand, Russ figured he'd be back in Fredericksburg in two days, max. He had now been away for five. At least success was in sight, thanks to Betty Blubber-Butt.

It had sounded like such a simple task: get Barbara's medical file from her obstetrician to prove that she had delivered the baby prematurely. Russ's word wasn't enough for the Hamiltons. Since it was vital to his ultimate goal that the Hamiltons had no doubts about the child, Russ drove up to New York City to get the evidence Decker requested. Besides, he had been down to his last hundred dollars and was in serious need of operating capital.

He figured he could break into the office over the weekend and be back Sunday night. But Dr. Roselli had moved her practice to Albany, and when he got there, he discovered that the files in the office only went back two years. A phone call Monday morning informed him that the file was in storage, but could be retrieved—with the doctor's approval—in two to three weeks.

The only solution he could think of was to seduce one of the office girls into getting the file for him, and unfortunately for him, only one was immediately available. So he zoomed in on Betty something-or-other, a middle-aged, grossly overweight, sex-starved divorcée, and all night had been prepaying for the favor he needed.

Part of his deal with Decker was a promise that he would keep an eye on Barbara and make sure she didn't skip town while Russ was away, or if she did, he would have her followed. Decker thought Barbara was Russ's only interest, and Russ certainly wasn't going to tell him otherwise.

As a backup, though, Russ knew his partner was sticking close to Barbara and the boy as well.

With his mind focused on Barbara and his newest plan to put her in his debt forever, he was able to give Betty one more wild ride on the Russmobile before asking her to perform a little chore for him.

"I miss you," Kyle said as soon as Barbara identified herself over the phone.

She glanced at her watch and noted that it was one-thirty, the same hour that he'd called on the previous two days since he'd been gone, only this time she had someone sitting in front of her desk.

Knowing the kinds of things he might say that she couldn't possibly respond to at the moment, she asked, "Could I call you back? I'm with a customer right now."

"No. I'm on my way out. I just wanted you to know that I was thinking about you."

She smiled at the elderly man across from her and pretended to be writing an important message. "Very good. We can discuss that later."

"Have you made arrangements for Friday night yet?"

"Um, no, I'm still working on it."

"What you're doing is stalling. Listen to me, Barbara. I'm not going to go away just because you're afraid of complicating your life. I want you in a way that I've never wanted a woman before, and after Sunday night, I know you feel the same way. You can set any kind of limits that will make you comfortable. Just promise to spend the evening with me."

"Please, I really can't get into that right now."

"Fine. I'll call you tonight. It might be a little late."

"That's okay. Bye." She hung up and smiled again at her customer. "I'm sorry. Now, you were telling me about how your housekeeper threw out your mail by mistake." As the man related his long explanation of why his checking account was overdrawn, Barbara kept replaying Kyle's voice in her head. Monday and Tuesday he had teased her about her hesitation to follow through with what they'd started Sunday night. Today he was annoyed.

When she was with him, there was no doubt in her mind. She wanted everything he had to give her. When she was alone, however, the relationship seemed hopeless. She knew she had to end it before it became more intimate. Then she would hear his voice over the phone and bounce back to being confused.

That afternoon, Matt unknowingly helped to push her toward a decision. The first words out of his mouth as he climbed into their car were, "Kenny asked me to stay over at his house Friday night. His mom already said it was okay, and to tell you she'd pick me up right after school, so you won't have to rush for a change."

Barbara thought that was the sign she'd been waiting for, until she saw a countersign parked in front of her house. As she pulled into her driveway, Simon Decker got out of his car and hurried to head her off before she and Matt could go inside.

"You will hear what I have to say, Miss Mancuso, or we will do our talking in a courtroom."

For a split second before she got control of her temper, she considered strangling the vile man. "I know a little about courts myself, Mr. Decker, such as how to get a restraining order against someone who insists on harassing me without cause."

"Let's see," he said, rubbing his jaw in an exaggerated manner. "That would be from your Russ

Latham period, I suppose. I must admit, I wasn't terribly surprised to learn how that relationship ended. That young man's temper had caused a number of problems on the estate."

"Is that why you suggested he *charm* me into signing that agreement after Howard left?"

His eyebrows lifted. "Latham told you about that? How interesting. What else did he tell you?"

"That you were a slimy little worm that would crawl on his belly if the Hamiltons told you to. Matthew, go inside and call the police. Tell them we have a trespasser." She was pleased to see Decker react with a step backward. "The police will be here within five minutes. That gives you four to say what you came here for and take off."

Decker's eyes narrowed as he watched Matt enter the house. "You're being very foolish. The Hamiltons only want what's best for the boy." He saw Matt give his mother a thumbs-up sign in the front window and picked up the pace of his speech.

"My investigator was able to uncover the fact that you gave birth to your son six weeks prematurely, following Latham's assault. That brings the time of conception in line with your meeting Howard.

"Of course, there is also the possibility of proving Matthew's inheritance through DNA testing, but the Hamiltons would prefer not to exhume their son's body after all these years. Instead, they are prepared to pay you one million dollars, with all taxes paid, if you will—"

"You're all insane!" Barbara shouted. "They cannot buy my child! What would make you think it was only a matter of raising the amount?"

"Might I remind you that you accepted payment ten years ago in the form of certain valuable gifts, which you promptly sold for cash?"

"I had no choice! I was abandoned, pregnant, too sick to work. Anyway, that wasn't the same. They were just things, and I had a baby to support."

"Nevertheless," he countered, maintaining his air of superiority, "you are still struggling to support that child. You've moved around like a nomad since he was born; you don't even own the house you live in. While the Hamiltons could provide him with every luxury available and a guaranteed future as a captain of industry. Think of the child."

Barbara straightened her shoulders and glared at the attorney. "That child is the only person I've been able to think of for a third of my life, and I am absolutely positive that turning him over to you and your clients would be the most despicable crime I could commit."

"I'm sorry you feel that way. It will only make it that much harder on you when the transfer of custody occurs. You will end up with nothing. No child. No fortune. I would have thought that your earlier experience would have taught you that when the Hamiltons wish for something to happen, it does. You weren't able to fight them then, and you won't be able to now."

He heard a car pull into the driveway behind him and was startled to see a police unit. Apparently, he had thought she was bluffing.

"You're going to regret this," he declared in a threatening tone that contradicted how quickly he started walking toward his car.

Dani stepped out of her car and held a black baton out in front of Decker. "Stop right there, sir," she said firmly. Keeping her gaze fixed on him, she addressed Barbara.

"Is this the man you had problems with in the past?"

"No. But this one has shown up here uninvited twice, and he just threatened me."

"That's a blatant lie," Decker said. "I am an attorney, attempting to deliver an offer to settle a dispute between Miss, er, *Mrs.* Johnson and my clients. I merely warned her that she would regret her refusal to mediate the matter."

The officer looked at Barbara for her response.

"That's his interpretation. I took it as a threat. However, I won't file any charges if he promises to stay away from me and my son."

The officer lowered her baton, but her attitude continued to hold him where he was. "All right, sir, you're free to go, as soon as you show me your identification."

"For what reason?" he asked warily.

Her mouth parted in a semblance of a smile, but no friendliness showed in her eyes. "I just want to make sure I spell your name correctly on my report."

Barbara could see him wanting to refuse, but he merely huffed his annoyance and showed the officer his driver's license. He wasted no time getting away as soon as she dismissed him.

"Do you have time to stop in for a few minutes?" Barbara asked Dani.

"Very few. We're backlogged tonight, for some reason. I was on my way to another call when I heard this one."

"Hi, Sergeant Pfeiffer," Matt said as they went inside.

"Hey, Matt. Dispatch said you did an excellent job with that call for assistance."

"No big deal," he said with an embarrassed smile. "I've done it before."

Barbara could see by Dani's expression that she thought that was a shame, but she said nothing.

"I was watching you from the window," Matt said to Dani. "I saw how you stopped that guy with your nightstick. Could I look at it?"

"Matt . . ." Barb warned.

"It's okay," Dani said, smiling, and drew the baton out of its holder. "In trained hands, it can be a lethal weapon, but it's no more dangerous than a stick to an amateur."

Matt took the baton by its handle, felt the weight of it, then imitated the action he'd seen Dani perform to stop Decker. "Sensei said he'd be teaching us to defend ourselves with sticks in a few months, but I don't think those are like this one. Have you ever had to use it on a bad guy?" His eyes were wide with fascination.

"Matthew . . ." Barbara warned again, and Dani shook her head in a manner that told her not to worry.

"Let's just say I could if I had to. In fact, I received a certificate for outstanding achievement with it in the police academy."

"Wow! Could you show me some moves?"

Dani ruffled his hair and retrieved her baton. "How about another time? I really need to visit with your mom before I go."

Matt looked a little disappointed, but took the hint to leave the grown-ups alone for the moment.

"Coffee?" Barb offered.

"Great." Dani took off her jacket and followed Barbara into the kitchen. "I don't have to know anything to file a report on this call, but I am curious."

It took Barbara less than a heartbeat to decide to confide in her new friend. As she fixed two cups of coffee, she gave Dani the missing pieces of her personal history.

"Geez! When it rains on you, it really pours, doesn't it?" Dani added more sugar to her coffee and slowly stirred while she digested Barbara's new information. "I'm not an attorney, of course, but from my experience dealing with them, I'd bet that he didn't really believe they had much of a chance in court. That's got to be why he's offering so much money and risking threats."

"I hope you're right. Plus, he admitted that they'd rather not exhume Howard's body. Anyway, from what I remember about them, I can't imagine the

Hamiltons wanting the publicity that kind of a court case would attract. I know I don't, for myself or Matt. But if they force me, I'll fight this time."

"I know you said you don't want to press charges, but if anything happens that changes your mind, just call."

"Thank you. I will."

"I assume you haven't heard any more from your stalker."

"Nothing," Barbara said with a frown. "It's got me really baffled."

"Unfortunately, the lab wasn't able to pick up any clear fingerprints off the roses, so I contacted every florist in the area. No one had a special order for eighteen Oceania roses, with or without thorns. I don't mean to question your story, but is there any chance it was a coincidence?"

Barbara rubbed her forehead. It was impossible to dismiss her certainty that if he was anywhere around, Russ would have contacted her. It was completely out of character for him to send the roses and not show up in person immediately afterward. "I suppose there's a slim chance, and believe me, I *wish* it were a coincidence, but I can't assume that. I keep getting the strangest feeling that I'm being watched and followed, even though I never see anyone suspicious."

Dani's radio had been emitting scratchy noise since she arrived, but suddenly she heard something that made her shoot up from her chair. "Gotta go. I'll come back when I can."

As she grabbed her jacket, Barbara said, "Wait,

one second, please. Would you mind telling me whatever happened to your sister's stalker?"

Dani paused for a heartbeat, then finished donning her jacket. "He was beaten to death. Found naked in an alley behind a gay bar . . . with every bone in his body broken." On her way out the door she added, "He deserved worse."

Barbara thought the same thing.

Remembering Kyle's promise to call, she stayed up later than usual, but the phone never rang. It occurred to her that he may have given up on her in spite of his insistence that he wouldn't. She thought that should have given her a sense of relief, but that was no longer the case. She hadn't realized how much she had looked forward to hearing his voice until he didn't call.

She recalled her answer to Dani's question about marriage the first time she and the policewoman talked. Perhaps she hadn't fallen in love all these years for another reason: The right man, one strong enough to deal with the complications in her life, hadn't come along. Now it looked as though he may have appeared, and she had pushed him away by being too afraid to take a chance.

If she were a teenager, this would be the time when she'd call her best friend and talk about it until she felt better. But she hadn't allowed herself to get that close to anyone in years. Dani was the first person she'd encountered who might have filled the position, but she was too busy for girltalk. She knew she could call Tammy, but Tammy was too young to understand her reasons for putting Kyle off. The only thing she might say is "I told you so," and that was certainly not what Barbara needed at the moment.

She and Matt were walking out the door the next morning when the telephone finally rang. She hurried back to answer it just in case it was Kyle. "Hello?"

"You sound out of breath," Kyle observed.

"I was on my way out the door."

"Then I won't keep you. I just wanted to apologize for not calling last night. It was so late when I got back to my room, I was afraid I'd wake you and Matt up if I called then. But I didn't want this to wait until I got a break later today. I'm sorry I pushed you yesterday. I told you I would wait, then—"

"It's okay. I'm sorry I've been so . . . I don't know, uncertain, I guess. But I'm not anymore. I want to see you Friday night." She paused a moment, then decided to let him know just how certain she was. "Matt will be spending the night at his friend's house." Though he didn't say anything, she got the impression he was smiling.

"Maw!" Matt complained. "We're going to be late."

"I have to go," she told Kyle.

"I know." There was laughter in his voice. "I'll call later if I can, but today and tomorrow are packed with appointments, and after what you just said, I'm going to want to get through them as fast as possible. Just don't change your mind;

I don't think my heart could stand it, to say nothing for other parts of my body."

She was still smiling when she arrived in the cafeteria for her coffee and doughnut, and her friends immediately commented on it. She didn't feel comfortable announcing her secret to an audience, but at lunch she gave in to Tammy's nudging. The girl had been teasing her ever since she heard about Kyle, yet when she learned of Barbara's decision to give the relationship a chance to develop, she seemed disturbed.

"What's wrong?" Barbara asked. "I thought you'd be happy about that."

Tammy smoothed the frown lines out of her forehead. "Of course I'm happy. It's just that when I said you should get out more, I meant with different men, not just the first one who came along. I mean, Kyle's nice enough, but I don't think Matt likes him very much, and you really should consider his feelings before you start getting serious about a man."

"Whoa!" Barbara protested. "Who said anything about getting serious? It's just . . . well, it's just a strong chemical attraction. I may be ready to do something about that, but I'm certainly not ready for a permanent commitment."

Tammy raised a brow at her. "Maybe you don't think *you* are, but Kyle certainly sounds like he's looking for a wife. You know I'd be the last one to stop you from having some fun, but I'd hate to see you rushing into another bad situation."

"Don't worry," Barbara replied with a shake of

her head. "No man will ever rush me into anything again."

That brought a satisfied smile to Tammy's face. "Good. So, what time do you need me to sit with Matt?"

"Thanks, but he's gong to his friend Kenny's house after school."

Disappointment erased Tammy's smile again. "Oh. Well, give me a call if that falls through or if there's any other time I can help with him. You know how much I enjoy his company."

Barbara smiled her appreciation, but her mind was replaying the statement she'd made about not being rushed into anything. Despite her confident words, she began to worry that she had already given in to a bit of rushing. The question was, was it coming from Kyle, or was her own libido doing it? Either way, she wondered if she really was strong enough to slow it down before she got in over her head.

Chapter 10

As Barbara drove home from work on Friday, she wondered if the temporary insanity plea would work with Kyle. What could she have been thinking? After she had made it clear that the house would be all theirs for the whole night, there was no doubt in either of their minds as to what they were going to be doing in a few short hours. There would be no more putting off what seemed to be inevitable from the first glance.

From a purely physical standpoint, she wanted to spend the night with Kyle. She wanted it as much as she'd ever wanted anything in her life. If she could simply enjoy the physical part and remain detached emotionally, everything would be fine, but she knew she wasn't that type of woman.

If only he weren't so perfectly wonderful. If only Tammy hadn't gotten her thinking about how fast things were moving.

She glanced at the decorated bottle of champagne on the seat next to her. It had been delivered to her office that morning with an unsigned note that said only; *7:30 tonight or I'll pop my cork trying to get there*. Yesterday afternoon he'd sent a telegram that read: *Thirty hours and counting down. Love always, Kyle*. He had called at least once every day, just to let her know he was thinking about her. He was completely sure of himself and the fact that they would have a beautiful future together.

How could she not want to be with him tonight?

On the other hand, how could she be with him like that when he didn't even know her real name or how she'd become the person she was? She had told him the make-believe stories she gave to strangers or acquaintances who weren't important to her. Would he still think they had a future together when he learned that she had lied to him? Didn't he deserve to know the truth before they made love?

Questions were still bouncing around in her head while she got ready for her date. Kyle had told her to get dressed up without revealing where they would be going. To give herself a little more confidence, she had gone out at lunch that day and bought a black cocktail dress that would suit a wide range of functions. Recalling how early Kyle had been for their first date, she made sure she was ready well ahead of time.

At seven-fifteen the doorbell rang, and she bolted up from the sofa. Then she stopped and took a slow breath to try to compose herself. She didn't want Kyle to see how nervous she was. Determined to greet him as a confident, mature woman, she pulled her shoulders back, smiled, and casually opened the door.

It took her brain a moment to absorb the fact that it wasn't Kyle standing on her front porch, but *Russ Latham*.

That moment cost her. Before she could slam the door shut, he stuck his booted foot in the way.

"C'mon, babe. Don't be like this."

She pressed her weight against the door as hard as she could. He didn't push back, but he didn't move his foot out of the way, either. "You'd better get out of here, Russ. I've already warned the police about you. They're watching this house around the clock."

"I only want to talk to you. I swear. Just give me five minutes."

A flood of acid filled her stomach. How many times had he said those same words? Why wouldn't' he give up?

"You know you don't have the strength to keep me out here if I really wanted to get to you, so why don't you make this easier on both of us and invite me in so we can talk like two civilized people?"

She held back the obvious retort, knowing from past experience that insulting him only made things worse. She heard him let out a long-suffering sigh intended to make her feel sorry for him, but she knew his act too well to be fooled.

"Okay, I guess I deserve this," he said. "I've done some things that really hurt you. I know that, and I'm sorrier than you can imagine. That's why I spent every penny I had to hire a private detective to find you this time."

Though she was tiring, she maintained the pressure against his foot so that he'd know she was't relenting. Focusing on that helped to slow down the hysteria, but it wasn't enough. She knew it was her imagination, yet she felt his fingers around her throat, squeezing tighter and tighter. *Breathe!* she ordered herself. *Keep breathing and you won't black out.*

Her body began to perspire despite the cold draft, and the smell of her own fear filled her nostrils. No matter how far she thought she had come, nothing had changed. He still had the power to destroy her life whenever he chose. Why couldn't *he* have died in the car accident instead of Howard?

"Are you listening to me, Barbara? I said, I thought you looked real pretty when you opened the door, like you were all dressed up. Are you and Matt going somewhere special?"

Concentrating on his question helped her to remember that Kyle would be there any minute. What would he think was happening? Would he automatically react to protect her, the way he did with the mugger in the garage? Would Russ stand and fight or could he be discouraged if he learned she had a man in her life?

She swallowed and tried to make her voice sound calm. "I have a date. I thought it was him when I opened the door." It seemed to take him forever to respond, and when he did, it was the last thing she expected to hear him say.

"Good. I'm glad. I was afraid I had caused so much damage that you'd never let a man close to you again. I know you're not going to believe this right away, but I've changed. It took me a long time, but about a year ago, I met someone who convinced me to join a therapy group. It was as if somebody suddenly switched a big lightbulb on in my head and everything became crystal clear.

"I understand now that I was eaten up with jealousy over everything Howard had that I didn't, and sometimes it came out of me in really negative ways. That was why I wanted you so much. As part of my recovery, I had to see you again, apologize, and say good-bye."

"Good-bye?" Barbara wanted it to be true badly enough to give him her whole attention.

"Yes. If that's what you really want. But I need your help to do this. I have to spend some time with you to prove to us both that I've gotten over my obsession."

She was certain there wasn't a therapist on earth who would recommend a stalker spend quality time with his victim to aid his recovery. More than likely he'd read an article on the subject and memorized enough of the psychobabble to sound sincere. "Where was this therapy group?"

"Outside of Dayton."

At least that was the truth; she knew he'd hung around Dayton last year, hoping to get a lead on her. But that didn't mean he was being honest about anything else.

"You don't have to agree right now. The shrink told me it could take you a while to trust me again. That's why I gave you some time in between sending you the roses and coming to see you. I wanted to show you I wasn't trying to push you anymore. Wait a minute."

Barbara couldn't tell what he was doing until he tried to pass her a slip of paper through the opening.

"Please take it. That's the number of the motel where I'm staying. Call me after you think about what I said. Okay?" When she didn't take it from him, he let it drop to the floor. "There's one more thing I have to do as part of my recovery. I have to be completely honest with you and tell you all the things I lied to you about when we were together—a complete confession."

"I know about your lies, Russ. There's no need to dredge it all up again."

"You're wrong. You don't know everything. You don't know the part I played in breaking your engagement to Howard."

The part *he* played? What had Decker said about Russ being willing to do anything for money? It didn't matter. That was in the distant past and wouldn't make any difference today. Still, it took tremendous willpower not to ask him to explain.

"When you're ready to hear about that and some other things that you should know, call me at that number. We'll have lunch, maybe take in a movie. It'll be just like old times, only better. You'll see. You don't have to run from me ever again."

As soon as he retrieved his foot, she closed and locked the door. The years had taught her never to believe anything he said, especially when he sounded remorseful or made promises to leave her alone. They were all lies. He may have taken advantage of Howard's abandoning her, but he couldn't have had anything to do with it.

Could he?

She watched him walk across the street and get into a Volkswagen. The streetlight wasn't bright enough for her to make out the car's age or color, except that it seemed to be pale.

She picked the scrap of paper up off the floor, intending to call Dani to report the visit, when Kyle pulled into her driveway. Hurriedly, she stuck the note on the kitchen message board so she wouldn't misplace it before she had a chance to pass it on to the police.

Her initial case of nerves over seeing him was nothing compared to how she felt now. She no longer had the energy to greet him with a confident smile, nor did she have any desire to go out on a date, or even talk to another man, for that matter. However, she couldn't wish him away any more than she could Russ.

Before Kyle got to the door, she opened it and did her best to appear happy to see him. She could tell by the way his smile immediately turned to a frown that he wasn't fooled by her effort.

"What's the matter?" he asked, stopping short.

"I, uh, I was just a little worried that something had happened to you when you weren't here on time." The lie didn't sound the least bit convincing. She moved aside so he could come in, but he didn't move.

"I don't believe that's what's wrong. It's only seven thirty-two now. Would you rather not see me tonight? Have you changed your mind? I'll be disappointed, but I really won't die if you've—"

"Stop! Please, just come inside. I'll be all right in a minute."

He continued to scrutinize her face as he walked past her and took off his coat. "You're going to have to give me some direction here," he said, keeping several feet of space between them. "I've been counting the hours till I could hold you again, but I'm not sure if reaching for you would be good or bad at the moment."

She closed her eyes and let her heart decide. "Holding me would very definitely be a good thing right now."

"Thank God." In an instant his arms were around her, but that only served to make him more aware of a problem. "You're shaking." He leaned back and touched his palms to her cheek, then her forehead. "And your skin feels cold and damp. Why didn't you say you were sick? We don't have to go out anywhere. We can stay here, and I'll take care of you."

"No!" She backstepped out of his reach. "I don't need to be taken care of by anybody! I'm not sick." The look of bewilderment on his face told her she'd overreacted to his casual remark. "I'm sorry. Something very upsetting happened right before you arrived, and I haven't calmed down yet. Maybe you should leave. I'm not going to be very good company tonight."

"Too late. You missed your chance to work it out by yourself. I already took off my coat, and you admitted you needed to be held. Now you have to sit down and tell me all about whatever shook you so badly." He held out his hand to her and had to wait several seconds for her to accept it.

"I need to go take a shower and—"

He silenced her with a soft kiss. "Not now. I have a better idea." Looking around the room, he noticed the knitted afghan hanging over the back of the rocking chair. He got that and wrapped it around her. "The Boy Scout first-aid manual says to raise a shock victim's body temperature. This should help."

He then guided her to the sofa, but instead of sitting on it, he used it to support his back as he sat on the floor and pulled her down so that she was sitting between his legs with her back against his chest. Crossing his arms in front of her, he gave her a hug. "And this will help even more. Now talk."

She let the warmth of the afghan blend with the sense of security his body provided. It was almost as if he knew that, besides wanting to be enveloped by him, her story would be easier to tell if she didn't have to meet his gaze. "I'm not sure where to begin."

"As cliché as it sounds, how about the beginning?" She sort of laughed, and he gave her a little squeeze. "Start anywhere you'd like. I'll figure it out as you go."

She didn't expect Kyle to understand, only to listen, but he did so much more than that. For the most part, he let her talk without interrupting, except for a few questions that encouraged her to tell him how certain events made her feel. When she told him of Howard's death and what it had meant to her, she felt his chest tremble and turned to see him blinking moisture from his eyes. She nearly fell apart herself, but his empathy helped her to finish the account.

"Had you gotten here five minutes earlier, you would have met Russ on my front porch."

"Believe me, if I'd known a bastard like that was bothering you, I'd have broken all the speed limits to be here in time to greet him personally."

She shifted sideways in his arms and kissed his cheek. "I have no doubt you would have, but I didn't tell you about him so that you would get all macho on me. I've had to deal with him before. I'll do it again."

He narrowed his brows. "How? By running away *again*? Changing your names *again*? For God's sake, Barbara, haven't you had enough of being victimized?"

She was stunned by how quickly he'd gone from compassionate to condemning. "I had *enough* nine years ago, but I have a child to protect, and if I'm forced to run again, I will." She tried to pull away from him, but he held her tighter.

"Forgive me. I didn't mean it the way it sounded. Of course you'll do whatever you must to protect Matt, but I don't want to think about you going anywhere when I've just found you. I won't let this guy or anyone else force you away from me without a fight."

"That's very sweet, but it's not your fight."

"Like hell, it's not," Kyle stated firmly, then softened his words by stroking her hair. "The timing isn't right, I know, and I'm probably moving much too fast here, but I can't help it. I want you to know how I feel about you.

"I gave this a lot of thought while we were apart this week, and I came to the very logical conclusion that I had to wait awhile before saying certain things, but logic only works when I can't see your face or hold you in my arms.

"I love you, Barbara. It's as if I always have. I know I always will. You don't need to answer in any way tonight. I just wanted you to hear that at a time when you could be certain it wasn't lust making me say empty words."

It was good he didn't require an answer, for she had no idea what to say. At the moment she was too distraught over Russ's reappearance to even judge how his declaration made her feel.

"Now that I've said that much, I may as well

finish. I told you why I never got married. I was waiting for that one special woman who would make me feel all the things love's supposed to make a person feel. I don't need any more time to know that you're that special woman and that I want to spend the rest of my life with you."

Barbara heard his words and knew they would make most women very happy, but they only served to make her uneasy. No matter how wonderful he was, it was much too soon. "Kyle, I—"

His fingers pressed to her lips. "Hush. I said I don't expect answers tonight and I meant that. But I think, especially under the circumstances, that you need to know how deep my feelings are for you, and that it doesn't have to be you against the world anymore. I want to stand with you to protect Matt. I want that maniac to know you're no longer alone and vulnerable. I've met his type before. He's really nothing but a bully, terrifying a woman and a child, and that kind tends to crawl away if he's faced with serious competition."

"That makes sense, but I would never consider marrying a man just for protection."

Again he touched her lips to silence her. "Of course not. But if you loved that man, the protection would be a nice fringe benefit, wouldn't it? So, for the moment, I want you to put everything I said into some back corner of your mind and just bring it out when you're ready to think about it. Deal?"

She couldn't help but return his smile. "Deal."

"Do you need to talk about anything else?"

She shook her head no.

"How about any other little secrets I should know, like your mother's an ax murderer or your father's the head of the Mafia?"

She wrinkled her nose at him. "Smart-ass. Not all Italians are mafioso. It's only propaganda to keep all you WASP types in line. And no, I have no secrets left to tell. You now know every tiny detail of my life, and I'd very much like to avoid any further conversation about me or my problems for the rest of the night."

"Good enough. Now, correct me if I'm wrong, but I think a change of plans is called for here. I was going to take you into the capital for a very romantic dinner followed by some very romantic dancing, but we could do that another night."

He accepted the slight twist of her mouth as her agreement. "Didn't you say there's a Chinese restaurant nearby that delivers?"

"The Chinese Garden. I could probably handle some wonton soup."

"Sounds good to me. You mentioned wanting to take a shower. How about if you go relax in a hot bath instead, with lots of bubbles if you've got them. Then put on something warm and comfortable. I'll take care of dinner."

"I'd be insane to refuse such a generous offer," she said with a laugh. "The number of the restaurant is on the board by the kitchen phone."

As she closed herself in the bathroom and turned on the water in the tub, she wondered if any other woman ever had a third date with a man who compared to this one. When she first saw Kyle's car pull up, she was certain the evening would be a disaster because of Russ. Instead, Russ caused a change in their plans and, possibly, their entire relationship.

The best thing was that she could stop fretting over if and when and how to tell Kyle the truth, and how he would react to it. They were suddenly past it, and his reaction was far better than anything she had imagined it could be.

Sinking down into the bubble bath, she felt her tension float away in the steam. Kyle's romantic words replayed in her mind. *I love you, Barbara. I want to spend the rest of my life with you.* She had thought she never wanted to hear phrases like that again. With Howard, they represented a loss of independence and excruciating heartache. With Russ, they represented a twisted obsession that brought other kinds of pain.

What did those words mean coming from Kyle?

If nothing else, he had effectively distracted her from dwelling on Russ's visit. His words, his touch, his empathy had reduced the immediate threat to an annoyance that could be pushed aside.

He had assured her that she didn't need to respond tonight, but she knew her attitude toward having a man in her life had already begun to change, at least as far as Kyle Trent was concerned.

Kyle frowned at the piece of paper that had been added to the board by the phone. It only bore the name of a motel and a room number, but from what Barbara had told him, he knew where he could find Russ Latham.

If spending the night with Barbara weren't quite so important, he'd head over to that motel right now.

But, after all this time, renewing his acquaintance with Russ could wait another day or two.

"Barbara?" Kyle's voice broke into her thoughts from outside the bathroom door. "Dinner's ready whenever you are."

"I'll be right out." She could hardly believe it, but her watch showed that she'd been daydreaming for nearly an hour. She hadn't even noticed how cool the water had become.

No longer certain where their evening was headed, she put on some pretty underwear, but covered it with a long, *un*sexy terry cloth robe.

Kyle gave her a light kiss as she reentered the living room. The first thing she noticed was that he had taken off his suit jacket and tie, and unbuttoned his shirt collar and cuffs. It took her eyes a few seconds more to adjust to the dimly lit scene he'd created. He had apparently found her stash of emergency candles and lit every one of them. In the flickering glow, she could see that he planned for them to sit on pillows on the floor and eat at the coffee table. There were a half dozen Chinese take-out containers beside two neat place settings, and the bottle of champagne he'd sent her had been opened and was propped in a bowl of ice.

"You didn't tell me you were a magician," she said with a delighted smile. "This is probably more romantic than any restaurant you could have taken me to." She stopped and heard sounds of the ocean and wind chimes in the background. "You even found my new age tape to eat Chinese food by."

"I didn't think you'd mind my foraging a little rather than interrupt your soak every couple seconds to ask for directions." He eased her into his embrace and massaged her lower back muscles. "Feel better?"

"Mmmm. That's nice," she said, relaxing against him. "Can I keep you?"

He chuckled. "That's what I'm hoping for."

She tipped her head back to explain that she hadn't meant it literally, but his lips pressed to hers before she could speak, and then she forgot what she was going to say. As the kiss deepened, she felt his body changing, and hers instinctively responded to its invitation.

Parting their mouths a fraction, he murmured, "Did someone just turn up the heat in here?"

"It was probably Elliot." Kyle arched one eyebrow in question. "Elliot is Matt's invisible friend, who he blames for anything from a missing sock to spilled milk."

"I'm pretty sure Elliot wasn't to blame this time," Kyle said with a grin, then reluctantly separated their bodies. "Evidence to the contrary, I really don't want to rush this." He held out his arm in gentlemanly fashion. "May I escort you to the table, madam?"

Hooking her arm through his, she replied, "By all means, kind sir. I'm suddenly quite famished."

Not knowing what she might like besides won-ton soup, Kyle had ordered a variety of dishes. They both sampled every one without putting much of a dent into any of them. While they ate, Kyle told her how his day had gone, as he had nearly every day of that week.

She had no particular interest in the business and he didn't attempt to intrigue her with that sort of information. Instead, he told her stories about the people he'd met along the way. Always having been a student of people herself, she truly enjoyed listening to his descriptions of them and what he thought made them tick.

When she insisted she couldn't eat another bite, he unearthed the four plastic-wrapped for-tune cookies that had come with their order and held them out to her. "Pick two."

She selected one. "I'll save the other one for Matt. He actually eats these things." She waited for Kyle to take one and set the other two aside before opening hers.

"What does yours say?" he asked.

"Read yours first."

His fortune made him laugh. " *'You will be trav-eling in the future.'* Well, that's true. Now yours."

She looked at the slip of paper in her hand and considered making up a prediction rather than reading what it said, but she didn't want to tell him any more lies, no matter how small. " '*Confucius say, when love knocks at your door, answer it.*' "

"Wise man, that Confucius."

She smirked at him. "I could have just as easily gotten yours. Then what would you have said?"

"That's easy. You probably will be traveling . . . with me. Where would you like to go on our honeymoon?"

She narrowed her eyes at him. "I think that question could be classified under 'getting pushy,' and I distinctly remember you telling me I didn't have to give you answers tonight."

"You're absolutely right." He stood up and held out his hand to help her up. "Dance with me."

Her eyes raised to his. "Here?"

"There's enough room if we move the table."

She looked down at her robe and bare feet. "I'm not really dressed for it."

He took off his shoes and belt and pulled his shirt out of his pants. "Even?"

She giggled. Sloppy was definitely not his natural look. "Let me clean up the food first."

He stopped her from picking up his plate. "*I* will clear the table and move it. You pick out something slow to dance to."

She hadn't forgotten what dancing in public with him last Saturday had been like; she could only guess what dancing in private might mean. It called for nothing less than the sultry saxophone of Kenny G.

With the stage set and excuses eliminated, she stepped into his arms the moment he opened them to her. Instantly, she sensed the difference in his touch. He was no longer trying to comfort her or make her feel safe. In fact, the way his body felt pressed to hers was anything *but* safe.

Sometime between the second and third song her belt came untied and his hands slipped beneath the robe to stroke the bare skin of her back and trace the lace edges of her panties. Somehow the rest of his shirt buttons came undone and her fingers were free to discover the sprinkling of silky hair across his firm chest and down the center of his abdomen.

The music continued to play and their bodies still swayed gently from side to side, but their feet had stopped moving some time ago. Barbara felt lightheaded, as if she were more than a little drunk. Having purposely limited her intake of champagne to two glasses, she knew it was not alcohol, but Kyle working his magic on her.

She loved the way he was taking his time to seduce all her senses. It was perfect—exactly the way it happened in romance novels—and, like one of the heroines from those books, she thought she might burn up in his arms if he didn't progress to kissing her soon. "Kyle?"

"Hmmm?"

The sound vibrated through her. "Can we quit pretending that we're dancing?"

He stopped moving completely and whispered

in her ear. "This night is all for you, love. What would make you happy now?"

The question caught her off guard. He had initiated all the advances up to that moment, and she had expected him to continue to do so. "I . . . I'd like you to kiss me."

He smiled. "It would be my pleasure."

She hadn't thought it was possible, but within seconds he actually surpassed himself as the world's greatest kisser. Her knees were about to give out on her when he left her mouth to plant a trail of feathery kisses along her cheekbone.

"Is there anything else you'd like me to do for you?"

As he nibbled his way down her neck, the last of her inhibitions took flight. "I'm suddenly feeling a little tired. I think you should put me to bed."

Chapter 11

"That would also be my pleasure," Kyle said, sweeping Barbara off her feet. The next instant, his mouth recaptured hers, effectively cutting off any second thoughts she might have.

As he set her on the bed and lay down beside her, she was again aware that everything seemed to be going in slow motion. It was the exact opposite of having sex with Howard, which usually had been frenzied and quick, with almost no foreplay whatsoever. How could she have thought that was so wonderful?

Perhaps, it had only seemed wonderful because her two "experiments" before Howard had been so emotionless and unsatisfactory. The only other man who had ever touched her was Russ, and she had been repulsed by him.

She didn't need any more experience, however, to know that Kyle was the ideal lover. Not only did he take his time with each step and kiss with the skill of the devil himself, he clearly understood a woman's needs and had intimate knowledge of the female body. He knew how to undress them both without halting the sensual seduction that kept her from thinking about what flaws he might find. He knew how to make love to every inch of her body and which areas to save for last.

Before either of them got too carried away, she wordlessly retrieved a box of condoms from the nightstand drawer. Having gone through an unplanned pregnancy once in her life had been enough to give her the nerve to buy the protection at the same time as she had bought the dress.

Several times while he was arousing different parts of her body, she stroked him, wanting to return the pleasure, but he would only allow her the briefest touch before moving her hand or shifting his position.

Thinking he might still be playing the game where she had to voice her request to get what she wanted, she gathered her wits enough to speak. *"Please."*

He raised his head from her breast and smiled. "Please, what?"

Her body was screaming with such need she could barely think, let alone form an explicit command. "Make love to me."

"I thought that's what I was doing."

Frustration fueled her nerve. She grasped his shaft and held tight. "I want this." She touched her pubic hair. "Here. *Now.*"

He moved his body over hers so that the two parts met as she ordered, then rubbed himself up and down against her. "Like this?"

A spear of pleasure made her whimper. "Yes."

He did it again. "No. Kyle, please stop teasing me. I want you inside."

"No."

Her eyes flew open. His face hovered above hers for a moment, then he began inching his body down hers. In between burning her flesh with hot, wet kisses, he explained. "I have thought of little else but being inside you for a week. But then I heard your story and realized that what I wanted wasn't as important as what you needed. The last two men in your life only thought of what they wanted—one left you pregnant and alone, the other caused you horrible pain and years of suffering.

"I told you earlier, tonight is all for you. I want to prove to you that a man can think of your needs first."

"Kyle, you've already proven that. What I need—"

"Hush. I know what you need. Now pay attention. You'll be graded on your performance."

She would have laughed, but just then he moved the last inch downward and buried his face between her thighs. All at once his fingers were doing something incredibly exciting inside her and his tongue and teeth were doing other unfamiliar things on the outside. The phrase "zero to sixty in five seconds flat" came to mind as she grasped the sheets on both sides of her to keep from flying off the bed.

Her first climax was past before she was prepared for it. The second, following so closely behind the first, was an even greater shock. *What in God's name was he doing to her?*

He gentled his actions long enough for her to catch her breath, but her heart was still racing when he began arousing her again. Tangling her fingers in his hair, she moaned, "Kyle! You're killing me."

The expression on his face as he looked up at her was one of satisfaction. "Just once more, honey, and you'll have earned your A-plus."

By the time he was finished demonstrating just how well he knew what she needed, every bone in her body had turned to liquid. Fortunately, he came up beside her and drew her into his embrace, for she couldn't move a muscle on her own.

"You see?" he whispered. "That didn't kill you."

She might have debated that, if she had one ounce of energy to do so. Still intent on catering to her, he rearranged the bedcoverings over them and fit her spoon-fashion into the curve of his body. His erection pressed against her back and she made an effort to bring their bodies even closer, but he stopped her again.

"Sleep, love. We have the rest of our lives for you to satisfy me."

She wanted to protest, but his suggestion of sleep seemed to take control of her mind. The thoughts that normally kept her from getting a good night's sleep, her fears and nightmares, Simon Decker and Russ Latham, every big and little worry, were all banished because Kyle told her to sleep.

When she awoke sometime after dawn, she was still nestled in his arms, and he was still pretty much in the same condition he had been when she dozed off.

"Why didn't you wake me up?" she mumbled.

He gave her a soft kiss. "I was enjoying watching you dream." His hand skimmed over her hip and cupped her bottom. "You are the most beautiful woman in the world."

That made her chuckle. "I think that might be a slight exaggeration, but I won't argue with you." He went to kiss her again and she smelled toothpaste. "No fair. You've already brushed your teeth." She excused herself despite his assurance that she didn't have morning breath. When she returned to him, she felt much more comfortable and confident about what she planned to do.

"It's payback time," she said, crawling beneath the covers and back into his embrace. "What you did to me last night was . . . I don't even know a word to describe it. I've never had anything like that happen to me before."

He kissed her bare shoulder. "Good." His hand trickled over her stomach, then headed for more intimate territory. "Maybe you'll think of a word for it this time."

She gasped aloud as his fingers found their goal. Last night's exercise had left her extremely sensitive. She reached down and held his hand away. "You were very gallant last night, but this is a new day, and I'm only going to stay in this bed with you if you're willing to take as much as you gave."

He brought her hand to his sex. "I'm all yours, love. The only problem is, after holding back for so long, I'm not sure how much control I'll have."

She ran her hand over the length of him and smiled. "I wouldn't worry about how fast the first time goes. You'll still have two times after that to make it last."

Although Kyle attempted to explain the differences between a woman and a man's sexual capabilities, before the morning was over, he more than lived up to her prediction.

Barbara had promised to pick Matt up around noon and Kyle suggested they take him and Kenny out for the day. While Kyle was shaving, she called Laura and got her exuberant approval, which made Barbara wonder how badly the boys had behaved.

As she was hanging up, her gaze caught on the paper she had pinned next to Dani's card and called her home number.

"Yes?"

"Hi. This is Barbara Johnson."

"Hey, girl. What's going on?"

"Russ Latham showed up last night."

"Give me details."

"It was about seven-fifteen. I opened the door without looking—my mistake—but he didn't force his way in, just kept his foot in the door and insisted I listen to him." Barbara gave her a summary of the conversation. "He's staying at the

Wayward Motel and driving a light-colored Volkswagen bug. I'm sorry, I couldn't get a tag number."

"I'll go by the motel and check it out; then I'll add a note to the watch order on your house. You are going to go for a restraining order, aren't you?"

"Not yet. If there's even the slightest chance that he's really come to make amends, that could set him off all over again. I don't believe he's changed, but I want to give it a couple of days. I'll know soon enough. The old Russ wouldn't be able to wait that long for me to call him. If he contacts me even one more time, then I'll file."

Every minute of the next eight hours was filled with activities designed to entertain two rambunctious nine-year-old boys, but Barbara found herself having a terrific time as well. They had pizza for lunch in a noisy arcade and went through several rolls of quarters. An animated Disney movie came next, and they ended the day with cheeseburgers and fries at McDonald's.

Since the boys were still going strong when they got to Kenny's house—and Laura being a romantic soul—she insisted on keeping the boys there for another night.

The instant Barbara and Kyle were back inside her little house, he kissed her with a hunger that left her breathless.

"Oh, my," she whispered, feeling his strong physical response to her. "One would think you haven't been with a woman for an awfully long time . . . if one didn't know better." She shifted her hips against his.

He chuckled and pulled her down onto the couch with him. "It *has* been an awfully long time. Do you have any idea how hard it was not to touch you all day? I had to constantly remind myself that I couldn't hold your hand or kiss you whenever I felt like it, which was all the time."

She snuggled against him. "I know. I felt the same way, and I appreciate your being considerate of Matt's feelings, at least until he gets used to the idea of Mom having a male in her life besides him. Of course, the way you're spoiling him, I doubt if he'd put up much of an objection to anything you do."

With a wink, he said, "That was the general plan."

Unlike the previous night they spent together, this one was devoted to mutual satisfaction. By Sunday morning, Barbara wondered how she had survived so many years without even a fraction of the pleasure Kyle was determined to give her.

That pleasure was diminished somewhat when Laura brought Matt home around noon and he was clearly unhappy about something.

"Didn't you have a good time last night?" she asked with concern.

He submitted to his mother's hug, gave Kyle the minimum greeting he could get away with, and headed for his room.

Barbara excused herself from Kyle and followed

her son. "What happened? Did you and Kenny have a fight?"

He made a face at her as he plopped down on his bed and picked up a comic book from his nightstand.

Barbara closed his door and sat down beside him. "Matt, you're harder to read than that story. Tell me what's wrong."

It took him a moment to decide whether he wanted to talk to her or not, and when he did, four words explained everything. "Why is *he* still here?"

Though it sounded like his jealousy of Kyle had now moved on to cover her as well as Tammy, she didn't want to jump to the wrong conclusion again. "If you mean Kyle, he thought you'd like to go to the zoo this afternoon."

He started to react positively, then remembered that he was upset. "Did he sleep here last night?"

She nearly swallowed her tongue. "No. Of course not."

The lie was worth it since it seemed to lift part of the burden off his mind, but he wasn't satisfied. "Kenny said you two were probably . . ." He looked back down at his comic book. "You know."

Good grief. What had she ever done to deserve Kenny French in their lives? Should she refuse to respond, tell a half-truth, or be a hypocrite? She opted for a smokescreen. "There are different stages that men and women go through in a relationship. Right now, Kyle and I are in the dating and getting to know each other stage. How this one goes will determine whether we move on or not."

"You mean, like getting married?"

His body language warned her to be careful how she answered. "Sometimes people get married after dating, but not always. Is that what's bothering you? That I might get married?"

He thought about that for a few seconds. "I don't know. Maybe."

"Well, I can promise you that I'll never make a decision that important without getting your vote first. Okay?" That pleased him enough to give her a real hug.

Easing back, he asked uncertainly, "Do you love him?"

"I don't know yet. It's too soon. But even if I do fall in love with him someday, it wouldn't take away from how much I love you. At the moment, I'd have to say I like him. How about you?"

He shrugged. "He's okay, I guess, but I keep thinking how he's like this girl in my class. She keeps doing things for me and giving me her dessert at lunch."

Barbara made herself remain serious, since he was. "That's not so strange. You're a cute kid."

He grimaced. "Yeah, but she's only like that with me. To other kids, she's really mean. It's like she's a big phony around me just to get me to be her boyfriend."

"Hmmm. I can see why that would bother you. Kyle is obviously going out of his way to get us to like him. So, should I send him home? You and

I could spend the afternoon alone . . . here in the house . . . instead of going to the zoo."

There was no contest. "Oh, no. That wouldn't be nice."

"Good. But before we go, there's something I have to tell you, even though I wish more than anything that I didn't have to say this." She gave him a moment to prepare for bad news. "Russ came to the house Friday night, before Kyle got here." The worry that instantly filled his eyes made her stomach turn.

"He said he's changed, but I can't trust him. You're on full alert again. He's driving a light-colored Volkswagen bug. Keep an eye out for it, and carry Dani's card with you. She could probably get to you faster than I could if you need help while we're apart. Got it?"

"Got it." He placed his hand over hers. "You promised we could stay here and I'll do whatever I have to, to make sure we do. Remember, I'm not a baby anymore."

Smiling, she gave him another hug. "I remember. Now let's go see how much bigger that baby panda is since the last time we saw it."

By the time they got to the National Zoological Park, Matt appeared to be completely over his pangs of jealousy and was ready to enjoy himself. For the first hour, his attention was all on the animals, with only an occasional sideward glance at Kyle to make sure he wasn't standing too close to his mom.

Suddenly Barbara felt his fingers clamp onto

her arm. He was turned around, looking for something behind them. It had been a while since she had seen such a frightened expression on his face, but she remembered well what had caused it in the past.

"What is it?" she asked quietly, as her own gaze scanned the crowd.

"I . . . I thought I saw him . . . walking that way. He looked right at me and winked as he passed. But I don't see him now. Maybe it was somebody else, someone that looked like him."

For a second she wondered if he was just imagining seeing Russ because she'd prepped him for it before they left the house, but she immediately dismissed that thought. It was safer to assume Matt did see Russ and act accordingly.

"What's the matter?" Kyle asked.

"Russ Latham may be around somewhere. Matt, what was the man wearing?"

"Old jeans and a jeans jacket. I'm not sure it was him, though. This guy had a mustache and longer hair than Russ ever had."

"His hair *is* longer now," Barbara said. "And the mustache could have been a fake." To Kyle, she explained, "He sometimes disguised his appearance so that he could follow me without my knowing it."

Kyle looked over the crowd from his greater height.

"He's blond," she said to aid his search. "A little shorter, but, um, broader than you."

"I think I see him!" Kyle exclaimed. "Stay here."

Barbara and Matt watched him take off toward the enclosed aviary, but neither saw anyone who looked like Russ. It was nearly a half hour later before Kyle returned.

"Sorry," he said. "I was sure I saw him go in the aviary, but then I lost sight of him. I did a quick walk around every section of this place, but no luck. He probably left the zoo the second he realized a man was after him."

Whether the man Matt saw was Russ or not, their afternoon had been spoiled. Kyle took them to a family-style restaurant for an early dinner; then they headed back to Fredericksburg.

"I hate to end this weekend," he told Barbara after they got home and Matt went to his room. "But I still have a ton of paperwork back in my hotel room that has to get finished before I take off tomorrow."

She made her voice sound cheerful, despite the disappointment his words made her feel. "More sales meetings?"

"Just three days this time. Actually, the road trips are going to be a regular part of my work week, which, had I known I was going to meet you, I wouldn't have agreed to."

"Don't be ridiculous. You wanted this promotion, and we can see each other whenever you're here."

"That doesn't sound like much of a consolation at the moment. Look, I don't want to do anything that's going to make Matt feel like his mother's abandoning him, but do you think we could go out alone on Wednesday evening?"

Common sense told her to slow down, put him off until the next weekend, but then his fingers grazed her arm and his eyes reminded her of their hours alone last night. She didn't want to slow down; she wanted more, and wondered how she would stand waiting until Wednesday. "If I can arrange for a sitter."

"What about Kenny's mother?"

She shook her head no. "I can't ask for another favor until I reciprocate for this weekend. But I'll check with Tammy. She really seemed to enjoy spending time with Matt, and I know he enjoyed being with her."

He smiled and gave her a kiss. "Good idea. I never gave any thought to how single mothers manage a social life."

Saying good night to him was one of the most difficult things she had ever done, when what she really wanted was for him to stay. Nevertheless, her responsibilities as a good mother took priority, as always, and a good mother did not sleep with a man when her child was present, unless that man was her husband.

The phone rang as she watched Kyle back out of the driveway, and she let Matt answer it in her bedroom. When he didn't call her immediately, she assumed it was Kenny and headed for the kitchen to make a cup of tea. Ten minutes later, she was curled up on the couch, sipping her drink and flipping through the television channels, when Matt called for her.

"Pick up the phone," he yelled louder than necessary. "It's Dani!"

Her melancholy mood instantly lifted. She hurried into her bedroom with a smile and took the phone from Matt. Laughing, she said, "I thought he was talking to a friend of his all this time."

"I *am* a friend of his," Dani declared. "And he had a lot to tell me before I was allowed to talk to you."

"Oh, really? Like what?"

"Like how he has an incredibly beautiful girlfriend named Tammy, and Mom met a man that's trying real hard to get Matt to like him."

She laughed, then told her about Tammy, which made Dani laugh along with her.

"And the man?"

She heard the smile leave Dani's voice and wondered just how bad Matt made Kyle out to be. She briefly told Dani how she and Kyle met and had a few dates. "He's very sweet—in fact, he's pretty incredible—but things are happening a little fast for my comfort. I don't want to make the same mistake twice just because I have a weakness for knights in shining armor." Her words sounded as uncertain as she felt, and she let out a sigh.

"What's wrong?"

She smiled at her new friend's insight. "Nothing. Everything. I need to be seventeen again and hang out in a tree house for a few weeks with my best friend."

"If you close your eyes and stay very quiet, you can still go there. I do it all the time."

"You had a tree house, too?"

Dani chuckled. "Not exactly. My sister and I had an old parachute draped over some chairs. But I'm sure it worked the same way. Tell me how you feel about him."

Barbara sighed again. "I really do want to be cautious, but when I'm with him, my brain gets all fogged up with hormones. It would be a lot easier if he just wasn't so very, very perfect."

"Sounds a lot more fun than having your head fogged up with fear."

"*Hmmph.* The problem is, I've got plenty of that in there, too, and I'm experienced enough to know that makes me vulnerable to an offer of being protected from Russ, and the Hamiltons, and all the other bogeymen out there. It's a wonder I can remember my own name this week!"

"Remember when we first talked and I asked you if you'd ever gotten married?"

"Sure. And I told you I hadn't had time to fall in love."

"Maybe that was because no man ever moved fast enough to catch you."

Barbara laughed. "Nobody could accuse Kyle of dragging his feet."

"I haven't met this guy, so I don't want to sound like I'm endorsing a quick marriage to him, but I'd like to pass on something my sister's psychiatrist once told me. There are cases where stalkers continue to harass their victims after they've married another man, but that doctor believed that one of the reasons my sister's attacker had kept after her was that he was convinced that, as long as she didn't legally choose another man, she was still his for the claiming. In other words, had she gotten married to someone else, he might have focused his obsession on an easier target before hurting her.

"Think about it: Men who stalk and terrorize women are bullies; they rarely exhibit that sort of aggression with another man. If the woman takes a husband, she has a male protector, and the stalker is less likely to go up against him to get to her."

"Funny, Kyle said almost the same thing."

"And now that I've said that, let me play the devil's advocate here. Doesn't it seem rather unbelievable that your meeting with Kyle was very similar to your meeting with Matt's father? And doesn't it also seem awfully strange that after so many years of not being aggressively pursued by men, this one pops into your life right after your picture appears on the front page of every newspaper in the country? I truly hope for your sake that it's all an enormous coincidence, but just in case it's not, I want you to make me a promise."

Barbara knew that Dani had just said aloud what she had been afraid to even think. "Whatever promise you want, you've got it."

"I've been in police work long enough to know

that where there's smoke, there's usually fire. And, girl, you've got more smoke around you right now than a five-alarmer. I can't predict when the explosion's going to happen, but I'd bet my longevity bonus that it will. Until then, I want you to promise not to do anything crazy without calling me. Don't run away, don't sell off your kid, don't get married. Nothing. Just keep your eyes open and your guard up."

Chapter 12

Monday morning, Dani's words of warning were still buzzing in Barbara's head, but she kept up a light chatter with Matt to keep him from noticing that anything was bothering her. The moment they stepped outside, however, her efforts proved to be wasted.

A folded sheet of paper was stuck under her windshield wiper.

The second Matt saw it, he grabbed his mother's hand and tugged to keep her from going to the car. "Don't read it, Ma. Let me get it and throw it away."

She forced herself to appear calm and unafraid, for his sake. "It might not be from him. It could be a note from a neighbor or someone selling something." She didn't believe that any more than Matt did. Though she knew whatever Russ had written would upset her, she couldn't ignore it because his messages often gave a clue to his next move.

She felt the awful tremors setting into her limbs as she walked to the car and retrieved the paper.

She knew Matt was watching her face, but she was unable to hide the fact that she recognized Russ's angry scrawl the moment she unfolded the note.

"Let me read it, too," Matt said, moving to her side and putting his arms around her waist.

Knowing that the more he knew, the safer he was, she held the note so they could read it together:

> *You still don't recognize a WOLF in sheep's clothing when you meet one, do you? Don't you think spending every minute of the weekend with HIM was too much? You must think of Matthew's feelings. If you are going to force our boy to spend time with a man, it should be someone who really loves him, like a father. Call me TODAY. I'm looking forward to a long, REVEALING discussion.*

As much as she wanted to rip the paper to shreds, she knew she had to turn it over to the police. This was the evidence she had been waiting for to prove that Russ hadn't changed. He had been spying on them all weekend, and in his own twisted way, he still considered himself Matt's father.

For a brief moment, she considered rushing back inside, packing what they needed to survive, and escaping before he progressed from the spying and letter-writing stage to another attempt at kidnapping. However, she had run numerous times before, and it always turned out to be useless.

Even with all the precautions she had taken for the last move and the length of time that had passed, he had found them again.

But her circumstances were different now. This time, she had a female sympathizer in the local police department. This time, she had a male protector.

This time, she was going to stay and fight back.

Barbara turned on her heel and marched back inside. After calling her office to let them know she would be late, she unearthed her Russ Latham file. With the background information in hand, she knew there would be no problem in obtaining a restraining order. Determined to keep her courage up, she dropped Matt off at school and headed for the Stafford County Courthouse.

Filling out the affidavit for the order took relatively little time, but it would be at least three days before it was submitted to a judge and put into effect. She was told that the judge would set a hearing to review the case in about one month, and if she wished to keep the order in effect beyond that time, she would have to show up in court. She assured the clerk that if it became necessary, she would certainly make an appearance, although the last thing she wanted to do was face Russ in a courtroom again.

Regardless of how much Russ's note had upset her, she had trained herself over the years to keep doing what had to be done. A single, working mother had no time to fall apart.

Since she was late getting in to the bank, she told her supervisor she would work through lunch.

Though Tammy had told her that, as the receptionist for the insurance company, she wasn't permitted to take personal calls at the switchboard, Barbara thought a very brief one to let her know she wouldn't be meeting her for lunch couldn't get her into trouble. She looked up the number and dialed, expecting Tammy to answer, but the voice on the phone wasn't hers. "Hi. Is Tammy in today?"

"Tammy? What's the last name please?"

Barbara wondered how many Tammys there could be. "Garrett. She's the regular receptionist."

"I'm sorry. You must have the wrong number. I'm the receptionist, and my name's Gloria."

Could she have been mistaken about Tammy's position? "I'm sure she said she worked at Statewide Insurance. Could she be at another number?"

"We have several branches. If you'll hold a moment, I'll look her up in our employee directory."

Barbara was bewildered. Tammy worked in that building, not at a branch office. It was a huge company, however, and this woman might not know everyone.

"I'm sorry, there is no employee of Statewide named Tammy Garrett."

"That's impossible," Barbara said, her annoyance with the woman's incompetence beginning to grow. "She's worked there for two years."

"Well, I've worked here for six, and I never

heard of her," the receptionist snapped back. "Please excuse me now. I have other calls coming in."

Barbara stared at the telephone receiver as if it might explain what she'd just heard. Though she doubted it, there was a slim possibility that she had gotten the name of the company wrong; there were two other small insurance firms in the building. But she received the same responses when she called them—no one named Tammy Garrett worked there.

Not willing to believe that she had misunderstood the kind of company Tammy worked for, she called Tammy at home.

"H'lo?" a sleepy male mumbled.

Assuming it was Michael, but not wanting to take the chance of saying the wrong name, she asked for Tammy and had to wait about ten seconds before she heard the girl's voice greet her. She sounded groggy also.

"It's Barbara. Are you sick?"

"Sort of. What's the matter?"

"Nothing. I'm just confused. I had something important to tell you, but when I called upstairs to Statewide Insurance, the operator said she never heard of you. Did I misunderstand where you worked?" It took so long for Tammy to respond, Barbara was beginning to wonder if she'd fallen back to sleep, when she suddenly exploded.

"That bitch! They all warned me, but I didn't believe she was that evil. Damn her!" She let out a frustrated cry. "I'm sorry, Barbara. I shouldn't take this out on you, but it just makes me so-o-o mad.

"See, there's this man, one of the vice presidents, who was talking to me about becoming his secretary. I knew it was only because he thought it was a way to get into my pants, but I figured I could handle him after I got the promotion. Did the woman you talked to tell you her name?"

Barbara thought for a moment. "I think she said it was Gloria."

"I knew it. That's the bitch. She's been having an affair with him forever, and somebody told me yesterday she found out what he was up to. The personnel manager called me last night at home and told me I was fired . . . for socializing with the male clients too much.

"Now get this: When I go on breaks, guess who covers the switchboard? Yeah, *her.* I just can't believe she would tell you I never worked there. What nerve!"

"I'm so sorry, Tammy. What are you going to do?"

"Well, first off, after that call last night, Michael and I got very drunk, so I'm not going to be thinking about much of anything today. I might try to collect unemployment for a while. I wouldn't mind some time off."

Barbara listened to her complain a few more seconds, then had to hang up to take a call. Tammy's explanation should have cleared up her confusion, but she couldn't shake the feeling that something wasn't quite right about the whole situation, as if Dani's smoke had just gotten thicker. Then again, Gloria *had* sounded somewhat bitchy by the end of their brief conversation.

Unable to give it more thought at the moment, Barbara convinced herself she had been looking over her shoulder for so long, she was probably being overly suspicious.

"Of all the fucking times for you to answer the goddamned phone! You're lucky she didn't recognize your voice. Don't you have any brains at all?"

"For God's sake, Tammy, turn down the volume a little. My head's about to explode!"

"Good! You deserve it after what you pulled last night. Falling in the door at two A.M., when you aren't supposed to come here at all, drunker than an old wino, then passing out without telling me a thing of what you've been up to for an entire fucking week!"

He groaned. "Couldn't this wait another hour or two . . . just till my head stops pounding?"

"No."

"Five minutes, then. Get me some coffee while I take a quick shower, and I swear I'll tell you whatever you want to know."

Tammy threw the covers away from her and grudgingly agreed to the temporary postponement.

Russ scanned her perfectly shaped, naked body as she padded out of the bedroom—a view that had given him great pleasure over the last year— yet he felt little interest at the moment. It could have been the hangover that curbed his appetite for her this morning, but that had never stopped the hunger before.

He wondered if it had anything to do with how many times he'd come with Betty Blubber-Butt, but usually one look at Tammy's incredible ass was enough to get him hard regardless of how much "exercise" he'd had recently with anyone else.

He got up and went into the shower before Tammy could return and start nagging at him again.

Although several aspirins and alternating hot and cold water eased his headache, the glare Tammy shot at him when he walked out of the bathroom kept him from relaxing completely. He wrapped a dry towel around his waist and flopped back down on the bed.

She allowed him one long swallow of lukewarm instant coffee before beginning the interrogation. "Well?"

He grimaced at the liquid she called coffee, but took another gulp before speaking. "So, who's *Michael*?"

She clucked her tongue. "Lucky for you, I had already told Barbara all about my *boyfriend*, who, by the way, has been servicing me better than you have lately."

Rather than react to her complaint, he said, "Did she buy your story about being fired?"

"Of course. Lying on the spur of the moment is one of my greatest talents. Now I want some explanations or you're going to find out about my ability to torture the truth out of a man."

Since he already had firsthand experience with that ability, he wasted no more time, though he had no intention of telling her the whole truth. "I ran into an old high school buddy last night, and the drinking got a little out of hand. I apologize for coming here like I did, but nobody's following *me*, so I don't see what the big deal is."

"The *big deal* is that you've got to follow the plan, exactly the way I told you, for it to work."

"All I've done so far is exactly what you told me to do. I followed Barbara everywhere, without making contact. I have her complete routine nailed down, and she's jumping at shadows."

Tammy wasn't impressed. "That was last week, stupid. And speaking of last week, after you fucked up getting her keys, I managed to take care of that chore myself." She smiled, recalling how easy it had been to get Barbara to hand them over to her along with plenty of time to get copies made.

Russ considered slapping the smile off her face, but he wasn't up to dealing with the results of that action. "It took a lot longer than we figured to get that medical file for Decker." He gave her a rundown of the complications he'd run into, without getting specific about how he finally got his hands on the information. "He was happy, the Hamiltons should be satisfied, and I got enough cash to keep us going another month." Not wanting to give her a chance to demand more details about his trip, he asked, "How'd the week go for you?"

"I had no trouble keeping an eye on her, and the kid's mad about me, so we'll have no problems there. By the time I'm finished working him, he'll probably help us get rid of her so that I can step in as his new mommy."

Russ narrowed his eyes. "I'm still waiting to hear how you figure on getting her out of the way after the wedding."

Arching one brow, Tammy scraped one long fingernail down his whiskered cheek. "What's the matter, sweetie? Those old possessive feelings about her coming back again?"

He smirked at her. "Don't be a bitch. I just can't see going through all the other stages in your plan if you haven't worked out the final one."

"Well, it just so happens, I got it all worked out while you were gone. I decided to follow up on the comment I heard about that clinic in West Virginia."

Russ gave her his whole attention. "Was it true? Can we use it?"

"I think so. The psychiatrist that owns it is Dr. Emmanuel Phillips. From what I could find out, he was once used on a regular basis by criminal defense attorneys who wanted to prove that their clients were innocent on the grounds of insanity. It was rumored that he'd give any opinion they wanted to hear for enough money. Though he was never formally accused of it, the rumors were bad enough to destroy his credibility with the judges.

"That's when he opened his very exclusive asylum in West Virginia. Mostly it's known for the rich clients who go there to dry out, but it has a section for mentally disturbed patients as well. The word is he helps his wealthy guests along with their drug habit instead of breaking them of it, and, for the right payment, he'll accept anyone as a patient, whether they want to be there or not."

Russ nodded approvingly. "Sounds like Dr. Phillips is just the solution we were looking for. Should I make an appointment with him?"

"I already did," she said, giving him a cocky grin. "I drove over to West Virginia and had a preliminary meeting with the good doctor. Told him about my poor sister-in-law, Barbara Latham, and her paranoid delusions of being stalked by her own husband. He was very sympathetic. Even gave me a supply of Xanax to feed her to keep her zonked enough not to argue about being committed. He assured me she wouldn't notice if I mixed it in with well-spiced foods."

"It's perfect," Russ said, his eyes gleaming with feral anticipation.

"Yes, I thought so, too. Now all you have to do is convince her to marry you and let you adopt Matthew. Are you sure you're going to be able to stick to the script? I mean it, Russ, you can't pull any of that shit on her like you used to."

He looked confused. "What are you talking about?"

"You know damn well what I'm talking about.

She told me a few of the sick little tricks you played on her. And I'm warning you, if you do one thing that scares her now, the game is over. The only way you stand a chance with her is if you can convince her that you're completely cured of all your mental hangups and are really a nice guy whose first priority is caring for that boy."

"I'm not an idiot. I fooled her before. I can do it again."

Tammy wasn't reassured, but she let it go. "We may have to speed up the timetable, though. She's met a man, Kyle Trent. He seems to be moving in on her pretty fast. I tried throwing a pass at him myself to see if I could redirect his attentions, but he's only got eyes for her."

Russ rubbed his jaw. "What's this guy look like?"

"Sex on a stick—tall, dark, and handsome, with just a hint of preppy, in his mid-thirties."

The description made Russ's mouth twitch. "Yeah. I saw him with them yesterday, at the zoo. Don't worry. If he gets in the way, I'll take care of him."

That impressed her, as any suggestion of raw violence did. He watched the expression in her eyes change from business to lust as she imagined how he might carry out his promise.

"Considering how long that woman's been without a man, it shouldn't be that hard to seduce her into doing anything you want. Just remember what I told you, though. . . ." She slid her hand up his thigh, under the towel wrapped around his waist, and firmly twisted the soft flesh she found there. "*This* belongs to me. I don't care what else you do with her. You don't put this in anybody's body but mine."

He clenched his teeth against the discomfort between his legs, but he didn't make her stop, for this was also part of what excited him about her. "You don't know what you're asking—" He gasped as her fingers caught a pubic hair and yanked it out.

"Wrong. I know *exactly* what I'm asking. Your mistake with her before was that you were in too much of a hurry to fuck her. The only way you'll get the jackpot on this one is by being extremely patient. I told you how it works. You give them just enough to get them breathless; then you pull away." Her fingers soothed the hurt they'd caused. "Then you come back and give them another dose, but you never give them everything. In no time at all, you'll have complete control because she'll do absolutely anything to finally get your dick inside her."

He felt himself hardening and growing within her hand despite his earlier disinterest, and for the first time he resented the fact that she had even this small power over him. "Speaking of mindless control," he asked while he was still able to think, "have you checked in with Decker yet?"

"I plan to surprise him this afternoon. He thinks I'm hibernating at my parents', trying to decide what to do about him. I seriously doubt if he could ever convince Barbara to give up her kid, but I figure I better continue to keep tabs on his progress anyway."

As she went to work on him in earnest, he tried to prolong the foreplay by thinking his way through the maze this was turning into.

A little over a year ago, while he was still camped out in Dayton, he'd become friendly with a guy who visited the same bar he did after work. One night his new friend told him about a support group for sex addicts; how he first went to pick up chicks who couldn't get enough, and ended up solving a few of his own problems. Russ accepted his invitation to go to a meeting with him mainly out of curiosity. He'd always wanted to meet a real live nymphomaniac.

His wish came true in the form of Tammy Garrett. The first night they'd spent together, she almost killed him. In the next month, she taught him more about sex than he'd picked up in his entire life. Most important, she showed him how to increase the pleasure by delaying the climax and how to use pain to spice up the routine. She occasionally allowed him to spank her, or play the rape game, but more often it was she who punished him, and he both loved and hated her abuse and the explosive release that always followed.

It wasn't long before he had confessed all his secrets to her, and from that moment on, she badgered him about tapping into the Hamilton fortune. It had been her idea for them to move back to Boston and for her to get close to the Hamilton attorney to see what she could learn about the

Hamiltons' private affairs while she and Russ waited for Barbara to resurface or for Pop to die.

Although he repeatedly assured Tammy she had erased every trace of lust he'd had for Barbara, he had known all along what a lie that was. But as long as he had no idea where Barbara was, Tammy did keep him from aching for her. And she was smart. Smart enough to help him set a trap that would hold his little runaway for good this time.

They had figured on Decker and the Hamiltons trying to get to the boy, but Russ was confident that once he told Barbara all the shit they had pulled to break up her and Howard, she'd never give in to them. He, on the other hand, would be a hero for being honest with her about the past and protecting her from their evil clutches.

What Tammy didn't know was that he wasn't nearly as stupid as she thought he was. Once Barbara was hooked, it wasn't her he'd be getting rid of, but Tammy.

Which is why he didn't tell Tammy what Kyle Trent's real name was or the true reason he was moving in on Barbara so fast. Not only had he gotten in on the game at warp speed; he thought he could push Russ out of it with a death threat.

Russ massaged his temples as Tammy's efforts began to rob his concentration. What to do? What to do?

The last time he saw his old pal was in a bar where he had started a fight with eight bikers and almost won. Even though the man seemed fairly sane last night, Russ knew he could carry out his soft-spoken threat to kill him if he went near Barbara or Matt again.

And yet, wasn't the final reward worth any risk? He simply had to get to Barbara at a place and time when "Kyle" wouldn't see them together. He had to unmask him for her before she fell for his lies. A rush of pleasure zipped through him as he thought of how grateful she would be for his rescuing her. After that, she'd accept his protection on a permanent basis without another moment of hesitation.

Russ did not allow himself to think about Barbara being with his old pal all weekend. If he did, if he pictured them together, the way he wanted to be with her, he was afraid he'd end up killing them both.

And that would really fuck up everything.

Chapter 13

"*Tammy?*" Simon was stunned to see her instead of room service when he opened the door. He poked his head out and glanced up and down the walkway outside his room to make sure no one was nearby, then hustled her inside. She was almost completely covered by the full-length silver fox coat he'd given her for Christmas, her gorgeous hair was tucked up inside the matching hat, and her hands were inside the muff, but he still didn't want to take any chances. "I thought we agreed not to be seen together while we were here."

"Something happened," she said, pulling off the hat and shaking her long hair loose. She carelessly tossed the hat and muff on the bed. "I thought you should know—" A knock at the door prevented her from saying more.

"I ordered room service for dinner. It's not much. I didn't know you were coming."

"For God's sake, Simon, I didn't come here to eat."

"Of course not." He hated it when he said the wrong thing to her. "I only meant—"

"Just get your dinner and send the waiter away. I'll be in the bathroom."

Simon's hand was trembling as he signed the room service bill. He'd been dying to see her again, even knowing that every time they were together was another kind of death. Whatever happened, she could have told him about it over the phone or sent him a note, as she had for the past week. Could it be that she'd finally had enough of her waiting game, that their separation had convinced her to give up her virginal status?

He was glad now that he had sprung for a whole carafe of wine with his dinner. "You can come out now," he called to Tammy as he filled the wineglass and the water goblet from the carafe. When she reappeared, he handed her the goblet, then realized she was still wearing the coat. "I'm sorry. Let me help you out of this." His fingers grasped the collar from behind her, but she held it tightly around her.

"I'm chilled. I'll take it off later."

Her icy tone warned him that her patience was growing thin. He picked up the smaller glass and prepared to make a toast. "To us?"

"To our future," she said, finally giving him the smile he'd been nervously awaiting.

"Shall we sit?" he asked, gesturing toward the bed.

She purposely walked over and sat in one of the two chairs by the table instead. Following her lead, as he usually did, he took the other one.

"Barbara found out that I don't work in her building."

Simon choked on the wine in his mouth, and it took him a moment to be able to speak. "What did you tell her?"

"I had a story already made up in case that happened. It was bound to sooner or later. She bought it. But I'm afraid my playing her best friend and spending time with the kid isn't getting us anywhere."

"I told you, if the boy considers you his friend and knows that you'll be living near the Hamiltons, the move should go much more smoothly. Besides, the more time you spend with the boy, the more likely the mother will trust you. With trust comes sharing secrets and listening to advice. She still hasn't confided in you? About anything?"

"Oh, I know all sorts of things about her childhood, but whenever I open the subject of that boy's father, she gives me fairy tales."

"This plan worked on her once. It will work again. It just may take more time than it did then."

"Tell me again how you handled her before. Maybe there's something we've missed."

He took a long swallow of his wine and set down the empty glass. "It was very simple. While she was at the estate, she showed some affection for young Latham. He was a greedy, foul-tempered bastard, but he still managed to fu— excuse me, convince every girl within fifty miles to let him have his way with her. The Hamiltons couldn't get rid of him because young Howard considered him his best friend, and they didn't want to risk upsetting Russ's father, either. They considered him irreplaceable. For a moderate amount of cash, Russ left the estate and moved in with Barbara."

"Wait a minute. Exactly how did he con her into letting him move in with her?"

"I suspect she was somewhat attracted to him to begin with, but from what he told me, he played on her sympathies. She was a sucker for the underdog, and I'm sure Howard's unexpected departure made her vulnerable to Russ's persuasion. Within a few weeks, he'd convinced her to forget about Howard and sign the agreement."

Tammy stood up and paced back and forth. "I sure can't convince her to give up her kid, if she hasn't even admitted that he's the Hamiltons' grandson." She stopped and turned to him. "All right, she was a sucker for the underdog and she had her heart broken, big time. What if I go to her with a sob story about my boyfriend leaving me instead of marrying me like he promised? Maybe that would make her want to tell me how the same thing happened to her."

"Do you think you could be convincingly heart-broken?" He regretted doubting her abilities the moment he said it.

She let out a disgusted sigh. "If I can play the ditziest blonde of the century, why would I have a problem crying over being dumped? It's just another role."

"Of course you can do it. I don't know what I was thinking. It's worth a try, but I still think it's a matter of trust. Even if you can't talk her into turning her son over to the Hamiltons, as long as she admits to you that Howard was the father, you can serve as a witness in case we have to go to court."

"I thought you said Latham could do that much."

Simon made a face. "He could, although his record makes him less credible than you would be. That reminds me, he returned from that errand I gave him to keep him occupied while I took another shot at Barbara. Surprisingly, he came through, so I think I'll give him another task."

"And what might that be?"

He could see she was intrigued by his intelligence, and he preened a bit. "It occurred to me that Barbara may have kept her copy of the agreement between her and Howard. It's basically worthless, but it would be better if it disappeared completely. I thought perhaps Russ could break in—"

"No!" Tammy spat at him. "You mustn't use him to do anything that might frighten her into running away again." She took a calming breath. "I'll do it. I can search for it while I'm baby-sitting, and she'll never know the difference.

There's no telling what else I might find that you can use."

Simon would never have asked her to do it, but he preferred to rely on her rather than Russ. "Just be careful that the boy doesn't see you doing anything suspicious."

"You know, that kid of hers is really smart. He's more grown up than a lot of adults. It could be that he knows the whole story, but I doubt it. I mean, what kid in his right mind would live in a little two-bedroom house with one television when he could be a millionaire in a mansion and play his stupid video games on his personal big-screen TV? Maybe I could get him curious enough to demand the truth from his mother. I don't think there's anything he wouldn't do for me if I ask nicely enough."

Based on his own experience, Simon knew how accurate that statement was. He watched her glide over to the window and look outside. She was in one of those moods in which she doubted him. And with her doubt came the thought that she could do better. In his younger days, he might have cut her loose, knowing there were others he could have with a snap of his fingers, others who would appreciate him more than she did. But they considered him an old man now, and the women who would have him couldn't come close to comparing with Tammy.

He needed her in a way he had never needed a woman before. It was more than sexual, though that was a great part of it. She made him feel young and powerful again. He loved walking into a restaurant with her on his arm and introducing her to his colleagues at cocktail parties, knowing every man who saw her was envious of him.

Tammy continued speculating, though she was talking more to herself than him. "Once Matthew knows he has such an unbelievable alternative, he might *choose* to move in with his grandparents. If she thought that's what her son really wanted, I think she'd give in. The trick would be in making it look like it was his idea."

Simon nodded his agreement, but his attention was focused on how to restore her faith in him. As demeaning as it was, he acknowledged the fact that it was his wealth that she was most interested in. He forgave her greed, knowing about her impoverished childhood. He also forgave her for tempting him with her lush body to get him to buy her expensive gifts. It was something he would have done if he'd been born a female and looked like she did.

She claimed she was a virgin and wanted to remain one until her wedding night. She wouldn't even let him French-kiss her, since she considered that a form of penetration. The problem was, she hadn't yet agreed to marry him.

Occasionally, her behavior convinced him of her innocence. Most of the time, it didn't. Like when she played certain games meant to drive him out of his mind with sexual frustration, then refused to allow him even the smallest liberty. Her teasing bordered on torture, yet he had become addicted to it.

Would she toy with him tonight, or was she too annoyed with him and the part he'd asked her to perform?

"I spoke to Mr. Hamilton today," he said in a tone that let her know he had something interesting to share. "I told him Barbara was being difficult, and he raised my bonus."

She slowly looked over her shoulder at him.

"If I can pull this off without going to court, he'll pay me an amount equal to whatever Barbara gets, which at the moment would be . . ." he paused until she turned around and faced him, "two million dollars." He let that sink in, then said, "You remember that house you liked so much? It's yours, honey. Just as soon as we wrap up this deal." He watched her expression change from bored to intrigued and knew he'd secured her devotion once again.

"Two . . . million . . . dollars?" she repeated in a husky voice. "I could have the house? What about the sports car you promised? Can I have that, too?"

"You can have anything you want."

She closed the draperies and gracefully walked over to him. "And what will you get out of it?"

He licked his dry lips. "You know what I want." He made a move to stand, but she pressed her hands to his shoulders to keep him seated.

She leaned down and placed a brief kiss on his forehead. "Yes, I know what you want," she murmured, and gave him another light kiss on his nose. "And you can have it, anytime, anywhere . . . on the floor, up against the wall, in your car, or the steam room at your club, *anywhere* . . . right after the wedding."

He gulped. "The wedding? Are you saying you'll marry me?" With a mixture of joy and relief welling in his chest, he tried to pull her onto his lap, but she straightened up and backed a few feet away from him.

"I've been wanting to say yes, but I needed to be positive that you could make *all* my dreams come true."

Her suggestions of where they would make love had taken him from being semi-aroused to erect, but her acceptance of his proposal caused a drop of semen to dampen his stomach.

As he shifted position in his chair to lessen his discomfort, her gaze drifted down to the bulge between his legs. "I know how hard it can be for a man to wait, so I thought of a way to give you a little something to hold you until the night you make me your wife."

He rose, but she held up her hand to stop him from coming closer. "You have to agree to do this my way, or we don't do anything."

His heart was already pounding dangerously in his chest and all she'd done was talk, but he was willing to risk anything to possess her. "All right. Whatever you say."

"Good," she said, looking very much like a cat

with a mouse trapped in her paws. "Take off your clothes."

"Everything?" He wasn't at all anxious for her to see his pale, sagging flesh or the varicose veins in his legs.

"If you're going to question every one of my orders—"

"I'm sorry," he said, hurriedly unbuttoning his shirt cuffs. "It's just . . . wouldn't it be more romantic to turn off some lights?"

"No."

Figuring she would see his physical shortcomings eventually, he proceeded to get naked and hoped that his erection would be impressive enough to help her overlook the rest of his aging body. He'd been as randy as a teenager for the past six months, since he met her at the American Bar Association conference in Boston. Now that the moment seemed to be at hand, however, he felt himself going limp beneath her critical stare.

"Do you have a problem I should know about?" she asked bluntly.

"No! Not at all. I was hard as a rock a minute ago. I'm just a little nervous. I mean, you've put me off for so long and . . . and taking my clothes off, while you stand there bundled up in that coat, isn't exactly arousing for me." He normally enjoyed it when she played the bitch, but this was far more than she'd ever done before. A fantasy image of what she might be planning came to mind, and his sex stirred to life again.

"I suppose you'd rather watch me take my clothes off."

The mere thought stole his breath away. She had previously only allowed him glimpses of forbidden skin by wearing low-cut blouses or very short skirts with no underwear. At least he thought that, because she would bend over in front of him for one reason or another and give him a peek, but his view was always too brief to be sure. A bit more blood collected in his shaft as he recalled it.

"Sit down, Simon, with your legs spread wide apart and your hands gripping the arms of the chair.

He quickly did as she demanded. "From here on, I only want to see one muscle move until I tell you otherwise. Understand?"

He nodded, though he understood very little.

Running her hands down the front of her fur coat, she sighed and said, "Do you have any idea what wearing this coat does for me, Simon? It *warms* me. In fact, right now, it's making me so hot, I'm wet between the legs. And since I'm not wearing any panties, I can feel my juices smearing all over my thighs when I walk." She laughed when the one muscle she gave permission to move gave her a standing ovation.

"Very good," she said, admiring his response. "Now remember, no squirming or closing your thighs, and keep your hands on the chair, or I'll leave.

"I'll bet you'd like to know just how good this

fur feels against bare skin." She got the muff off the bed and put her one hand in it while her other hand continued to hold the front of her coat closed.

He no longer believed she could still be chilled. What was the coat hiding? The question left his mind when she ran the muff up his one arm, around his neck, and down his other arm. As she moved on to tickling his chest, he shivered in response, and by the time she grazed his genitals with the exquisite fur, his body was covered with goose bumps. The light contact was so arousing he thought he might explode from the need for something, *anything* more solid.

She backed away again, obviously pleased with the results of her torture.

"Since you've been such a good boy so far, you get to see that I'm telling the truth about not wearing any panties."

In extremely slow motion she opened the coat and let it slide down her arms to the floor. Simon nearly fainted from the rush of blood from his head to his penis. There she stood, like a goddess, with her blond hair flowing around her shoulders. Around her neck was the gold choker she had begged for last week. He swallowed hard as he took in the white lace merry widow that barely covered her nipples, and the long garters that held up white stockings. On her feet were white shoes with very, very high gold spike heels and gold ankle straps. And, as she had claimed, between her thighs was nothing but pink, clean-shaven flesh, just asking to be devoured.

"What do you like to look at better?" she asked. "The front?" She lifted her breasts so that they nearly escaped the cups of the lingerie, then ran her palms down her abdomen to her thighs. "Or the back?" She turned and brought her hands up to her bottom and kneaded the cheeks.

Simon took his eyes off her only long enough to confirm that another drop of moisture had formed on the top of his straining, twitching manhood.

"I'm waiting, Simon," she said impatiently, keeping her back to him. "Make your choice."

"The front. Please, Tammy, let me touch you."

"No." She bent down and got a plastic bottle out of her coat pocket, then turned around. "Touching is forbidden until the wedding night."

"For God's sake. Are you trying to kill me?"

Her low laugh sounded as demonic as her eyes looked. "Don't be silly. I'm going to satisfy you."

"Without touching?" he asked incredulously.

"Hush, now, and do what I tell you." She came forward until she was standing between his knees.

Her beautiful pussy was so close he could smell her muskiness blended with her perfume. It was all he could do not to lean forward and— He felt something wet run down his penis and looked to see her pouring a clear fluid over its swollen head.

"It's only baby oil . . . with a little something extra," Tammy assured him. "Catch it with your right hand and rub it all over."

He circled the base of the muscle with his fist and spread the oil up and down. A second later, he felt an odd, tingly sensation and his erection strengthened. He wanted to ask what the "little something extra" in the oil was, but decided he was better off not knowing.

"Again," she said, pouring a little more.

"It's too much."

"No, it's not. You're going to give some of it to me."

He smiled and shifted his hips forward, certain that she meant to straddle him, but she surprised him again.

"Hold out your hand." He reluctantly released his grip and obeyed. With another one of her cat-like smiles, she placed her right hand over his well-oiled palm, then slowly slid it back and forth several times in an imitation of the sex act until perspiration dotted his forehead and her hand was as slick as his.

"Now do it," she whispered, and stepped back to where she was before.

He frowned in confusion. "I don't know what you want me to do.'

"This." She slipped three of her fingers between her thighs, parted the lips, and played with herself. "Do this to yourself while I watch, and you can watch me."

He felt his heart clenching in his chest, but nothing could stop him from continuing what she'd started.

"Good boy," she said when he obeyed her command. "I had no idea you had such a big dick, or that you'd be able to get it so stiff. A lot of men your age can't, you know. I can hardly wait to feel you shove that thing deep inside me." She picked up the pace of her massage to match his. "This is good, but that's going to be better. Are you imagining it, Simon? I am. In and out. In and out. Oh, God, I'm almost there. Come for me, Simon. Come like you never have before."

Again, he did precisely what she demanded. Watching her bring herself to climax accelerated his own. And when he had no more to give, he slumped in the chair, barely able to breathe, let alone clean himself up.

Between the pain in his chest and the overdose of sexual satisfaction clouding his brain, it took him a moment to realize she had put on her coat and hat. "Why?" was the only word he could get out as she gave him a peck on the top of his head.

"Must go, sweetie," she replied in a cheerful voice. "Call me tomorrow if you have any more ideas. I'm sure you'll think of something to speed this matter along now. Just remember, the sooner you get your bonus, the sooner we can be married. Oh, one more thing. Barbara's had a few dates with a man she just met, and she might be falling for him. His name's Kyle Trent, works for IBM out of Richmond. It might be a good idea to check him out. Maybe you know someone who could arrange for his transfer to Hong Kong before things get serious between them."

He watched her float out the door as if what

they had just done hadn't burned up one bit of her energy. It probably hadn't. She could probably play sex games twenty-four hours a day and never get tired. The mere idea of what it was going to be like after they were married was enough to kick his brain back into action.

He had to think. There had to be some way to force Barbara Mancuso into giving up her son.

From the dark side of his mind came the thought that if she couldn't be bribed or coerced, perhaps she could be gotten out of the way entirely. He wondered whether there was any limit to what Russ would do if the payment was high enough.

Chapter 14

Wary of what might be waiting for them at home, Barbara delayed their return by taking Matt to the mall for dinner and buying the new sneakers that his growing feet required. Her concern seemed unwarranted until she entered her bedroom and saw that her answering machine had taken four messages. After Russ's note that morning, one call would have been enough to start her stomach acid churning. Four was an extremely bad sign. Again she was reminded of Dani's comment about her being surrounded by smoke.

She stood there, staring at the blinking light, not wanting to press the play button, yet knowing she had to in case it was something important, like a call from her parents. With that possibility in mind, she extended a very shaky hand and played back the messages. The first voice made her teeth clench.

"This is Simon Decker. I stopped by to see you this weekend, but you were out. I have a very attractive offer to present, one that is entirely to your benefit. Please call to set a time when it would be convenient for us to meet and I will put myself at your disposal."

She couldn't imagine how any offer he had to present could be to her benefit, but he had sounded more respectful than he had during any of their previous conversations. She quit thinking about Decker when she heard Kyle's voice next.

"I called your office this morning, and they said you weren't in, and now you're not home. After everything you told me . . . God, Barbara, I don't know what I'd do if something happened to you. Please, call my beeper number as soon as you get in. I'll call you back immediately no matter where I am."

Guilt washed over her. Nellie had told her that Kyle had called, but she had so much to do, she hadn't thought to beep him back right away. It had been such a long time since she'd checked in with anyone other than Matt that it hadn't even occurred to her that he might be worried. A woman's mournful sob followed the next beep.

"Oh, Barbara [*sniff*], where are you? The most awful thing happened and [*sniff*] I really need to talk to you. I hope you don't mind, but I'm just going to drive up and hope you're home by the time I get there."

Barbara wondered what thing more awful than losing her job could have happened to Tammy since they'd spoken earlier. According to the machine's display, she had called over a half hour ago, which meant she could be here at any time.

She pushed down the annoyance that made her feel as the final message began to play.

"It's Kyle again. It's now . . . eight o'clock. If I don't hear from you in the next hour, I . . . I'm going to have to do something. I don't know what . . . something."

Barbara recognized the mix of emotions in his voice from personal experience—fear, panic, and frustration, all barely held in check by the hope that he was worrying for nothing. As quickly as possible, she located his beeper number and dialed it.

"What were all those calls?" Matt asked from the doorway.

She sat down on the edge of the bed to await Kyle's return call. "Two were from Kyle. And Tammy called. She's on her way here."

"Cool," he said with a smile.

"I'm not sure how *cool* her visit will be. She was very upset—" The ring of the phone cut her off, and she snatched the receiver off its cradle. "Kyle?"

"No. Simon Decker. I was hoping we could get together this evening."

She felt like screaming, but she kept her voice level. "I don't know how much simpler I can make this, Mr. Decker. I am not interested in hearing anything you have to say. Good-bye."

"Wait! Don't hang up. If you'll let me present the final offer in person, I guarantee I will not call or visit you again."

If that promise had come from Russ, she would

not have believed it, but as an attorney, Decker couldn't afford to continue to harass her. "I'll agree to listening to your *final* offer in exchange for that guarantee, but only over the phone. If you say anything of interest to me, then I might agree to a personal meeting. Otherwise, I'll give you five minutes of my attention right now. Then I never want to hear from you again. Understood?" She heard him let out an exasperated sigh. "Take it or leave it, Mr. Decker."

"Your attitude is making this more difficult—"

"The clock is ticking."

"All right. The Hamiltons wish to extend an invitation to you and your son to live with them in Boston."

"*Live with them?* You've got to be kidding!"

"I assure you, I am quite serious. Mr. and Mrs. Hamilton understand your refusal to part from your son. Therefore, in exchange for your granting them legal guardianship of Matthew, you will be permitted to reside in one of the cottages on the estate, for as long as he resides in the mansion. They also understand your, uh, reluctance to accept their money, but once you move there, you would have no means of support. Thus, they are willing to establish an account in your name with a balance of two million dollars, which you can use or leave for Matthew when he comes of age."

Barbara's blood was rapidly reaching a boiling point. "Is that it?" she asked through gritted teeth.

He paused, then said, "Yes. That's everything, and, as I said before, it is their final offer. Though

I will tell you that if there is a fine point you want clarified, there is some slight room for negotiation."

She slammed the receiver down without responding. When it rang again seconds later, she hesitated, but decided she'd better pick it up in case it was Kyle.

"You impudent little tramp! How dare you hang up on me!"

"I agreed to listen, and you agreed to leave me alone afterward. I did not agree to have a discussion with you. This is the last time I am going to say this. Neither my son nor I are for sale for *any* amount of money!" She started to hang up again, but his next words stopped her.

"Wait! You said you'd give me five minutes, and there is something else I have to say, something you don't seem to understand. The Hamiltons can do anything they want to anybody. So far, they've been trying to deal with you fairly. But there are other ways."

As she had learned to do when Russ harassed her over the phone, she pressed the record button on the answering machine. "Are you threatening me, Mr. Decker? The policewoman you met will be very interested to hear that."

"No threat. Just a few facts to help you put this into perspective. They wanted you out of Howard's life ten years ago, but all the usual methods of manipulating their son hadn't worked. It was very upsetting to them to have him stand up to them and refuse to break his engagement to you.

So I presented him with photographs of you and Russ Latham having sex in his cottage and an accompanying tape recording on which you bluntly told him you would keep him on the side, but you were marrying Howard for his money."

Barbara gasped. "That's impossible. Nothing like that ever happened, and I know damn well I never said anything to him about Howard's money. I *never* cared about that."

Decker snickered. "Technology is an amazing thing, isn't it? With a little ingenuity, an expert can make one woman look and sound so much like another that even her fiancé can't tell the difference."

He had just given her the missing piece to the puzzle that had plagued her for ten years, and it fit together to create a truly ugly picture. She remembered how jealous Howard had been when he had heard that she and Russ had spent an afternoon together, and how readily he had believed the servants' rumors.

They had used his jealousy to kill his love for her . . . and Russ had been the executioner. What had Russ said the other day? That he had played a part in breaking the engagement. Decker's explanation was too awful to be a lie, but it was still difficult to accept. "Howard was shown fake photographs, and he believed I would do that to him? Why didn't he come to me, give me a chance to deny it or at least explain?"

"Oh, he was going to, but there was that sudden emergency of his mother's, so all he had time to do was confront Latham. That young man really earned his money with that scene. He took quite a beating before admitting that the two of you had the hots for each other and that it was your idea to go ahead with the wedding anyway."

Barbara had a flash of Russ in her apartment in Queens, his face bruised and swollen. Russ had been Howard's best friend his entire life, while Howard barely knew her. Had she been in Howard's shoes, who would she have believed? The truth left her feeling more depressed than she could ever remember, but Decker wasn't finished torturing her yet.

"Months later, after Howard came back from Europe, he was talking about finding you again— he was having a hell of a time forgetting you, even started drinking pretty heavily—so Latham cooperated again with some new photos. Maybe you'll remember the day I came to visit you and Latham, and he carried you up the stairs to your apartment? That made a touching picture. But it was the ones taken with the hidden camera, showing the two of you sleeping together in your apartment, that did the trick, or rather, those and a document bearing your signature in which you agreed to break it off in exchange for an enormous amount of cash—obviously not the agreement you did sign. Unfortunately, rather than forgetting about you, Howard chose to drink more."

The world was spinning out of control for Barbara, but one question rose above the rest. "Was he drunk the night he . . ."

"The car accident? Yes, it was alcohol-related, although that detail was kept out of the media. As I said, the Hamiltons have more power than you can imagine. You can't win against them. It's just plain stupidity to try. I'll give you one more week to accept their final proposal. If you don't contact me by the end of that time, I will begin legal proceedings against you."

"Legal? Like forging agreements and touching up photographs? Do you intend to make me look like an unfit mother the way you made me look like an unfit fiancée? Even if you could, it won't do you any good if you can't prove who my son's father was. They'll have to exhume Howard's body to learn whether Matt's related to them or not, and you already said they didn't want to do that."

Decker was silent for a moment, then responded in a more controlled voice. "The Hamiltons will do whatever has to be done. And when it's all finished, your precious son will belong to them, and you'll be nothing but a bad memory to him."

She sat there with the phone next to her ear for some time after he hung up, partly because she didn't have the strength to move and partly because she wasn't prepared to leave her bedroom and face Matt until she knew what she wanted to say to him.

All these years, she had successfully avoided telling Matt the whole truth without actually lying to him. He knew that his father had died and his parents had loved each other very much. So far, he had accepted her refusal to speak his father's name or talk about him at length, but she knew the day was coming when saying it made her too sad would no longer end his questions.

She had been planning to tell him the truth when he turned twelve. Somehow that had sounded like an age when he would be able to understand. But now she was worried that she had waited too long. What if he learned it from someone else first? What would he think of her if Decker fed him the Hamilton version of the past?

They might be able to turn Matthew against her if they were determined to. If Howard, a grown man, could be fooled by their tricks, wouldn't it be that much easier for them to convince a nine-year-old boy that she wasn't who or what he thought she was? Then again, how hard would it be for them to prove she was an unfit mother without any lies? Had she ever provided her son with a stable, secure environment?

On the surface she was a flighty creature, bouncing from city to city, job to job, constantly uprooting her child. How long would it be before Decker found out why they had lived like that? And when he learned that they were victims of a crazed stalker, how hard would it be to prove that Matthew would be safer with the Hamiltons?

How ironic that the man they had paid to destroy her relationship a decade ago was still in a position to help them destroy what was left of her life.

The enormity of the threat Decker had just

made countered the fact that she had recorded it. That was probably why he didn't worry about what he said. The truth put her in deeper jeopardy than it did him. Slowly she set the phone down and tried to find enough equilibrium to rise.

"Ma? Is something wrong?"

She was shocked to see Matt still in the doorway. How much had he heard? She was about to lie, then decided the time for total honesty had come. "No, I'm not okay. There's something very important I have to tell you. Come sit down with me."

Matt's eyes were wide and filled with worry as he went to her side. "I wouldn't have listened in if it was Kyle, but I heard you say Mr. Decker, and you told me he was a bad guy, so—"

"It's okay, honey, I'm not going to scold you for eavesdropping."

"What did you mean about us not being for sale? People can't really buy other people, can they?"

She pursed her lips and tried to find a beginning point that he'd understand. "Some people have so much money, they think everything's for sale, even people."

"That's really dumb. You'd think they'd be smarter if they got that rich."

His logic made her smile despite the sadness she felt. "Sometimes people don't have to be all that smart, because they're born rich."

He nodded. "You mean they inherit it."

"Yes, that's right. Where did you learn that word?"

Making a face, he tried to remember. "Oh, yeah, Tammy was telling me a story, but I didn't really understand it."

"Well, the story I have to tell you has to do with inheriting money, too." She screwed up her courage, but the doorbell rang before she could begin.

Matt jumped up. "That's probably Tammy." He stopped at the doorway. "Is it okay if you tell me that story later?"

She forced a half smile. "Sure, kiddo. Later."

The visitor was Tammy, as Matt had hoped, but as Barbara had warned, she was too upset to give the boy more than a brief greeting. Barbara was shocked by her pitiful appearance; her eyes were bloodshot and puffy, with smears of mascara beneath them; her hair looked as though she'd been trying to pull hanks of it out. Whatever had happened was no minor annoyance.

Barbara placed her hand at the small of Tammy's back and guided her toward the kitchen. "Matt, honey, go on to your room and study your spelling words."

Before Tammy could begin, she asked for a hug, which Barbara gave; then she used a paper napkin to wipe her eyes and blow her nose. Eventually she pulled herself together and murmured, "Michael broke up with me."

"Oh, Tammy, I'm so sorry. Did you have a fight?"

"No. That's what hurts so much. We'd been talking about getting married. Then all of a sudden this afternoon, he just says it's not going to happen. He wouldn't even give me a reason."

Tears started to fill Tammy's eyes again, and Barbara got her a box of tissues from the bathroom. Michael's departure on top of losing her job was a lot to handle in one day. Barbara had plenty of her own problems tonight, but she temporarily shelved them and tried to think of how she could cheer up Tammy.

"You know, sometimes things that look horrible turn out for the best. Maybe there's a wonderful new man, even better than Michael, waiting right around the corner. Maybe you'll meet him when you find a new job."

Tammy shook her head. "I'll never find anyone better than Michael." She blew her nose again. "I bet his mother was behind this. She never liked me."

Barbara couldn't remember Tammy ever mentioning Michael's mother in any previous conversation. She couldn't help but think of how it sounded similar to her experience with Howard. She was tempted to talk about how she survived his abandoning her, but she always hated it when a person insisted on telling his or her story when she was trying to relate her own. It always ended up sounding like a game of one-upmanship. Even when Tammy asked her if she had ever had her heart broken by a man and how it felt when

Matt's father left them, Barbara refrained from focusing the conversation on herself.

She did her best to lift Tammy's spirits, but nothing worked. Even worse, by the time Tammy went home, she actually seemed irritated with her and even snapped at Matt on her way out. Barbara decided to give the girl a couple days to adjust on her own before offering any more advice or sympathy where it wasn't appreciated.

Shortly after Tammy left, Barbara got Matt off to bed and was wondering if she had the wrong beeper number for Kyle when he finally called. The phrases "What happened?" "I was so worried" and "I'm sorry" overlapped each other from both ends of the phone line.

"I was caught in a traffic jam because of an accident when you beeped," Kyle explained. "I've always refused to have a phone in the car on sheer principle, but I'm getting one tomorrow!"

"It's okay, really. It was my fault for not realizing you'd be worried. First there was the note from Russ, then I had to go to the county courthouse for the restraining order, but it's going to be three days before they serve him, then Matt needed shoes, and Decker called, and Tammy—"

"Whoa! Could we run through all of that one more time, a little slower maybe?"

She took a deep breath and summarized her day for him. When she finished, she apologized again. "I really didn't mean to dump all that on you."

"That wasn't dumping. That was sharing. I just

wish I'd been there to help. I miss you so much, love."

That one sentence somehow balanced all the negatives. "I miss you, too."

"I hope you're thinking about everything I said the other night. You don't have to go through this alone. I know I could make it all easier for you if you'd let me."

"I know. It's just that I wanted so badly to do it on my own."

"And you did. For years. Now it's time to relax and let someone love you again."

She hesitated a moment before answering. It was almost too tempting to resist, yet her common sense made her hold back. "I'll try." A yawn slipped out before she could stifle it.

"You've had a long day, and I'm making it longer," he said with a smile in his voice. "Get some sleep, and I'll see you when you get home from work tomorrow."

"Tomorrow? I thought you said you wouldn't get back here until Wednesday."

"Your situation requires a change in my plans. I don't want you staying there alone until the restraining order goes into effect."

"But—"

"No arguments. Say good night, honey."

Barbara chuckled. "Good night, honey."

"I love you."

She heard the soft click of him hanging up the phone and sent him a mental thank-you for not insisting on a response to his declaration.

Another yawn overtook her. As Kyle had said, it had been a long day. She had meant to call Dani about Russ's note and the restraining order as soon as she got home, but the evening had flown by, and now she could barely keep her eyes open. She supposed tomorrow would be soon enough to update her.

As tired as she was, however, the conversation with Decker kept replaying in her head.

He was right. She couldn't win. Not if they wanted her to lose. After all, the Hamiltons had watched their own son drink himself into a grave rather than allow him to lead his life the way he wanted to.

She had tried to survive on her own, do everything without depending on any man's help, and where had it gotten her?

Nowhere. She had no home, no husband, no close friends. She rarely saw her parents. And now she could lose her son. Perhaps the time had come to try a different path.

Kyle's words echoed in her mind and wrapped around her like a warm blanket. Perhaps it really was time to share the burden with someone who loved her.

Only once in his life had Kyle been this frustrated. His plan had started out so simply, but with every day that passed, more complications were piled on. The lies were eating at his gut, yet he didn't know how to undo them without destroying himself.

He should have guessed that Russ wouldn't be pushed aside with something as incidental as a death threat. Obviously, only action was going to get through to him.

One thing at a time. First he had to rearrange his schedule so that he could get back to Barbara. He picked up the phone and dialed his executive assistant's home number. Her sleepy hello increased his guilt. "Carol, it's Ham. I'm sorry to call you so late, but I've got an emergency. I need you to cancel tomorrow afternoon's board meeting."

Carol groaned. "Mr. Ivanovich will have a cow if he flies in and you're not here!'

"That's why I want you to call him tonight. He'll still have a cow, but he'll have it in Chicago."

"I know how anxious you've been to get the board's approval on the new stock option. What happened?"

"I can't explain now, but I will soon. After you notify all the directors, I need you to do two more things in the morning—reserve a seat for me on the twelve-thirty flight out of LaGuardia to Richmond, and get me a cellular phone."

"Did I hear right? Hamilton K. Treadwell is actually going to leap all the way into the nineties?"

"Not entirely. I don't want anyone in the company but you to know I have one, and if you call me on it for any reason except a dire emergency, you'll be out of a job." He heard her laugh at his empty threat. Fortunately, he knew he could trust her to follow his directions implicitly.

"You got it boss. Richmond again, huh? Boy, whatever deal you're putting together down there must be pretty damn big."

Kyle sighed. "It's the biggest deal of my entire life."

Chapter 15

There was no note on her car's windshield the next morning, nor did Barbara get any sense of being followed on her way to work, yet she knew better than to let her guard down. Though Russ wasn't behaving in his usual manner, that didn't mean they were safe.

She had just finished opening an account for a new customer and was about to call for the next person on the sign-in list in the front of the bank's lobby when Russ suddenly stepped in her path. Her heart slammed against her rib cage, but there was little she could do without creating a scene.

"Please go away," she said in a low voice that quivered from the fright he'd given her. "I have a lot of people waiting for help."

He gave her his most innocent smile. "I know. I'm one of them. I came by to take you to lunch."

Barbara glanced around the busy lobby until she caught the eye of the security guard. At her nod, the man casually began moving closer. To Russ, she said, "I'm busy for lunch. Just say what you want, then leave."

"I told you before," he replied, still smiling. "I need your help, and I have some important facts you should know about." He walked over to her desk so that she was forced to follow.

His phony smile vanished as soon as they were seated across from each other. "I wouldn't have had to come here if you had called me like I asked you to. I waited all last night, but you never called. I'm starting to get the impression you don't want to help me with my recovery."

She clenched her hands in her lap and took a breath. "I know you've been following us again. Why would you do that if you've gotten over your obsession with me?"

He leaned forward with his elbows on her desk. "I just wanted to see Matthew. You know how I feel about our boy. That's one of the reasons I want to make up with you. I'm still the closest thing he has to a father. I want to be able to spend time with him and have him know how I helped you through that horrible pregnancy."

"How you *helped* me?" Realizing that they were attracting curious attention, she lowered her voice, but anger had brought a flush to her cheeks and an unusual hardness to her voice. "Simon Decker told me all about how much you *helped* me. You're lucky I don't hire an assassin to pay you back for all the help you gave me. And if you don't stay away from me and my son, I may do that yet."

He studied her eyes for a moment, then said, "I came to Virginia to apologize for all that, but I can see that you don't have enough goodness in your heart to hear my side of it." He rose and bent forward with his hands braced on her desk and his face an inch from hers. "You're even a bigger bitch now than you were then. And bitches always get what's coming to them sooner or later."

"Do you need assistance, Mrs. Johnson?" the bank guard asked with a hostile glare at Russ.

She was struggling not to give in to the panic gnawing on her stomach, and the question gave her something solid to hang on to. "Yes. Would you please escort this man out of the bank, and if he comes here again, I'd appreciate your calling the police. I have a restraining order against him."

Russ's eyebrows raised in surprise, then narrowed in fury as he decided she wasn't bluffing. When the guard grasped his elbow to move him along, he shook off the man's hand. "I'll leave on my own, but not before I say one more thing. You think you don't need me, but you're wrong, and I'll prove it."

The guard unsnapped his holster and placed his hand over the butt of his gun.

Russ saw the move and started backing away. "Your new boyfriend's name isn't Kyle. It's Hamilton. And all he wants from you is the same thing Decker wants—control of Matthew!" Without another word, he whirled around and stormed out of the bank.

Barbara thanked the guard for his help and accepted his offer to escort her to her car after work.

Russ's last statement proved that he would say

or do anything to get her attention, but to suggest that Kyle was a Hamilton was ridiculous. Even if she stretched her gullibility far enough to consider that, it wouldn't make sense for the Hamiltons to be offering two million dollars to buy Matthew if another relative could be named as heir for free.

She no longer had a single doubt about Russ changing. He still believed she and Matt belonged to him, and he would undoubtedly believe that until the day he died . . . unless she found a way to show him otherwise.

Dani's comment about a stalker backing off when his victim married another man came back to her, but when she allowed herself to think about marrying Kyle, she still felt they hadn't known each other long enough for her to hand over her and Matthew's life to him, no matter how wonderful he was.

Russ's tires squealed as he tore out of the bank parking lot. He wanted to punch something . . . *somebody*. Another restraining order! He hadn't been served yet, but the bitch wouldn't have said it unless she had really filed for one. The last thing he needed now was to get himself thrown in jail, and out of the game.

He probably shouldn't have blurted that out about Ham without being able to prove his claim. Now Barbara would probably tell her *boyfriend* and he might follow through with his death threat.

And if she blabbed it to Tammy, that one would

probably make an attempt on his life as well, or at the very least cause him some serious damage. Not that he really cared what she thought. He was sick of her lording it over him, as if she were the only one smart enough to have a plan. He'd begun to suspect that her "plan" was meant to keep him away from Barbara instead of setting her up to marry him.

Jealous bitch! Sometimes she acted like her pussy was gold-plated. It was obviously time to show her once and for all who was the boss. The confrontation with Barbara had put him in exactly the right frame of mind to do it, too.

As soon as he got back to his motel room, he would call Tammy and demand she get her sassy ass over there pronto. Thoughts of what he could do to straighten her out stirred a ripple of excitement that swelled his dick.

In the meantime, he had Decker's latest offer to think on—a hundred thou to get Barbara out of the way. Rather than use the word *murder,* he had suggested some sort of 'permanent abduction'—a scenario in which Russ would get the mommy all to himself and the Hamiltons would be able to discreetly take possession of the son.

Since he had no intention of letting that happen, but wanted to get hold of some of that cash Decker was waving around, he tried to think of a way to kill two birds with one stone.

While he tried to sort out his options, a news item on the radio broke into his thought process. There had been another drive-by shooting in a suburb of Richmond—the third this month. As the idea that news triggered developed into a plan, he revised the old saying about the two birds. If he just killed *one* bird, named Ham, he'd solve two problems. He'd be rid of his competition and, if it looked like the attempt had been against Barbara, Decker might be convinced to fork over an advance chunk of the payment to Russ on good faith.

He had an untraceable gun, but it had been a decade since he'd fired it. He was certain, however, that with a little target practice, he'd be as good as he was when he and Pop used to go hunting. It wouldn't do to get caught practicing around here, though, considering the restraining order.

Then there was still the matter of proving to Barbara that he was the only one she could trust.

In a flash of brilliance, the solution came to him. He hated losing the couple of days it would take to drive home and back, but in doing so, he could collect all the evidence he needed for Barbara, get in the necessary target practice, and avoid being served until he was ready to carry out his plan.

That settled, he went back to fantasizing about how he was going to deal with Tammy before he left on his trip that night.

After Russ's departure, Barbara began to fret that he might go by Matt's school and try to get to him. Under the circumstances, she was of no use to anyone, and her supervisor gave her permission to go home for the day.

The moment she and Matt walked in the door, she knew someone had been in their house.

"Stay here, honey," she told Matt, leaving the door ajar. "I want to start doing our entrance check again, the way we used to." Matt made a face, but he obeyed, even though he didn't notice what she saw.

It was so subtle, the average person probably would have overlooked the clues. But she had trained herself to pick up on the little things. Each morning before she left the house, she did a walk-through and made sure there were no crumbs on the table, clothes and towels were picked up, and so on. Everything had its proper place, and she enjoyed coming home to a neat house after working all day.

One thing out of place she might have attributed to absentmindedness on her part, but there were quite a few. In the living room, the door to the cabinet where she kept her music and videotapes was closed. Since it tended to stick, she never shut it completely. A chair in the kitchen was at a slight angle instead of squared off with the table the way she liked it. At first glance, Matt's room and the bathroom seemed to have been left alone, but her bedroom and closet showed small signs of tampering.

"Okay, Matt," she called after she was certain the intruder wasn't still in the house. "All clear. I'll be out to make us some lunch in a sec." There was no reason to frighten him any more than he already was at this point.

It only took her a few minutes to determine that nothing was missing. She had very little of value anywhere in the house, but if it had been a burglar, surely he would have taken the stereo or Matt's video game system.

If it had been Russ, he would have taken something personal of hers, but all her underwear and toiletries were accounted for. Nothing had been added, either, as Russ often did to let her know he'd been there. Then again, nothing he'd done lately had followed his old patterns.

It didn't look as though frightening her was the motive. Instead, it appeared that someone had been searching for something and had tried to put everything back in its place so that she wouldn't notice that he'd been there. What could she possibly have that someone would want to steal? Who wanted something that he thought she had?

The only answer that came to her was that Simon Decker and the Hamiltons wanted her son. To get him they needed proof that Matthew was Howard's child. She couldn't picture Decker sneaking around her house, but after everything he'd revealed to her, she could easily imagine his hiring someone else to do it for her. He already knew what it said on the birth certificate, but perhaps he thought she had some other document or personal letters he could use.

She moved her vanity chair into the closet, stood on it, and rearranged several shoe boxes on the top shelf until she could retrieve the one that didn't have shoes or a purse in it. Taking it to her bed, she quickly flipped through the contents. It was impossible to tell if anyone had gone through the various receipts and legal documents, and it wouldn't make any difference if they had. There was nothing in there that revealed who Matt's father was.

Her gaze touched on the white envelope in the bottom of the box. Inside were the only items she had left to prove that she had ever known Howard Hamilton IV. She couldn't remember the last time she'd looked at them, and she didn't think she wanted to now, but her fingers pulled the papers out and the past was suddenly staring her in the face.

Regardless of the painful memories they called up, she had never been able to throw away the cartoons Howard had drawn for her. She had told herself it was something positive that she could show Matthew when she finally told him the whole story, but there was more to it than that. She had needed to keep them to remind herself that Howard had loved her enough to ask her to be his wife, and that she had loved him enough to have his child even after he abandoned her.

Decker's revelations had slashed open the old wound and poured salt into it. She and Howard had had a chance for the kind of happiness very few people ever experienced, and his parents had coldheartedly stolen it from them.

All these years she had thought Howard had

given in to them because he was a spineless boy, but that hadn't been the case. In his attempt to impress her with his power, Decker had admitted that Howard had resisted the attempts to break them up. His only weakness had been in not knowing how ruthless his parents could be.

Barbara recalled Decker saying that the Hamiltons never got over the loss of their son. She hoped to God they thought about it every single day . . . the same way she had for years—like a knife twisting in their chests.

They should burn in hell for what they did. Under no circumstances could she allow those bastards to get their hands on Matthew.

She swiped the tears off her cheeks and set the cartoons aside. The only other "souvenir" she had kept was the agreement she had signed. From what Decker had revealed, Howard was shown a different agreement, one that stated that she received a large sum of money. Either they had changed the wording after she signed it, or they forged her signature to a separate document. If they had forged her signature, they probably also had forged Howard's on the agreement she had.

Looking back on it, Russ had helped them with that as well. Apparently, the only truth he had told her was that Decker had offered him money to convince her to sign the agreement. If only she had realized that everything else he said had been a lie. If only she had refused to let him stay with her. If only she'd—

She stopped herself from continuing along that

route. It was negative thinking, and she couldn't afford even one second of that.

Her eyes scanned the agreement and darted back to the one sentence Russ had used to convince her to sign it: *Barbara Mancuso and Howard Hamilton IV shall be henceforth absolved from any and all promises made or implied to one or the other*. When she had first read it, she wasn't sure that could be applied to their child, and she wasn't any more certain now, but it was better than nothing.

"Ma? Are you okay?"

Barbara's head jerked up. Matt looked both concerned and annoyed. "I'm sorry, honey. I had to look something up." She still wanted to have that talk with him, but she decided to put it off until her nerves calmed down a bit. She slid the drawings and agreements back into the envelope and put everything back in the box. "Why don't you do your homework while I warm up the leftover casserole."

"I don't have any," he said, still looking at her curiously.

"Good. Then you can set the table."

After lunch, she encouraged Matt to go play a video game while she cleaned up the kitchen. As soon as he seemed sufficiently occupied, she called the police station and left a message for Dani to contact her. She wouldn't have bothered to call the police to report a break-in with such flimsy evidence, but she knew Dani wouldn't dismiss it with a smug expression like some other, male police officers had in earlier years. Dani would know she wasn't just another paranoid woman.

Barbara was pleasantly surprised when Dani showed up in person a short while later. After the officer took off her jacket and exchanged greetings with Matt, Barbara led her into the kitchen and poured them both cups of coffee.

"I was planning to stop by tonight anyway," Dani said, sitting down at the table. "I finally got a good look at Russ Latham yesterday. I made a few passes by the motel where he told you he's staying, but I hadn't had any luck up till then. He was backing out of a parking space just as I was pulling in, and I noticed he had a burned-out taillight. It gave me a convenient excuse to stop him and ask for his license and registration. Unfortunately, everything was in order, and he was a perfect gentleman. The only thing I could ticket him for was the light. So, what's going on?"

Barbara let out a long sigh and filled her in, beginning with Russ's note on her windshield and ending with her belief that Decker had had someone search her house. "The restraining order should be served on Russ Thursday, Friday at the latest, but I'm no longer sure he's the worst of my problems."

Dani shook her head. "Let's take this one problem at a time. I can't do anything officially about Latham until he's served, but I can keep a watch out for him. I'll check on the status of the order tomorrow and see if I can't move it along a little faster. After that, maybe I can make it too uncomfortable for him to stick around.

"Next, that attorney is a real piece of work. I can't give you professional advice, mind you, but if it was me he was harassing, I'd have another meeting with him and tape-record the conversation. It might not give you anything you can legally use for your defense in court, but if he says enough, it could give you some leverage. Maybe you could get him in trouble with the Bar Association, or something like that."

"As a matter of fact, I did tape the last conversation, but I have no idea how I could use it to hurt him without hurting myself."

Dani frowned. "Even so, I'd hold on to it in case the opportunity arises. On a more realistic level, if he broke into your house and we could prove that, we've got him committing a crime. How did your intruder get in?"

"I don't know. I was more concerned with the who and why than how. Russ was so good at that sort of thing, I quit having the locks changed. One time, while I was at work and Matt was at school, he convinced a locksmith that it was his apartment and he'd locked himself out."

Dani cocked her head. "Wouldn't he have to show some sort of proof of residence?"

"That's the best part," Barbara said, grimacing. "All he had to do was go to an office supply store, buy a blank lease form, and fill it out to show that he had recently moved in, which is why his driver's license would have an out-of-state address on it. I don't remember what his excuse was as to why he happened to have a copy of the lease on him, but I'm sure it was very convincing."

"Yeah. I got the impression he was real good at sincerity . . . as long as you aren't aware of what's underneath that charming smile."

"There was a time when I blamed myself for being too naive to see through his act, but everyone who met him was fooled. I can't tell you how many times police officers believed his story over mine."

Dani grimaced. "I know exactly what you mean. But I promise you, he won't win *me* over."

Barbara placed her hand over Dani's. "Thank you. That makes me feel better."

Dani smiled and stood up. "Good. Now it's time for me to do some actual police work here. Does anyone have a key besides you?"

"Just the owners, and they live in Florida."

"What about Matt? Does he carry one?"

"No. I only keep one set of extra keys to the house and the car, and they're well hidden."

"All right. Let's check points of entry."

It didn't take Dani long to give her opinion. "I don't see any sign of forced entry. If you're willing to make a formal report, I could have the place checked for fingerprints."

"On what basis? That the chair in my kitchen wasn't in the exact position I'd left it? Anyway, if Decker hired a professional to break in here, I'm sure he would have been careful not to leave fingerprints. It's seems like a waste of time and it makes such a mess."

Dani shrugged. "Let me worry about how to word the report, and the tech won't have to brush the whole house, only your bedroom. Have the two of you ever been fingerprinted? It would be helpful to have your prints to eliminate from any picked up."

"Yes. I had that done years ago. I'll pull the cards out of my file tonight."

"Has anyone else been in the house who might have left prints recently?"

Barbara quickly ran through the possibilities. She hadn't let Decker or Russ inside. "A friend of Matt's and a woman named Tammy Garrett have been in the house, but they wouldn't have gone into my bedroom. The only other person whose prints should be in there would be the man I told you about, Kyle Trent."

Dani grinned. "So *that's* what you meant when you told me things were moving too fast for you."

Barbara gave an embarrassed shrug. "You know that expression 'He swept me off my feet'? That pretty much sums it up."

"Congratulations," Dani said with a wink. "I hope it works out for you." She asked a few other questions to complete her report, then stopped when a call on her radio caught her attention. "What an interesting coincidence. Someone just reported a disturbance at the Wayward Motel. It sounds like a domestic, but I think I'll check it out anyway. Who knows? Maybe we'll get lucky and Latham will be involved." She was on her way in a matter of seconds.

Dani stayed in her police car as the show played out in the Wayward parking lot. She intended to have a few words with Latham, but not in front of an audience.

She waved at a man on her squad who didn't seem to be doing anything but observing. "What's the story, Harris?"

He leaned down to her level and smiled. "You're gonna love it, Sarge. See the blond couple over there?"

Dani recognized Latham, but not the woman. "Hooker?"

"Not that we know of or that she'll admit. There was so much screaming and shouting when our guys arrived, they didn't bother to knock. Just broke the door in. There they were, both buck naked, but she's stretched out on the bed on her stomach with her wrists handcuffed to the headboard and her ankles tied to the frame, and he's whipping her with this stringy leather thing, like you'd find in—"

"I get the picture," Dani said holding up her hand. "Is she willing to press charges against him?"

Harris laughed. "Of course not. She says she's going to sue us for intruding on their privacy. Apparently their idea of foreplay is bondage and beatings. Looks like the only thing that's going to happen here is the guy's been told to pack up and check out."

Adding the girl's refusal to press charges to Latham's history with Barbara, Dani decided she was a hooker he'd picked up in Richmond or D.C., and she dismissed her from the collection of people she was keeping track of. She also gave up the idea of speaking to Russ at the moment. It would be too easy for him to claim police harassment. She would simply have to wait until he was served with the restraining order. The only problem with that was that he would no longer be where they expected to find him.

Dani parked her car in the restaurant lot next to the motel and waited for Russ to make his move. When he pulled out, so did she, but he didn't drive to another motel down the road. She followed him at a distance until he crossed the Virginia state line. He was heading north, which she knew was home for him, but she also knew his type didn't give up this easily.

He'd come back. And when he did, she'd be right on his ass. Her fingers found the baton at her side and stroked its length. Whatever it took, she was going to prevent what happened to her sister from happening to Barbara.

"Simon? It's Tammy."

"Tammy? You sound awful."

Keeping her fingers tightly clamped on her nose, she said, "I've picked up a cold, and I'm running a fever. I just wanted to let you know I won't be able to get over there tonight." She pictured his sagging cheeks drooping even further.

"I could come there . . . bring you some chicken soup . . . cold pills . . ."

"Please don't. I hate being fussed over when I'm sick. I just wanted you to know that I searched Barbara's entire house today. If she kept her copy of that agreement, it's somewhere else."

"Damn. All right. The fact that she hasn't used it up to now probably means she didn't keep it. How did your visit with her go?"

"Not good enough. I'm going to concentrate on Matthew next. What about the boyfriend?"

"I put my investigator on it this morning, but it may not matter. I've given Latham another assignment. If he pulls it off, our problems will all be solved."

Tammy was so surprised, she let go of her nose. "You gave Latham an assignment? What was it?"

"Nothing I want you involved in, my love. Why don't you call me in the morning, after you've gotten some rest. Perhaps you'll feel like spending some time with me then."

"Bastard," Tammy hissed at the phone after she hung it up. He knew she'd be too curious about what he was doing to play sick for long. The problem was, she wasn't really playing.

She adjusted the cold water in the shower so that it came out in a fine spray, then stepped under it. Uncontrollable shivers vibrated her body as the icy water hit her burning back. She was going to repay Russ for this if it was the last thing she did. A little spanking was exciting, but under no circumstances would she tolerate having her body scarred. The welts would go down, but the skin on two of them had been broken. If they didn't heal smoothly, Russ's punishment would be castration!

Barbara had been right all the time. He was crazy. And a liar. He had said he was going home to see his sick stepfather, insinuating that he might die, thus releasing Russ from his promise to his mother not to do anything that would embarrass that man while he was still alive. But Simon had just let her know that he had sent Russ off on an assignment. The whole story about being the illegitimate son of Howard Hamilton III was probably just another one of Russ's lies.

It was obvious to her now that Russ was never going to be of any use to her. Barbara wouldn't marry him if he was the last man on earth, and even if she did, he was still too obsessed with her to have her committed. Tammy had no doubt that *she* was the woman Russ was planning to get rid of rather than Barbara.

As old and repulsive as Simon was, he was now the front-runner in the race for the Hamilton fortune, and the kid was her ticket to ride along.

Tomorrow night she would stop wasting time with Matthew and get down to some serious manipulation of his attitude. If that failed, she could always fall back on the plan she had suggested to begin with: the one both Russ and Simon had rejected as too dangerous.

Chapter 16

Barbara made one last spot-check of her bedroom and was satisfied that it was back to normal. The technician Dani had sent to the house had been neat as well as quick, although he warned her that getting the results could take as long as a week. That didn't bother her, however, as she was still of the opinion that it had been a waste of time.

"*Ma!* Kyle's here."

Barbara made a face at her mirror image and decided it was too late to worry about her hair or makeup. She hadn't even gotten dinner started.

She found Kyle and Matt in the kitchen, unpacking a box filled with Chinese takeout containers. Smiling, she said, "And once again, superhero Kyle Trent comes to the rescue of the poor maiden." He returned her smile with a look that made her breath catch in her chest.

"Just trying to make up for not being around to help yesterday."

Barbara caught sight of the sour expression on Matt's face and tried to soften it. "No problem. I had Matthew to protect me."

"Yeah, sure," Matt said, still frowning. "If you really thought that, you'd have told me why that man was in your bedroom."

Kyle's eyes opened wide as his gaze darted between mother and son, hoping for a reasonable explanation. Barbara had the distinct impression that Matt had purposely worded his statement to sound suggestive. "I was trying not to worry you in case it was just my imagination."

"See what I mean?" Matt exclaimed. "You're still treating me like a baby, but *he* comes in after it's all over and you call him a superhero!" He gave Kyle a shove to get him out of his way, then ran out of the kitchen.

Barbara's shoulders slumped in frustration. "I'm sorry. He usually has the best manners, but it's been a very difficult day and—"

"And he's just a little worried that I'm trying to take his place with you. Let me to talk to him. If I can't put him at ease, I'll leave."

Barbara sighed. "I don't know if you should—"

"Please," he said taking her hands in his. "Let me try." He kissed her knuckles and started to move away, but turned back to kiss her mouth. "I love you."

She stood there as Kyle left the room, wondering how big a mistake this was. Then again, Matt wanted to be treated like a grown-up, and what could be more grown-up than a "man-to-man" talk?

But Kyle had no experience dealing with children, other than entertaining them, and Matt didn't seem to be in a mood to be bought off tonight. She decided to give Kyle five minutes while she set the table; then she'd check to see if they needed a referee.

"Hey, Matt," Kyle said from the doorway of the boy's bedroom. "Can I come in?" Matt shrugged indifferently and Kyle sat down on his desk chair. "I think we need to talk."

Matt sat upright on his bed and crossed his legs and arms. "So, talk."

Kyle cleared his throat. "You know, we have a lot in common—we like the circus, the zoo, the arcade, pizza, adventure movies, collecting baseball and football cards—"

"And your point is?" Matt interrupted with a bored look.

Kyle pinched the bridge of his nose and organized his thoughts. "The point is, there's something we have in common that's a lot more important than any of those things."

He gave Matt a second to look at him. "We both love your mother very much and would do anything in our power to protect her from every bad thing in the world. From what I can tell, she has more than her fair share of bad things to deal with, so she should have more than one man to protect her. I was hoping the two of us could team up. That way she'd almost always have at least one protector, and when she needed more, she'd have us both."

Matt twisted his mouth from side to side. "I

guess that makes sense. But what about when neither of us are around? Like today, when Russ bothered her at the bank."

Kyle shot up from the chair. "Russ was at the bank? That son-of-a—" He cut himself off. What had Russ said to Barbara?

"You can cuss in front of me. I call Russ names like that all the time. Well, not in front of Mom."

The humor in Matt's comment brought Kyle back to the discussion at hand, and he sat down to deliver his conclusion. "Anyway, the main thing I'm trying to say is that I don't want to change anything between you and your mother. I just want to be added on." He could tell by Matt's expression that he needed to reword that. "Let's see. Think of a motorcycle."

Matt brightened. "A Harley?"

"Okay, a Harley," Kyle said with a grin. "Imagine your mom is the front wheel and you're the back wheel. You need each other to keep going, and you could go along fine by yourselves as long as you keep moving. But if you stop, there's a chance you could lose your balance. I want to be a sidecar to your cycle. That way, I'd get to ride along with you, while helping you both keep your balance even if you're standing still. And sidecars have lots of other advantages, too, if you'll just give me a chance to show you."

Matt tilted his head up at Kyle. "You're pretty smart, aren't you?"

Kyle became very serious and shook his head. "Not always. I've made some really bad mistakes, and there are a lot of things I don't understand. Like why two incredibly terrific people like you and your mother have had such a tough time of it."

"Okay," Matt said simply.

"Okay?"

"We can try teaming up . . . for a while. But you're gonna have to learn all the signals and codes and swear to keep them a secret."

Kyle solemnly agreed, and Matt proceeded to fill him in on the special language only he and his mother had previously shared.

When they returned to the kitchen, Kyle could see that Barbara was dying to know how the discussion went, but he figured he'd leave it up to Matt to decide what to tell her. Meanwhile, he had questions of his own. As soon as they sat down to eat, he began. "Matt said Russ paid you a visit at work this morning."

"Yes, but the bank guard helped get rid of him."

That wasn't exactly what Kyle needed to know. "Did he have, um, anything in particular to say?"

Barbara glanced at Matt, then shook her head. "No. Same old, same old. I let him know I filed a restraining order against him, but he hasn't been served yet."

Kyle was certain there was more, something she didn't want to say in front of Matt, but whatever it was, she wasn't angry at him because of it, and that was all he cared about. "And what about the man who was in your bedroom?"

Barbara arched an eyebrow at him, then

laughed when she remembered Matt's earlier comment. "He was taking fingerprints. Dani sent him by after I told her I thought an intruder had been in the house this morning. Which reminds me, do you know if your prints are on file anywhere? If not, they might need you to go down to the station and have them taken to compare with what they picked up."

Kyle felt the egg foo yung turn into cactus on its way down his throat. He tried to keep it moving, but only ended up choking. After some vigorous back-pounding from Matt and several sips of water, he finally got it under control, but it was another minute before he could speak.

Fingerprints. Not only would his real name be revealed, but his arrest record along with it. His voice had a croaking quality when he finally responded. "I've been fingerprinted before, for a, uh, job application. Did they say how long it would take to identify the prints?"

"The technician said about a week," Barbara said, watching him closely. "Are you sure you're all right?"

He patted his chest. "Fine now. Must have gone down the wrong pipe." *A week.* It was far less than he'd counted on; he would just have to move up his timetable. "Would the two of you mind if I stayed on your couch tonight? With everything that's happened around here in two days, I'd be too worried to sleep anywhere else, except maybe in my car in your driveway."

Barbara almost said yes without thinking, then looked to Matt for his decision.

"Sure," he said. "Or you could have my room and I could sleep on the couch."

Barbara winked at him. "Nice try, kiddo, and while we're asleep, you'd stay up and watch television all night. I don't think so."

Rather than admit that she was right, he changed the subject. "Can we play Monopoly tonight?"

"If you agree to a two-hour time limit," she returned. "You can set up the game while I put away the leftovers."

"I'll help," Kyle said, closing a container.

She noticed a glint in his eye and guessed at what he was thinking. "It will be faster without your *help*." His phony pout proved her intuition was right.

"Fine. Then I'll just go bring in my suitcase."

Since it took at least ten minutes for Barbara to put the kitchen back in order, she was surprised to discover that Kyle hadn't come back in from going to get his bag.

From the front window she could see him sitting in his car with the interior light on. Concerned that something might be wrong, she went out to check on him. As she drew closer, she realized that he was talking on a cellular phone with his attention on the seat beside him. Only when she was right beside him did he notice her.

He smiled, ended the call, hurriedly pushed some papers back into his open briefcase, then closed it. Barbara thought his smile looked a little shaky as he climbed out of the car, phone in hand.

"My new toy," he said, showing her his phone. "I swore I'd never have one of these things. A beeper was bad enough. But after yesterday's scare, I gave in. Then when I came out to get my bag, I remembered I left the thing in my briefcase, and I needed to let the office know where I was staying, and when I called in, they had messages for me."

She accepted his hand as they walked back to the house, but the little voice in her head was yammering at her. They were alone outside, but he didn't jump at the opportunity to take her in his arms, as he had seemed to want to do in the kitchen. He was nervous, as if she had caught him at something. He gave too many unnecessary details. He was talking to a girlfriend, or worse yet, a wife that he had denied having.

She found it nearly impossible to keep up a happy front for the entire two hours while they played Monopoly, and as soon as Matt was securely bedded down, Kyle let her know that he wasn't fooled.

"I've never been very good at reading women's minds," he said when she sat on the sofa a good two feet away from him. "But I'm better than average at analyzing facts. Despite everything that's happened, you were happy to see me and in a fairly up mood . . . until you saw me on the phone." She didn't bother to deny that. "I see.

Well, the only thing I can say in my own defense is that I'm really trying to break the habit."

Barbara's mouth fell open. "I beg your pardon?"

"I told you when we first met that I'm a workaholic. Every woman I ever dated complained about it. But I swear, since I met you, I've cut my hours in half. That was one of the reasons I didn't want a cellular phone. I figured if I had one of those, I'd never stop working."

"Wait a minute. Are you saying that you were embarrassed that I caught you making a business call in your car instead of helping Matt set up the Monopoly board? And you figured I'd resent that?" His guilty expression was her answer. "Then you weren't talking to . . ." she had to make sure, "another woman?"

He let out a laugh and quickly covered his mouth for fear he'd wake Matt. "You thought . . . Oh, God, Barbara, I can't tell you how happy that makes me." He closed the space between them and pulled her into his arms. He hugged her hard, then held her away so that he could see her eyes. "You love me. You may not have said the words, but this proves it."

"Kyle . . ."

"Admit it. You were upset because you thought there was someone else."

"Well, maybe a little."

He kissed her hard on the mouth. "There is no other woman in the world for me but you." He kissed her again, a little softer, a little slower. "There has never been another woman in my life who meant anything to me." His third kiss was long, lingering, and thoroughly seductive. And when he spoke again, he was on his back and she was on top of him, moving with the need he made her feel. "There will never be another woman in my life but you. I love you, and now, whether you're ready to say the words or not, I'm satisfied that you love me, too. Unfortunately, if you keep squirming like that, I'll forget who's sleeping down the hall and—"

"*Oh!*" Barbara squeaked, and brought them both upright again. "I don't believe how easily you can do that to me. That kind of power should be illegal."

He touched her chin with his finger and gave her the lightest possible kiss on her nose. "The only power I have is the power of love, and you're the one who activated it."

"And that's another thing. How do you manage to say things like that without sounding corny?"

The corners of his eyes crinkled with laughter, but he held back the sound this time. "Things like that only sound corny when they're lies. Now, in order to save my sanity, I'm going to suggest we do the last thing I actually want to do. You'll probably deny this, too, but you're exhausted. Let's watch the news and go to sleep—in separate rooms."

Barbara thought there was very little chance of her falling asleep with him so close by, but she must have, for when she heard a high-pitched ring, it took her a moment to figure out that it was neither her telephone nor the alarm. She squinted at the illuminated digits on her clock. It was only twelve-thirty. What had awakened her?

She told herself it was a dream and rolled over, but a man's voice came to her from a distance. She sat up and listened with both ears.

"Tough . . . more complicated than . . . power of persuasion . . . no, no . . . a hundred sixty-five million . . ."

Barbara strained her ears, but she couldn't hear anything else. Kyle was definitely talking business rather than romance, but why would a sales manager get a call so late at night? She tried to make sense of the words she'd heard, but they didn't fit into the context of his job as she understood it to be. In spite of the confusing questions in her mind, though, she was asleep again minutes later.

"Did you get a call last night?" Barbara asked Kyle over breakfast.

Before answering, Kyle washed down a bite of toast with a gulp of orange juice. "Yes. I couldn't believe it. I've only had the phone one day and I already got a wrong number in the middle of the night. I was hoping you hadn't been awakened by it. Sorry."

"It's okay. I went right back to sleep." Barbara couldn't remember exactly what she'd heard him saying, but she hadn't thought it sounded like the response to a wrong number. Considering how quickly she fell back to sleep, however, there was a good chance she'd been dreaming.

"Are you sure you and Matt should go to work and school today?" Kyle asked with a worried look.

"Yeah, Ma," Matt quickly added. "I probably oughta stay home today."

Barbara smirked at him, then said to Kyle, "Yes, I'm sure. Whenever possible, we try not to let Russ stop us from living somewhat normal lives. Anyway, both the bank guard and school officials are looking out for him, so we should be okay."

Kyle didn't look convinced, but a phone call kept him from debating the point. Barbara let Matt answer it, since he moved first, but it was Dani calling for her.

"I have semi-good news. That disturbance yesterday did involve Russ Latham and some hooker. He got thrown out of that motel, but rather than moving to another one, he went north, out of Virginia. I've left word with the front desk of every motel and hotel in the area to notify me if anyone checks in matching his description or with his vehicle, and so far, there's no sign that he's returned. I wouldn't suggest a celebration quite yet, but I'm keeping my fingers and toes crossed that he's given up."

Barbara took a deep breath. "Thanks, Dani. I just wish there was something I could do to repay you for all your help."

Dani chuckled. "Maybe you'll pack me another lunch someday. In the meantime, the biggest thing you can do for me is to find yourself some happiness."

Barbara relayed the news to Kyle and Matt with

her own warning to Matt not to let his guard down yet.

"Even semi-good news demands a semi-celebration," Kyle said. "How about dinner and a movie tonight? An early one, of course."

Matt and Barbara accepted his invitation, but as they were all leaving the house, she wondered if she should have clarified the matter of where Kyle was planning to spend the night.

The day was blissfully uneventful for Barbara and Matt, until the doorbell rang while they were getting ready to go out with Kyle.

"It's Tammy," Matt exclaimed after looking out the window.

Since Barbara had told Kyle about the girl's last visit, he completely understood the unhappy expression on her face. However, Tammy seemed to be back to her old, bubbly self, as she greeted all three with cheek kisses.

"Before anyone says a word, I want to apologize for my megaboring bad mood the other night. You were absolutely right, Barb. I got a better job this morning, and I already met *several* fascinating prospects. So I came to take you and Matt out to dinner to celebrate." She looked at Kyle as though she just realized he was there. "Oh! I'm interrupting something, aren't I?" Her lively expression died in two blinks of her big blue eyes.

"Ma?" Matt tugged on her sweater and looked up at her pleadingly, but Kyle replied before she could.

"Please join us. We weren't planning anything special."

Tammy instantly became animated again. "I've got a better idea. Let me take Matt out and you two can have the evening to yourselves. Or the two of us could stay here and order pizza and play video games. Your choice, Matt."

"Pizza and games!" he declared without hesitation.

The change of plans had occurred so swiftly, Barbara felt a little dizzy. "Are you sure?" She felt Kyle's fingers scratch her back three times and glanced at him curiously. He had just used one of her and Matt's signals for "run as fast as you can."

"Absolutely," Tammy stated firmly.

"Positively!" Matt seconded.

She went through all the predeparture reminders twice as she put on her coat and checked her purse for her keys. "Are you absolutely positive—"

"*Out,*" Tammy ordered Barbara with a dramatic wave of her arm.

"Yeah, Ma," Matt said, laughing. "Get out before we have to throw you out."

Kyle tugged on her arm. "I think they want to be alone."

"All right, all right," Barbara said, shaking her head. "But if anything happens, you have Kyle's cellular phone number and his beeper number—"

"Is she always like this?" Tammy asked Matt, and he rolled his eyes.

Barbara knew when she was hopelessly outnumbered. After one more hug for Matt, she and

Kyle finally left the house. When he opened the passenger door of his car for her, he had to move his briefcase before she could sit down.

"What kind of leather is this?" she asked, running her hand over the slick black finish as he lifted it out.

"Eelskin. It doesn't get ruined if it gets wet." He waited for her to get situated, then hurriedly put the briefcase in the trunk and got behind the wheel.

As he was backing out of the driveway, she asked, "What does the *H* stand for?"

He quickly glanced at her and continued out into the street. "The what?"

"The *H* of *HKT* . . . the initials on your briefcase. My goodness, Kyle, you're blushing. Is it that awful?"

"I think so. Why don't you guess?"

"Harold? Hector? Harvey? Herbert?" He shook his head and his smile widened with each of her guesses. "I've got it—Horatio!" She just prayed it wasn't Howard.

"You're not even close."

"Okay, let's see. Harrison? Homer? What are you doing?" She couldn't imagine why he pulled into the parking lot of the first shopping strip they came to. As he brought the car to a stop a good distance from any stores or restaurants, her curiosity rose.

Kyle answered her unspoken question by drawing her into his arms and pressing his lips to hers. With each heartbeat, the kiss went from saying

"Hello," to "I missed you terribly," to "I need you," to "I don't want to wait until we're somewhere more private, the backseat will be just fine."

They were moments away from mindlessly following through with their urgent desire when a blast from a car horn jolted them to their senses.

Kyle grinned at her. "I guess that pretty much sums up what I've been thinking about all day." He raised her hand to his lips and kissed her palm. "Where would you like to have dinner?"

She angled her head to inhale the cologne on his neck, then kissed his earlobe and whispered, "How does room service sound?" He responded to her suggestion with a low growl and another long, hungry kiss.

"Kyle?"

"Hmmm?

"What's your first name?"

"Ha—Hannibal."

"Hannibal? As in Missouri?"

Kyle made a face. "As in the man with the army of elephants. My father was a history buff."

Rather than drive all the way to his hotel room in Richmond, he decided to head toward Washington and take advantage of the first decent-looking place they came to. It still took them nearly a half hour, with every stoplight offering an excuse to touch and taste a little more. By the time they got inside a private room with a king-size bed, the foreplay had already gone on much longer than either of them could stand.

The French twist she had so painstakingly

forced her hair into came undone in seconds. Kyle barely noticed the new sexy lingerie in his rush to get it off her body. His neatly pressed shirt and slacks were carelessly dropped to the floor.

Unable to tolerate any more delays, he lifted her and joined their bodies where they stood. She welcomed him with a sigh of relief, but as he raised and lowered her hips, her relief was replaced by another building need. He quickly brought them both to climax, yet neither was fully satisfied. Without separating their bodies, he moved to the bed and resumed the rhythmic demonstration of his deep love for her.

That second release relaxed them both sufficiently to think about ordering food, but once dinner was finished, Kyle carried her back to bed again.

After a soul-wrenching kiss, he asked, "What time does Matt get up for school in the morning?"

"About six a—" She gasped as his mouth closed over her nipple and sucked.

He lifted his head to see the clock on the nightstand. "Six, huh? That gives us another eight hours before we have to get home."

"That's not fair to Tammy. Remember, she just started a new job."

He made a face at her. "All right. We'll get home by midnight. She wouldn't expect us to be back before then." Before she could voice another objection to staying a little longer, his extremely skilled tongue went to work on her other breast.

It was the first time all over again as he slowly

aroused every nerve in her body until there wasn't a thought in her mind, only physical sensation. Each time she began to peak, however, he moved his attentions to a less sensitive area. She tried enticing him in return, but he had been so well sated, he wasn't having any problem controlling his response. Pleading failed as well. She finally resorted to threats to get him to stop teasing her.

"Are you frustrated, love?" he murmured against her mouth. "Is your skin on fire?" His fingers lightly tickled the flesh around her navel. "Is a drum pounding between your thighs? Do you think you might explode if you don't soon feel me inside you?" His fingers slipped into the center of her heat and pressed upward.

She managed to nod her head as she bit her lower lip.

"Good. Then you know how I've felt since Sunday morning after we made love the last time. I thought being with you over the weekend yet not being able to touch you in front of Matt was torture, but I didn't have any idea how bad it could get until all I had was your voice over the phone."

He went back to kissing and stroking her until she was reduced to kittenish whimpers. "Before you know it, we're going to have to leave this room and go back to being frustrated and sleeping alone. How long will it be this time? Two days? Three? Five again?" His fingers drew another anguished moan from her. "I love you so much. I don't want to hide how I feel about you. I don't want to sleep alone anymore."

He repositioned his body over hers and eased his way inside. She tried to move her hips, but he held her still. "I want to be free to do this every night, love." He slowly withdrew from her, then pushed forward again, causing her nails to dig into his back. "Tell me you want the same thing, and I'll be the happiest man in the world. Say you'll marry me, Barbara, and I'll make sure you never have another worry for the rest of your life."

"Oh, Kyle, I—" The slightest shift of his hips took her breath away once more.

"I need you in my life. Please, love, just say *yes*."

She could no longer remember any of her logical reasons for maintaining her independence, not when Kyle was everything she could ever ask for in a husband. As he expertly drove her back to the place where her mind stopped functioning entirely, she whispered the word he awaited.

"Yes."

Chapter 17

Barbara's mind slowly refilled with little things: Kyle's warm breath on her neck, his heart pounding heavily close to her own, the monumental decision she had just made while her hormones were in control of her brain.

Last night she had just begun to admit that she might be in love with Kyle. Matt was just beginning to warm up to him. Perhaps, in time, she would have agreed to marry him anyway. But this wasn't the way she wanted it to happen. How could she marry someone whose first name she hadn't even known until a few hours ago?

Your new boyfriend's name isn't Kyle. It's Hamilton.

You still don't recognize a wolf in sheep's clothing when you meet one, do you?

Barbara knew better than to trust anything Russ said, but did she really know Kyle well enough to trust him with her and Matt's life? They had only met two weeks ago . . . under extremely strange, yet oddly familiar, circumstances. Not even two weeks, actually. And her photo had appeared in the newspaper less than a week before that.

Was he really embarrassed about being caught making a business call in his car, or was it something else? The words she heard him say during the night came back to her. She hadn't dreamed them; it hadn't been a wrong number. She clearly remembered the phrase "a hundred sixty-five million." Big money. Not the kind an office equipment salesman would deal in, but the kind the Hamiltons possessed.

Girl, you've got more smoke around you right now than a five-alarmer.

Dani was right. There had been far too much smoke blinding her lately, but she was about to blow some of it away.

She sat up and tried to see the truth in his face. He opened his eyes and smiled. Either he loved her with all his heart, or he was as good at lying and acting as Russ was. "Why did you do that?"

His smile faded as he realized she was upset rather than happy with him. "I wanted to please you."

"Maybe, but that's not what it feels like to me. I feel like I've been very expertly pushed—no, *seduced*—into agreeing to marry you. Why is that, Kyle? Why are you in such a hurry for me to say yes?"

A muscle in his cheek twitched, and he pulled himself up beside her. "I love you too much to be patient."

She took a slow breath as she felt her heart freezing up in her chest. "You were right. It does sound corny when it's a lie. Just like the wrong number in the middle of the night. And Hannibal. Funny thing about that. Russ said your name was Hamilton. Naturally, I assumed he was lying, since I thought he meant your last name."

He closed his eyes and rubbed his forehead. "I can explain everything. I was going to as soon as I was sure—"

Awareness that he really was hiding something slammed into Barbara like a punch in the stomach. *"When you were sure of what?* A legal commitment? Or . . . oh, my God . . . after you adopted Matthew? Did Decker hire you to—"

"Nobody hired me!" He grasped her shoulders to stop her from rising. "I know it looks bad, but it's not. It started out as repayment of a debt, but, as crazy as it sounds, I fell in love with you the moment I saw you. If I'd told you the truth up front, you would never have given me ten minutes of your time. Then one lie led to another—"

"Shut up. I don't want to know what lies you told me. I don't really want to hear why you did any of what you did." She pulled away from him and scrambled for her clothes.

"Barbara, please, let me explain."

"No." She stepped into her dress and shoes, and stuffed her underwear and stockings in her purse, but Kyle reached the door before she did. "Let me by, or I will scream so loud the police in the next county will hear me."

"No matter how angry you are right now, I can't let you walk out of here like this. Your dress isn't even zippered. Were you planning to hitchhike home half naked?"

"I'll get a cab."

"Maybe. In an hour or so. Or you can be rational, finish getting dressed, and I'll drive you home. What if Matt's waiting up? Do you want him to see you looking like you just rolled out of bed? Or worse, that you were raped again?"

She glared at him. "I was, wasn't I?"

"How we feel about each other is not a lie! I've never had to force myself on you."

She didn't like it, but letting him drive her home was more reasonable than what she was about to do. Without verbally agreeing, she went into the bathroom to straighten her hair and finish dressing.

"Let me get your zipper," Kyle said quietly, coming up behind her.

She stepped away from him with a snarl on her face. "Don't you *ever* touch me again." He looked crushed, but he backed away. Less than ten minutes later, they were in his car driving back to Barbara's house.

"My real name is Hamilton Kyle Treadwell."

"If you insist on talking, I'm getting out." She tried to open her door, but he had locked it from his side.

"You're not that stupid, Barbara. Nor do I believe that you're so secure that you don't need to know why I appeared in your life when I did." He paused, but she gave him no encouragement; she just stared out the side window.

"I thought you'd recognize the name. That's why I didn't use it when we met. I needed to get to know you without your knowing who I was. I once suggested you tell me your story by starting at the beginning. So I guess that advice holds here, too." He took a delaying breath. "I'm Howard's cousin."

Barbara's head jerked toward him automatically, but she stopped herself from expressing her shock aloud. As she looked away again, he continued.

"I figured he would have told you about me."

"The Three Musketeers," she murmured.

"Howard, Russ, and I were inseparable when we were growing up, but after I left for college we only got together on holidays. I was working in Chicago when you and Howard met, and since our parents didn't communicate with each other, I didn't find out about you until Howard came back from Europe. Aunt Edith was so upset about Howard's drinking by then, she lowered herself to invite me to the estate for Christmas.

"I stayed for a week. I'm sure you can imagine the picture my aunt and uncle painted of you, but Howard never had a bad thing to say. No matter what they told him you'd done, he would have forgiven you, but he believed you had chosen Russ over him . . . because he wasn't man enough for you."

Barbara closed her eyes against the remembered pain.

"Naturally, it never entered his mind that his parents and their attorney had fabricated everything, as we now know they did. My parents, on the other hand, had told me enough stories about the Hamiltons' cutthroat ways of controlling people and events so that I wondered if you were really as horrid as they claimed.

"It didn't really matter to me one way or the other. I just wanted to help Howard forget about you and straighten up his act."

He inhaled deeply and when he spoke, his voice was strained with emotion. "We went to a party New Year's Eve. He got so drunk he could barely crawl to his car, but he fought with me over the keys. Ironic, wasn't it? I was afraid he'd get us both killed, so I drove."

Barbara's eyes opened wide. "*You* were driving the car the night Howard was killed?"

"Most of the details were kept out of the media, but I thought you might have known that much. I had only had one glass of champagne, but the roads were covered with ice. I swerved to avoid an oncoming truck and lost control. The car went off an embankment and rolled over. We were trapped inside for a couple hours, both hurt, but Howard . . . was cut up really bad. He . . . he bled to death in front of me . . . and . . ." He took a shaky breath. "I had to watch him die, Barbara. I couldn't do a thing to help."

The tears in his voice caused her own eyes to water, but she was determined not to care about anything he had to say.

Several seconds passed before he spoke again. "Before he died, he made me promise to do something for him. He, uh, asked me to find you, tell you he never stopped loving you, and to make sure you were happy. If you needed anything . . . anything at all . . . I swore I would provide it for you. When I look back on it now, I think he had something like a vision about you needing help."

The tears flowed down her cheeks, but she refused to turn to him.

"I was pretty messed up for a while after he died, both physically and mentally. Suffice it to say, I was so crazed with guilt, I did some pretty self-destructive things. I even spent some time in jail. What saved me was remembering the promise I'd made. The problem was, when I finally got around to looking for you, you'd disappeared. Twice, an investigator I hired tracked you down, but by the time I went to visit you, you'd taken off again. Through the investigator I learned you had a son, but I had no way of knowing if the child was Howard's or Russ's."

A huff of annoyance came out before she could stop it.

"Regardless of what an angel Howard thought you were, remember I didn't know which story was closest to the truth. I loved Howard like a brother and intended to keep my promise to him if I could, but I also wanted to judge for myself whether you deserved his devotion.

"The picture in the paper was the first clue to your whereabouts that I'd had in years. Between the photos my investigators had taken and how much Matt now looks like Howard, I was almost positive of who you were, and then the investigator confirmed your name change. I found out where you worked and—"

"And had me *mugged*?"

"No! I had this neat little plan worked out to bump into you at the bank. I just lucked into the mugging, I swear."

She turned away again.

Kyle banged his fist on the steering wheel. "Damn it, Barbara! Give me a little understanding here. What else could I do? Walk up to you and say, 'Hi. I'm Howard Hamilton's cousin. You know, the one that killed him. Are you an angel like he said, in which case I'll grant any wish you have, or are you really a two-bit, gold-digging whore?' And if you were what his father claimed, isn't it conceivable that you would lie to see what you could get out of me? I couldn't think of any other way to judge you fairly except to pretend that I was someone else."

"And you couldn't possibly judge me *fairly* unless you first fucked my brains out, right?"

He didn't say another word until he stopped at a red light. Shifting toward her, he stroked her cheek, and she instantly slapped his hand away.

"I told you not to touch me."

He withdrew his hand and gripped the steering wheel with tense fingers. "Falling in love with you at first sight was the last thing I could have anticipated. But after hearing how it happened to Howard with you, I didn't stay surprised for long. He and I used to be alike in so many ways. I kept ordering myself to tell you the truth, but the more I learned about you, the more I realized how many reasons you'd have to hate me. Instead of getting easier, it just kept getting more complicated.

"I know how stupid this is going to sound. But I convinced myself that if you loved me enough to marry me, you'd have to forgive me for all the lies. I was hoping I could tell you everything tonight."

He pulled into her driveway and turned off the car, but didn't unlock her door.

"Let me out." Her voice was calm, not at all the way she felt.

"Ask me anything, and I'll explain it. The call last night—"

"Don't bother. I wouldn't know if it was the truth or not. I can't seem to tell the difference. Now unlock the door and get out of my life."

He released the security lock, but got out as quickly as she did and hurried to intercept her. Despite her order to the contrary, he grasped her arms. "I don't know how to fix the mess I've made, but I need to. If you don't believe what I just said, what *do* you believe? Why in God's name would I have gone through such a masquerade?"

She tilted her head back and met his gaze. "For the money, of course. Marry me, adopt Matthew, and cut yourself in on the Hamiltons' millions."

His mouth opened, then widened into a smile. "If that's the main reason you won't believe me, it won't hold up. My family has more money than they do!"

"That's ridiculous," she said, and pushed him out of her way so she could continue walking to her door. "No one has more money than—" Two terrifyingly loud explosions made her whirl back around.

A truck was speeding down the street.

Kyle fell to his knees, put his hand over his shoulder, then stared in bewilderment at the dark stain on his palm. "I think I've been shot."

Russ lifted his foot off the accelerator and slowed Pop's truck down to the speed limit despite the adrenaline pumping through his body, demanding that he keep flying.

Talk about luck! He'd driven straight to Barbara's from the expressway, saw Tammy's car in the driveway, and stopped to look around. It only took a few seconds of listening at the window to determine that Barbara was out with Ham.

It was too perfect an opportunity to pass up. He simply had to wait for the lovebirds to return to enact the "random" drive-by shooting.

From what he had witnessed, they seemed to be having quite an argument—another bit of luck for him.

Unfortunately, he would have to wait to hear tomorrow's news to learn whether or not it had truly been a successful night. He saw Ham go down, but had either of the bullets finished him off?

"Is it really necessary to have a police car parked in front of the house? Wasn't it enough that you grounded Matt and me?"

"Humor me," Dani said with an understanding smile. "A detective in an unmarked car will replace that one by this evening and your neighbors will quit talking about you. As far as your staying home today, until I'm convinced that last night's shooting was a random drive-by, I'm assuming the two of you are in serious danger, and we can protect you better if you stay put."

"You think it was Russ, don't you?"

"Ninety-nine percent sure, based on my intuition, but I have yet to confirm that he was even in the area last night. None of the motel people called me, but he could have slipped in unnoticed. I'll be spending most of today recontacting them, plus I put out a BOLO on him and his car. That's an advisory for police to be on the lookout. If he's back, we'll find him. In the meantime, you and Matt can put up with a few restrictions."

"What about Simon Decker?"

"He's the other one percent, not that I can picture him pulling the trigger. Hiring a hit man would be more his style, I'd think, but then, from what you've told me, there's a possibility that Russ Latham could be the man he'd hire. At any rate, I had a conversation with Decker this morning. He behaved properly shocked and upset. He can't prove he was in his hotel room all night, but we can't prove otherwise. We're keeping a loose watch on him just in case."

Dani scrutinized Barbara's face. "Try to take a nap this afternoon. You look like you were the one shot instead of him."

Barbara smirked at her. "For some strange reason, I had a little trouble sleeping after everyone left the party."

"Speaking of everyone leaving, your friend Tammy Garrett wasn't home when the detective went by her apartment to get her statement, and she hasn't returned the messages left on her answering machine. If you hear from her, try to convince her to stop in at the station, or at least give me a call. I'll be glad to handle it personally, out of uniform, if she's really that phobic about talking to police."

Barbara rolled her eyes. "I think phobic might be an understatement. The instant she realized police were on their way, she was gone. I can't help but wonder what could have happened to her that would terrify her that much."

"Hard to tell, but it usually means the person either is, or once was, on the opposite side of the law. Although, the way Matt talks about her, it's unlikely she'd fall into that category."

Dani hesitated a few seconds before moving on to the next person on her list. "I checked on your other friend before I came here. It was only a flesh wound—hurts like hell, but he'll be out of the hospital by tomorrow morning."

Barbara's expression hardened. "Too bad."

"Yeah," Dani said with a slow nod, then continued in a clearly sarcastic tone. "Too bad he wasn't killed. Better yet, too bad he wasn't set on fire and slowly cremated. That would have been a lot more painful."

"You think I should feel some sympathy for him?"

"I think you should feel something. I know our friendship is very new, and I may have over-stepped my bounds, but you were falling in love with this guy, and suddenly he's the devil incarnate, to the point where you didn't even ask about his condition. The thing is, I think your emotional antennae are very finely tuned when it comes to men, and the fact that you trusted him as much as you did shouldn't be ignored. Anyway, I had a talk with him."

Barbara clucked her tongue and sighed. "Don't tell me you were sucked in by his chemistry."

"I'm pretty sure any natural chemistry he has was canceled out by the shot of morphine he was given while I was there. He was a little out of it, but he managed to tell me an interesting story about who he is and why you now hate his guts."

"And you believed him?"

Dani chuckled. "A man pumped full of narcotics is usually fairly truthful."

"But did he admit that he planned the whole thing to get his hands on Hamilton money through Matthew?"

"He doesn't need their money."

"Are you sure they didn't give *you* some hard drugs while you were there?"

With a shrug, Dani said, "You'll believe whatever you want, so I'm going to save my breath, except for one suggestion. Get yourself a list of the wealthiest people in the world and see whose name ranks above whose."

When she was alone again, Barbara tried to busy herself by reorganizing the kitchen cabinets, but Dani's suggestion kept haunting her. What if Kyle had told the truth about having more money than the Hamiltons? What other reason would he have for seducing her?

"Ma? Could I talk to you for a minute?"

Barbara withdrew her head from the cabinet under the sink and smiled at Matt. "Did you sleep all right?"

He nodded and sat down on the floor next to her. "Is Kyle going to be okay?"

"Yes, he'll be fine. Dani checked on him earlier." They had talked about the shooting for a while after the police left, but she was willing to go over all of it again if he needed more reassurance. Barbara gave Matt time to ask for more details, but he didn't. "Is that what you wanted to talk about?"

"No. I mean, I wanted to know if he was okay, but that wasn't it." Rather than say what *it* was, he untied and retied the shoelaces on his new sneakers.

"You know you can ask me anything." He stopped playing with the laces, but he couldn't seem to find a comfortable position. "Should I start guessing, or will you give me a hint first?"

Though Matt stopped fidgeting, he kept his eyes downcast. "I've just been wonderin' about . . . stuff."

From the embarrassed look on his face, she thought she'd figured it out. Once upon a time, nine-year-old boys didn't know about sex and didn't want to. Today, they had knowledge forced on them at an early age. Either that or being around Tammy was playing havoc with his prepubescent hormones. "Is this about boy-girl stuff?"

He wrinkled his nose at her. "Naw. I told you I know all about that junk."

"Oh, that's right. I forgot. Come on, kiddo. I can't fill in the blanks if I don't know the questions."

He went back to playing with his laces, as he asked, "Did you and my real father ever get married?"

Her stomach clenched. So that was the problem. He wanted answers to the questions she'd been putting off. Evasion would no longer do, and she couldn't lie. "No, we weren't married."

He let that sink in, then went on to the next question. "Is he really dead?"

"Yes. He died in a car accident the night before you were born."

"Why didn't you two get married?"

Again, honesty seemed to be the best policy. "We loved each other very much, but we were from two different worlds. His family was very wealthy and didn't think I would fit into their social circle, so they . . . did things to convince him not to marry me."

"Huh?" Her explanation clearly made no sense to him.

"His mom and dad didn't like me," she summarized more simply.

"Oh. They must have been real assholes. *Oops!*"

"Matthew!" She was about to scold him, but the devilish grin he was trying to hide made her laugh. "Yes. They were royal assholes, but I don't want to hear that word out of your mouth again."

"Sorry." He started to retie the lace, then abruptly looked directly at her. "That means I *do* have another gramma and grampa, just like Tammy said I did. How come I never saw them? Are they dead, too?"

"No, they live in Boston in a big, stuffy old mansion with lots of servants who aren't allowed to smile. You've never met them because they didn't know about you. I always figured, when you got a little older, you could decide if you wanted to meet them. But as long as you brought it up, you may as well know it all. That gray-haired man, Simon Decker, works for them. Through him, they've offered to buy you from me."

"Huh? That's dumb. You can't buy kids from their moms." He paused and cocked his head at her. "Can you?"

"Not legally."

"Then they're bad people, too."

"Yes, but they're very rich, and they think that makes it okay to do whatever they want."

"I don't want to meet them. Ever. Tammy's wrong. I don't care if they could buy me virtual reality and fly me to Disney World every weekend in a private jet."

Barbara felt a chill run through her. "What did you say about Tammy?"

He had to think for a second. "Oh. We were talking about rich people last night. She thinks being rich is the coolest thing. She said if I had a family with lots of money, I could have everything I ever wanted and so could you, and Russ would never be able to scare us anymore."

There was something terribly unsettling about Tammy bringing up wealth *and* grandparents with her son on the same evening. "And what did you say to that?"

"Wel-l-l, when we were talking, I thought it might be cool to have piles of money. I mean, I'd like to have all that stuff, and for you not to have to work so hard. But if being rich turns you into the kind of creep who thinks you can buy somebody else's kid, I don't want to be like that. Kyle isn't rich like that, is he?"

Barbara's brain was still focused on Tammy and the odds of her casually discussing the benefits of having rich grandparents with Matt.

"Is he?"

"Oh, I'm sorry, baby. What did you say about Kyle?"

He made a face, but didn't complain about the endearment. "I was just wondering if he was rich, but I guess not, 'cause he doesn't even drive a fancy car. Can I ask one more question?"

"Of course."

"What was my father's name?"

After years of careful answers and guarded secrecy, it took a lot of courage for her to fill in the final blank, but it now appeared as though she needed to arm him with all the facts for his own protection. "Howard Hamilton IV was your father, and you look just like him."

Having cleared his mind of puzzling questions, Matt went off to play a video game. Barbara tried to get back to her project, but she now had even more to wonder over than before.

She didn't really care what Kyle's financial status was, but Dani had roused her curiosity, and the conversation with Matt had given her an idea how she could get the facts. She vacillated for several more minutes, then called Simon Decker.

"Why, Ms. Mancuso. What a pleasant surprise. But I heard you had a bit of an unpleasant surprise last night. Awful business, these drive-by shootings. Just awful. Believe me, I was appalled that that policewoman thought to question *me*, as though I would stoop to such a level to convince you to be reasonable."

Barbara listened to him ramble for a little longer. It was reminiscent of how Kyle had gone on and on the other night after she caught him making a phone call from his car. "Mr. Decker, excuse me for interrupting, but I didn't call about the shooting. I called to let you know I have considered the Hamiltons' final offer."

"Really?"

His surprise and excitement were exactly what Barbara counted on to get what she wanted. "But

I wonder if you would help me with a little problem I have."

"Anything. Anything at all."

"Good. I assume you were told who was shot last night."

"As a matter of fact, I was, but it was quite bewildering to me how Hamilton Treadwell happened to be in your front yard."

"Then you didn't know he was here and had spent the last two weeks trying to seduce me into marrying him?" She heard Decker gasp. "You sound surprised. When I found out who he really was, I assumed you had hired him."

"H-hired him? My dear lady, Hamilton Treadwell would never . . . has no need . . . oh, my, no. I haven't even seen him in a decade. Since . . . since young Howard's funeral. His family and the Hamiltons do not associate with one another. Oh, my, no. If Mr. Hamilton ever heard a rumor that I . . . well, I just wouldn't."

"Are the Treadwells rich?"

He let out a nervous laugh. "Oh, yes. Very."

"So, Kyle, or rather Hamilton, wouldn't need to marry me and adopt Matthew to get his hands on millions."

Another high-pitched laugh preceded his response. "I should say not. If he was pursuing you, his motives would have been for an entirely different reason."

"Oh. What other motive could he have?"

"Revenge."

Chapter 18

"Revenge? I thought Howard and Ky—Hamilton were best friends."

"Oh, they were. The dispute goes back to the prior generation. Treadwell Enterprises was Hamilton-Greene's stiffest competitor in the food industry at one time. Howard the III's sister, Celeste, fell in love with the founder, Kyle Treadwell, and married him despite all her brother's threats and warnings, thereby thumbing her nose at her family. Howard cut her out of his will and has never spoken to her since. It is believed she named their first son Hamilton to annoy her brother even more.

"It was only at Edith's insistence that the two boys were permitted to play together so that her son would learn to associate with children in his social class rather than someone like the gardener's son.

"Under Hamilton Treadwell's leadership, their company diversified into a number of other industries, allowing Hamilton-Greene to reclaim the lead in the food industry."

"I'm not sure I'm following you. Are you saying that Hamilton Treadwell made some bad business decisions, but blames Howard Hamilton for getting ahead of him, so he would get revenge by gaining control of the only Hamilton heir?"

"Oh, my, no. You misunderstood. Hamilton Treadwell's decisions were far from bad. He multiplied the company's net worth thousands of times over. The revenge would be for the rude treatment of Hamilton's mother and father by Howard Hamilton III all these years."

"I see." In truth, she didn't see at all, but she had learned long ago that rich people thought differently than she did.

"And now that I've answered your question, are you ready to give me mine?"

She could hear the confidence in his voice and wished she could see his face. "My dear Mr. Decker, I've been ready for some time. My answer is this: You can take the Hamiltons' offer, roll it up real tight, stick it up Edith's blue-blooded ass, and tell her to spin on it."

Simon dropped the phone into its cradle and felt the blood rush to his face as his heart reacted to the insult.

"She said no, didn't she?" Tammy said snidely. "I told you she wasn't going to go for cash."

"I . . . I . . . she didn't exactly say—"

"Can it, Simon. That road's closed." She grabbed her sweater and walked to the door.

"Where are you going?" He couldn't stand it if he lost her now.

"It's obvious that I'm going to have to take care of this myself. I have a few errands to run, things to organize, that sort of thing. I'll call you when it's time for you to do your part."

"But Tammy—"

The door slammed before he could warn her about that policewoman.

"I'm sorry to bother you again so soon, but—"

"Don't you dare apologize," Dani gently scolded her. "As long as we're talking, I know you're alive. What's up?"

Barbara related the Tammy portion of the conversation she'd had with Matt. "Under different circumstances, I wouldn't have given it much thought, but I got to thinking more about her vanishing act when the police were coming. Did I ever tell you I also met *her* for the first time after our picture appeared in the paper?"

"Holy shit, not another one!"

"I don't know. I thought I was just being paranoid, but when I put all the little oddities about Tammy together, I'm not so sure it's all in my head anymore." By the time Barbara told her about the insurance company where Tammy had either been employed for two years or not at all, Dani had heard enough.

"I can't begin to guess where she fits into any of this, but I'll bet she does. I know Matt thinks she's the most beautiful girl in the world, but can you give me a little more detail?" Even before Barbara completed her description, Dani cursed again. "I think I've seen her."

"Really? Where?"

"I'll let you know if I'm right. Anything else?"

"Just that I had a final conversation with Simon Decker and he confirmed that Kyle is very wealthy and was not seducing me for the Hamiltons' sake or to get in on their money. He said his motive was revenge for how Howard's father treated Kyle's parents."

"Bullshit. Plain and simple. Now listen to me, girl. Remember what I told you about there being way too much smoke around you and how one of these days there's going to be a major explosion? Well, it's coming fast, I can guarantee it, and you don't have so many friends that you should count Kyle out as one of them."

Barbara shook her head in denial even though Dani couldn't see the movement. "Everything he told me was a lie. I can't forgive that."

"Maybe not. I'm only suggesting that you give it some thought. If you still can't believe his story and forgive him after a few days, then you're probably better off without him. Okay? Will you at least do that?"

"Sure. I'll give it some thought," she said, without any intention of doing so. She liked Dani and considered her a smart woman, but she seemed to have a blind spot when it came to Kyle. Perhaps he had seduced her as well.

While he was in the hospital, injured, and stoned

on morphine? the annoying little voice in her head asked.

Why not? she answered. Considering the effect he'd had on her, she would believe he was capable of any number of miracles.

The fact that she had double-checked every door and window and knew there was a police officer watching her house didn't remove the anxious feeling that something else was about to happen. Only sheer exhaustion allowed Barbara to let go of the fear enough to fall asleep that night.

She was dreaming, or at least she thought she was. Her body weighed a ton. No, she was being weighed down. She could barely breathe for the pressure on her chest. Had she been buried alive? She pushed upward to free herself and felt the weight shift.

"That's it, babe, move with me, just like you used to."

Russ's murmur in her ear jolted her to full consciousness. He was lying on top of her, gyrating his hips against hers. She opened her mouth to scream, but he swiftly clamped his hand over it, muffling the sound.

"Don't be mad, babe. I couldn't help myself. You just looked so beautiful lying here with your nightgown twisted up around your hips, like you were expecting me."

She felt his erection poking at her body, blindly seeking entrance, and concentrated all her energy on keeping her muscles locked against him.

"C'mon, babe, relax. It's been a long time, but you gotta remember how good it was between us."

Knowing he was too strong for her to win a physical contest, she stopped struggling and made a pleading sound.

"That's better. Now, if you'll promise not to scream or fight, I could use my hands to make it even better."

She nodded her promise and controlled her panic as his hand eased off her mouth, then slid down her throat to her breast. As he kneaded her flesh, she whispered, "You'd better hurry, Russ. The moment you entered this house, you triggered a silent alarm direct to the police department. They'll be here any second, and they're very anxious to have a talk with you after last night's shooting."

His body ceased all movement except for the sharp rise and fall of his chest; then he abruptly jerked upright and slapped her across the face. "You fucking bitch. You just don't learn, do you? You're mine. And that boy's mine. And I'm tired of waiting for you to admit it."

He got up from the bed and yanked on his jeans. "I brought you something to look at. It's on your dresser. When you see what's inside that envelope, you'll know once and for all that I'm the only one you can trust." He raised her window and pushed the screen out of the way. As he climbed out, he said, "I'm the only one can keep you both safe from the Hamiltons. Oh, I had to change motels, so when you realize what a mistake you made tonight, you come to room 208 at the Sheraton, and we'll finish this."

Barbara's brave front disintegrated the instant he was out of sight, but she had one thing to do before she could fall apart. In a heartbeat, she leaped from the bed and ran to Matt's room.

She saw him stretched out diagonally across his bed and moved close to assure herself that he was breathing normally. Matt was safe. Nothing else mattered.

She tiptoed out, closed his door, and made it back to her own room before the tears started to flow. She nearly sat down on the bed, then jumped away from it. She could never use that bed again.

Her strength gave out, and she collapsed to the floor. Wasn't there anything she could do to stop Russ from contaminating their lives?

She gathered her energy and picked up the phone to call the police, then remembered that there was an officer parked in front of her house. A lot of good that had done. Rather than dial 911 or the police station, she called the one person she knew she could trust to help.

As soon as Dani heard Barbara's hysterical tone, she went from sound asleep to alert.

"I woke up . . . and . . . God, Dani . . . he was . . . on top of me . . . and—"

"Just hold on, girl. I'll be there as soon as I can. In the meantime, I'll radio for your so-called guard dog to get out of his car and go sit inside with you till I can get there. His name is Harris.

He's a big black man, and he'll be in plain clothes, but make him show you his ID before you open the door anyway. Did Latham let you know where he was staying?"

Barbara sniffed. She felt more secure already. "The Sheraton, room 208."

Russ's smile spread across his face when he heard the soft knock at his door. He'd known she'd come once she saw what was in that envelope, but he hadn't expected her quite so fast. He snuffed out his cigarette and pulled on a pair of boxer shorts to answer the door, though he didn't intend to keep them on long after she was inside.

He was so certain his visitor was Barbara that it took him a moment to switch gears when he saw who it was. In that moment's delay, he felt the slam to his diaphragm that stopped his ability to inhale while forcing his upper body forward. A powerful blow beneath his chin catapulted his body backward again. His spine hit the floor as the door to his room was silently closed.

With the taste of fresh blood in his mouth, Russ staggered to his feet, only to receive the third strike between his legs. The paralyzing pain forced him back down, but the assault didn't stop. His knees, shins, forearms, ribs, and nose cracked and broke beneath the methodical battering.

He begged for mercy—first for the beating to stop, then for unconsciousness, and finally for the killing blow that he knew, without a doubt, was coming. "Why?" he croaked. "For Christ's sake

. . . just . . . tell me . . . why?" Through eyes blurred by bloody tears, he looked up into his attacker's face, but there was no answer there.

Instead, he saw the lethal weapon being raised one last time.

Barbara's state of shock kept her from noticing whether minutes or hours had passed between the time when she spoke to Dani on the phone and the time when Dani arrived at the house. She may have even dozed off on the couch for a while after Officer Harris came inside; she wasn't sure. She was just relieved that Matt had remained peacefully asleep and that Officer Harris wasn't the type who insisted on conversation.

She did notice, however, that, for the first time since she'd met her, Dani was not in uniform, and had brought a man with her. He was of medium height and husky build, had light brown, regulation-cut hair, and was wearing a jacket and tie. Barbara thought they made a very nice-looking couple.

Dani took a close look at Barbara's pupils and frowned. "Maybe this should wait."

Barbara blinked at her. "I'm fine. I'd rather get it over with while it's still fresh in my mind." She noted the way the man glanced at Dani, as if her comment had surprised him.

"Barbara Johnson, this is a good friend of mine, Detective Neil Butler. He needs to ask you some questions, and I've promised to try not to butt in."

"You have the right to remain silent—"

"For God's sake, Butler," Dani interrupted him. "That's not necessary."

"It's for her protection."

"I hope you'll forgive Detective Butler," Dani said to Barbara. "He just made the grade, and he's still in the doing-it-by-the-book stage." Butler looked like he had a retort to that, but he kept it to himself.

Barbara listened to the detective state her rights to her, but couldn't fathom why he would do that when she was the victim.

When he was finished with the Miranda, he took a pen and small notebook out of his inside jacket pocket, revealing his shoulder holster to Barbara in the process. Somehow, the concealed weapon looked much more sinister than the one Dani openly carried.

"Mrs. Johnson, could you tell me where you were between one and two o'clock this morning?"

"I told you," Dani said. "She was on the phone with me; then Harris was sitting here with her. Right, Harris?" The officer glanced from Dani to Butler, clearly uncertain about who had more authority.

"*Sergeant*, I warned you . . ." Butler said, narrowing his eyes at her.

Dani tried to look contrite, but didn't quite succeed. Nevertheless, she sat down, folded her hands on her lap, and closed her mouth.

"Do I need to repeat the question, Mrs. Johnson?"

"I was here all night. I'm not sure what the time was when I woke up and—" She looked at Dani.

"Tell him everything, exactly as you remember it."

Barbara took a slow breath and described her encounter with Russ. "Then I called Dani at home."

"Why didn't you call 911?" he asked in a suspicious tone.

"Because they'd ask a lot of questions, then send a stranger out to ask some more, and more than likely no one would actually *do* anything to help me. Dani knows the history and knows I'm not making it up."

"Was there penetration?"

"Irrelevant question under the circumstances, Detective Butler."

"Hush, Sergeant Pfieffer, or I'll have you removed from the premises."

"No," Barbara said. "He tried . . . but . . . no, there was no physical penetration of my body."

"What time did he climb out your window?"

Barbara rubbed her eyes. She knew these details were necessary for the report, but she'd been so upset . . . "I think it was twelve-something."

"She called me at twelve thirty-five," Dani said.

This time Butler didn't reprimand her for interrupting. "Harris, what time did you get the radio call to come inside?"

Harris opened his report case and scanned the top sheet. "Twelve-forty."

"Was Mrs. Johnson out of your sight at any time in the three hours since then?"

"No, sir. Oh, except for when she checked on her son, went to the bathroom, and made us coffee."

"You see?" Dani said sarcastically. "There was absolutely no way she could have done it."

Butler cocked his head at her. "Unless the time of death was earlier, and she was out and back before she called you."

"You're being a dickhead, Butler. Harris will confirm that she never left the house."

"She could have climbed out the back window, the way she said Latham did."

"And then what? *Jogged* to the Sheraton and back? The time of death couldn't have been that much earlier, not by the looks of the body! I specifically requested that you be assigned to this case, because I thought you'd be more understanding. She's my friend—"

"Excuse me!" Barbara exclaimed to stop the debate. "What are you two talking about?"

Butler straightened his tie and his expression. "Sometime between one and two A.M., Russ Latham was killed in his motel room."

Barbara gasped. "*Killed?* You mean he's . . . he's *dead?* How . . . who . . ." Suddenly she understood the purpose of all the questions Butler had asked. "You think *I* could have done it?"

"You have the obvious motive. I had to question you first."

Barbara wrung her hands as her gaze darted

between the three police officers. "I hated him for what he's done to us. I'll even admit that I wished him dead more than once. But I could never have killed him. I can't even kill insects. Matt has to do it for me."

Dani moved to sit next to her and covered her clenched hands with one of her own. "Use your gut instinct, Neil. You used to have one before your promotion. Not only is she genuinely shocked to learn of the murder, look at the size of her. Do you really believe she could have beaten a man Latham's size and strength to death and not even get a scratch on her? And before you ask, she does not have a black belt in karate."

Dani turned to Barbara and answered her other question. "After I talked to you, I decided we had more than enough to pick Latham up and hold him for a long while. Before I called the station, though, I wanted to verify that he was where you said, since no one at the Sheraton had reported his check-in.

"Not only had he checked in shortly after last night's shooting, but he had arrived in a truck—possibly the one you saw drive by. No one at the front desk would admit to having overlooked the BOLO on him, but somebody obviously did, because Latham didn't even try to hide his identity. Cocky son-of-a-bitch.

"At any rate, whoever killed him was apparently waiting for him to return. The fact is, it probably happened while I was arguing with the night manager in the lobby."

"Who else . . ." Barbara's mind called up other possible suspects. "Maybe Decker . . ."

"He claims he never left his room, and physically he couldn't have managed what was done to Latham. But if they had some kind of deal going and Latham double-crossed him, he might have hired a pro to do the deed. He's been warned not to leave town until further notice."

"What about . . ." She couldn't even say his name.

"I already called the hospital. Besides the fact that he's in no condition to even defend himself, let alone commit assault, Kyle was in his assigned bed asleep the entire time in question. Unfortunately, there's one more person in this bad soap opera that has to be considered."

Barbara narrowed her brows in thought. "Edith Hamilton?"

"No. I'm talking about Tammy Garrett. After we talked yesterday, the fingerprint analyses came back. One of the sets found in your bedroom belonged to Tammy Wheatstone. The prints were all over the place, as if she'd gone through every drawer. She was arrested in Boston a little over a year ago for running a scam on elderly men.

"The physical description matches the one you gave me for Garrett. It also matches the woman involved in the domestic disturbance with Latham— the one I thought was a hooker. The two of them were interrupted while he was in the process of whipping her. Maybe it wasn't foreplay like we figured. It could be that she decided to retaliate with a lead pipe. She certainly looked big enough to do a thorough job of it. Better yet, maybe she and Latham's partnership went beyond sex, and he double-crossed her."

It took Barbara a few seconds to correlate this new deceit with all the others. "Dear God in heaven. She was . . . with Russ . . . and I left Matt with her. . . ."

"It's only supposition," Butler declared. "But we're looking for her. If she's still in the area, we'll find her."

Dani stood up, and the men did as well. "In the meantime, I'd like you and Matt to stay here. I'll have another officer relieve Harris at shift change."

Barbara felt as though her brain was working in slow motion. "You think . . . whoever killed Russ might come after us?"

"I hope not," Dani said. "But the fact is, you stand between the Hamiltons and something they want very badly. Someone fired shots at you last night, and Latham was murdered a few hours ago. The smoke's thinning out, girl, but I'm afraid the explosions have just started."

Before Dani and the detective left, she murmured to Barbara, "Just so you know, the only other prints in your bedroom besides yours, Matt's, and Tammy's belonged to Hamilton Kyle Treadwell, and they were only found on the lamp next to your bed and your telephone."

Barbara wasn't at all hungry, but fixing breakfast for Harris gave her something to do. The routine task seemed to calm her mind enough to sort out everything that had happened. The horror of being questioned in connection with a murder had nearly overshadowed the realization of the crime and what it truly meant to her.

Russ Latham was dead.

Although someone had committed a brutal murder, he or she had given her a gift beyond compare: *freedom.* She would never have to look over her shoulder again. She could go home to Dayton whenever she wanted without worrying about Russ frightening her parents. Matt could ride his bike down the street without her accompanying him, and he could take the bus to school.

She wondered how long it would take before she got used to the idea of being free again.

By the time the sun was rising, she felt sufficiently comfortable with Harris to get cleaned up while he was in the living room. She would have to tell Matt what happened when he woke up, but she felt it would go better if her appearance looked less frazzled.

She was looking for the pink rosebud earrings he'd gotten her for Christmas when she saw the white envelope. She knew Russ had left it there, but that knowledge had been overwhelmed by everything else. What had he said about it? Something about keeping her and Matt safe from the Hamiltons?

She was tempted to burn the whole thing without looking inside, but what if it really did contain something important? If not to her personally, perhaps there was a clue to his murder. With that possibility in mind, she opened the envelope and emptied it.

On top was a letter to her from Russ. Beneath that was a photo of three smiling young men with their arms around each other, plus several letters in different handwriting. She guessed the names of the threesome, but still turned the photo over and read the dated inscription: *Russ, Howard & Ham—The Three Musketeers.* Russ had obviously expected to earn a few points with her by revealing Kyle's true identity.

The first paragraph of his letter confirmed that much. He had written it all out in case she continued to refuse to listen to his story. One sentence made her inhale sharply and she reread it: *He threatened to kill me if I went near you or Matt ever again, but I would risk facing the devil himself for the two of you.*

Russ had definitely faced the devil, but according to Dani, Kyle was in the hospital when the murder took place. Then again, perhaps it wasn't Decker who hired an assassin, but Hamilton Treadwell. She would have to turn this letter over to Dani as soon as possible. But she decided she needed to finish reading it first.

The second paragraph switched to another story, one that had her flipping back and forth to the other letters:

I know this is going to come as a big surprise, but I've enclosed the letters so you'll know I'm not making any of it up. When you read them and understand how important they are to me, you'll understand how hard it is for me to let the originals out of my hands, but it is the best way I can think to show how much I love you. The first one is to me, from my mother. A friend of hers gave it to me along with the other letters after she died twelve years ago. I know once you read them all, you'll see why you should marry me. We can use them to blackmail the old man into leaving you and Matt alone. He'd never want any of it to go public. Poor Edith would die of humiliation. (Once, I almost turned them over to a society reporter just to see that happen.) Then together we can claim the whole damn Hamilton estate and they won't be able to do a fucking thing about it.

Hoping his mother's letter would make more sense, Barbara picked it up and read the slightly shaky writing:

My darling son,

Now that I am gone, I have a secret to share. I beg you to hold your temper until you have read the entire story I have to tell. I suppose there is no good way to say this except in a straightforward manner. Pop is not your real father. Howard Hamilton III is.

Before you condemn any of us for lying to you, please keep in mind the age in which this all happened. Young people today are not as confined by class as we were then. Howard and I met in the drugstore where I worked. At that time, he was engaged to Edith Greene, the daughter of his father's business partner. We both knew it was wrong, but we couldn't stay away from each other. When I told him I was pregnant, he was so very happy. He intended to break his engagement so we could be married immediately.

How foolish we were to think we could change the world because we were in love.

To make a very long story somewhat shorter, I will simply say that his father convinced him to go through with the wedding to Edith as planned, and Pop was convinced to marry me. In exchange for accepting a pregnant bride and pretending to be the father, he was assured of a lifetime job and home on the grounds, and I was promised a lifetime of security for myself and my child—as long as I kept the name of the real father a secret. Edith never knew how close she came to public embarrassment or that her husband's mistress and bastard child lived on her property. If Pop ever guessed the truth, he never said it aloud.

I can see you raging, Russ dear. Please don't. I know you well and will assume you are already considering how to avenge me, but let me say this first. It was very pretentious of me to reach beyond my station, and I was much luckier than other young girls who found themselves in a similar situation. I had a good life with Pop, and I satisfied my need for revenge by resisting every advance Howard made to resume our intimate relationship after he was married.

As to your own need for revenge, I ask only that you consider Pop's feelings. He has always treated you as his own and I know you love him as I do. You will do what you must to claim the heritage that was stolen from you, but I beg you not to do anything that would hurt or embarrass Pop while he is still alive. On my deathbed, I am holding you to that, my last request.

Barbara had to work a little harder to read the writing in the other letters, but she didn't need to read every word to comprehend that they were love letters from Howard Hamilton to Russ's mother. His desire to make her his wife was repeated several times, and in one he clearly stated how ecstatic he was that she was expecting their child, and that if it was a boy, he would be named Howard Hamilton IV.

Her Howard's father had once been a young man, very much in love, but when history repeated itself with his son and Barbara, that man took the same intolerant path his father had. Was it bitterness that had driven Howard III to destroy his son's happiness, or had he really believed he was doing the proper thing?

Barbara spread all the letters and the photo out on her dresser and stared at them. Russ thought they would prove his love for her, but what she saw was the explanation that had eluded her all these years. Yes, Russ had wanted her because Howard had, but it had gone far beyond simple envy on Russ's part. Howard's entire life should have been Russ's.

But now they were both dead.

And she had possession of the letters.

Chapter 19

"I'm sorry if I woke you, Mr. Decker, but I didn't want this to wait another hour."

He coughed, cleared his throat, and coughed again. "Excuse me. If you're calling about Latham, the police spoke to me hours ago."

"Actually it's partly about Latham, but not the way you think. I want you to call your client—Howard, not Edith—and tell him Russ gave me some letters before he was murdered. Tell him the letters are solid proof of something that occurred before his marriage that would be extremely embarrassing to him and his wife.

"Tell him I said that if he ever tries to make contact with me or my son, personally or through an intermediary, I will turn the letters and an incriminating photograph over to every sensationalist tabloid publisher and see to it that the story is smeared on the front pages in every supermarket in the country where his products are sold."

"Ms. Mancuso—"

"I'm not finished. Within forty-eight hours, I want delivered to me a handwritten letter from

Howard Hamilton III, repeating to me what you told him and a sentence stating that he is completely convinced that my son is not related to him in any way. And don't bother to write the letter for him. I have several copies of his handwriting and I plan to take the letter to an expert to confirm that it's not a forgery."

"This is really—"

"Not yet. You're next. I tape-recorded the conversation in which you threatened me and offered money for my child. If *you* ever bother me again for *any* reason, or if you do not do exactly as I have requested, copies of that tape, with an explanation, will go with the letters I spoke of, as well as to the Bar Association and your esteemed client."

"This aggressive hostility is hardly necessary—"

"I disagree. I think it is long overdue. Just do as I say, and your dubious career will continue uninterrupted, by me at least, and Mr. Hamilton's secret will remain so."

"I'm bored," Matt complained after lunch. "How long do we have to stay inside like this? And why can't Kenny come over after school?"

Barbara closed her eyes and massaged her temples. If she could just take a short nap, maybe then she could come up with answers to satisfy him. "You know what? I'll bet Officer Kravitz is bored, too. Why don't you see if he'd like to play a game or watch a movie with you?"

As she had hoped, the very young man who

replaced Harris was relieved to have something to do, and she quickly took advantage of the break to lie down for an hour. She pulled the quilted spread off the bed, folded it in half, and arranged it on the floor with the spare pillow she kept in her closet—one Russ hadn't touched. It wasn't as comfortable as a mattress, but it was good enough.

After she was rested, she was going to have to talk with Matt again about Russ's death. His reaction was too indifferent considering the fact that the man had been like a terrifying shadow looming over their lives since he was born. Perhaps she and Matt should seek counseling to readjust to life without Russ in it.

One thing was very clear to her. She couldn't tell Matt the truth about Kyle or Tammy until the events of the past two weeks faded a bit. He had more than enough to digest already.

As her eyelids closed, the computerized music of Matt's favorite video game filtered through the closed door of her bedroom. Despite the irritating sound, it comforted her to know that he wouldn't even notice her absence for the next hour or so.

Matt handed the game controller to Officer Kravitz. "Go ahead. You try it for a while. I'm gonna go see if I can find my *Game Pro* magazine that has the password we need to get to the next level."

He was leafing through the colorfully illustrated pages when he heard tapping on his bedroom window. To his surprise and bewilderment, Tammy was standing outside, trying to get his attention. As soon as he saw her, she put her finger to her lips to keep him quiet. He didn't understand, but her big smile made him feel good inside. Whatever game she wanted to play was okay with him.

When she motioned for him to open the window, he became more curious, but didn't hesitate to do it.

"I have a surprise for you," she whispered. "And I don't want the policeman to know I'm here."

"Why not?" Matt asked quietly. "He's cool."

Tammy lowered her head. "I know it's silly, but police really scare me."

"Oh," Matt said, though he did think it was silly. But then, lots of girls were afraid of things that he wasn't. "Do you really have a surprise for me?" She gave him another beautiful smile that made his stomach all shaky.

"Yup. But I need to come in there to give it to you. Help me, okay?" At his nod, she dropped a canvas bag on the floor beneath the window.

He swallowed hard as she boosted herself over the sill and her T-shirt pulled way down in front. He wanted to help, *a lot*, but he didn't know quite where to put his hands. The best he could manage was to hold on to her elbow as she climbed in.

As soon as both her feet were on the floor, she leaned close and put her cheek next to his. "Where's your mom?"

Her whisper tickled his ear and made him shiver a little. "She's asleep in her room."

"Cool. Now close your eyes real tight and put your hands behind your back."

When he hesitated, she gave him a kiss on the forehead that made his stomach feel like he was going down in a really fast elevator.

"C'mon, honey. It's part of the surprise. You're going to love it."

He couldn't imagine what the surprise could be, but he could see she was really excited about it. He stared into her pretty eyes for a second and decided to follow her instructions, even if they did sound strange.

"Good boy. Now don't move."

He opened his one eye a crack and saw her getting something out of the canvas bag, but he squeezed it shut again as she turned back to him. The next instant he felt something being drawn over his head, which made him a little nervous, and when it suddenly tightened around his neck, his eyes popped open. "Hey—" The sight of a gun barrel pointed at his nose stopped his complaint.

"That's right, brat," Tammy told him in a hushed voice. "You're in big trouble. But if you behave yourself and do everything I say, I won't kill you or your mummy. Got it?"

Her smile had changed. It looked very scary now. He nodded.

"Good. Put your hands behind your back again."

He obeyed, and she pressed a piece of wide brown tape over his mouth. The shaking in his stomach was replaced by a terrible cramp, and he was afraid he was going to pee in his pants. He felt something tighten around his wrists and quickly realized that that binding was connected to what was around his neck. When he tried to move his hands, he choked himself. As bad as Russ was, he never did anything like this to him. Tammy must be even crazier than he was. He wanted to warn Officer Kravitz somehow, but he didn't know how without risking all their lives.

Tammy moved to his side and attached one end of a long leather strap to a band on her left wrist and the other end to the part around his neck. "I think that'll do it. Let's go say hello to your watch-dog." She pressed the gun against the back of his head and nudged him forward. "Go. Remember, you try anything funny and you're dead meat. And your mummy will be right behind you."

Officer Kravitz was having such a good time with the video game, Tammy walked right up behind him and tapped him in the head before he turned around.

"Aw, shit!"

Matt thought the policeman was going to wet *his* pants. His hand moved toward his holster, but when Tammy cocked her gun and pointed it at him, he raised his hands over his head.

"Smart boy. Now, nobody will get hurt if you do everything I say," Tammy told him in a bossy voice. "Take off the gun belt and put it on the table. Slowly. Then go sit down on the floor next to the recliner."

Matt had to move along with Tammy to keep

from being strangled as she got the officer's hand-cuffs, wrapped them around one of the metal bars of the recliner's footrest, then clamped them on the man's wrists.

"Lady, this is nuts," Kravitz protested. "The whole police department is looking for you. They've been in and out of here all day—"

Tammy slapped a strip of the brown tape across Kravitz's mouth before he could finish his sentence.

"I think we can take care of Mummy now," she told Matt with that excited look in her eyes again.

Before she went into his mother's bedroom, however, she tucked the officer's gun into the waistband of her jeans, then went back to his room for her bag. Matt had told his mother a hundred times that he wasn't a baby anymore, but that's what he felt like, being dragged helplessly behind Tammy.

He was also helpless to do anything but watch while Tammy used two more leather things to tie his mother's wrists to her bedposts. She couldn't say anything to him, since Tammy put tape on her mouth as soon as she woke up, but he understood what her eyes were saying: *Do whatever she says. Don't be a hero.* But he had to do something! If Kyle was let out of the hospital, and if he came by, and if he remembered the sign . . .

"Okay, brat," Tammy said, pushing him out of his mother's bedroom. "It's time to make a phone call, and I can't have anybody listening in. Let's see . . ."

Matt stayed close to her as she got a kitchen chair and put it in the living room, but before she could tie him to it, he pretended he heard something outside.

"What?" Tammy asked suspiciously.

He shook his head no and shrugged, but glanced pointedly at the front window.

"You heard something, didn't you?"

She jerked on his leash as she went to peek out the front window. The moment he was close enough, he kicked the ceramic elephant across the windowsill as hard as he could, causing it to shatter against the wall.

Just as quickly, the back of Tammy's hand struck his cheek. "You little bastard! I have no intention of putting up with any temper tantrums from you." She yanked on his leash so hard, he stumbled and fell, only to have her pull on it again to get him back on his feet. He blinked back the tears that filled his eyes and let her strap him onto the kitchen chair without any further problems. He'd already done the only thing he could.

Simon had to stop half a dozen times during packing to catch his breath, but the pain in his chest wasn't easing. In fact, it seemed to be extending into his left arm. He'd been thinking about seeing the doctor for months now, but somehow that would have been akin to admitting that he had a serious problem, and with Tammy in his life, he didn't even want to admit he was aging, let alone had a weak heart.

And look what it got him! A man of his stature being questioned in connection with a murder, involved in a shooting by association, and now this! How could he have guessed that either Russ or Tammy would go to such extremes? With Russ dead, that miscalculation would not be discovered. But Tammy! To hold three people hostage in hopes the Hamiltons would pay a five-million-dollar ransom was completely insane. He could only hope denial and the information he'd just called in to the police would save him if Tammy chose to implicate him.

He wasn't certain he would ever recover from the humiliation of having to deliver Barbara's ultimatum to Mr. Hamilton and simultaneously admitting that he'd failed to gain custody of the boy. The only saving grace was that he now knew that his client had a secret so horrid that he had agreed to the blackmailing bitch's terms without a moment's hesitation.

He lifted his suitcase and headed for the door, but a pain, greater than any he'd experienced before, seized his whole body and stopped him from taking another step.

"Dani? Thank God I reached you. This is Kyle—Hamilton—whatever. The elephant's not in the window."

"Maybe you'd better call for one of the nurses—"

"No, no. I checked out of the hospital after you were here this morning. I'm in front of Barbara's house. She and Matt have all these private signals they use, and Matt taught them to me. If the elephant's not in the window—"

"—there's trouble inside. Okay. We already know about it. Decker called in about fifteen minutes ago—"

"That son-of-a-bitch! What's he done?"

"We're not sure yet, but the hostage rescue team is preparing to head out there now. There was no answer when I called the house just now. What's it look like to you?"

"Quiet. There's a police car and Barbara's car in the driveway. Who's supposed to be in there?"

Dani took an audible breath. "Decker said Tammy called him demanding an enormous ransom for Matthew—"

"How much? Never mind. It doesn't matter. I'll pay it."

"It may not be necessary. Our team has an excellent success rate. You just get yourself away from there—"

Dani heard the line disconnect and slammed her own receiver down. *Damn!* She didn't need to be psychic to know what Kyle was about to do. In a heartbeat she was off to warn the team that an amateur had just jumped into the ring and that they'd better get their asses in gear.

Matt could no longer feel his fingers, but he felt sorrier for Officer Kravitz and his mom than himself: the officer, because he obviously felt really stupid, and his mom, because she was in the other room all by herself and couldn't see that he was okay. Not that there was much to see except Tammy stomping back and forth, waiting for something. When someone knocked at the front door, she practically jumped out of her skin.

"Don't either of you make a sound," she hissed.

Yeah, right. Like we could if we wanted to.

"Tammy! It's Kyle. Decker sent me."

Kyle remembered the elephant! Matt would have danced around the room if he could have.

Tammy peeked out the front window. "Why would he send you?"

Kyle laughed. "Because I'm his very silent partner—the Hamilton everyone forgot, or at least tried to. I'm surprised you didn't figure it out. In case he couldn't talk Barbara into selling Matthew, I was the backup plan, but she caught on to me, and that ended that. It looks like this ransom demand of yours may be the only way any of us are going to get our hands on the Hamiltons' millions."

Matt could hear Kyle's words clearly and his stomach started to hurt again. *Is Kyle a bad guy, too?*

Tammy opened the door and waved Kyle inside.

Matt's eyes opened wide when he saw Kyle enter and tug on his left ear—the sign that meant "Everything I'm saying is a lie just to get us out of this." Kyle did it again, and Matt blinked back at him. That wasn't one of the regular signs, but he figured Kyle was smart enough to know that it meant he understood.

Tammy looked Kyle up and down in a way that made Matt feel sick inside.

"Surprised hardly covers what I'm thinking right now," she purred. "But I can understand why Simon didn't tell me. Why would I want to play with him, when I could have been dealing with you?"

"From what I heard, you already had more than enough on your plate," Kyle said, looking at her the same way, like she was a huge stick of cotton candy.

"You mean Russ? He was just a distraction. I always knew he wasn't in my league . . . or should I say *our* league."

Kyle grinned at her. "So-o-o, where's the rest of the family?"

"You mean the lady of the house?" Tammy said with a laugh. "In her bedroom. Uh-uh," she said, stopping him as he took a step in that direction. "She can wait. First we talk."

Kyle nodded at the gun in her hand. "That's really not necessary. These guys aren't going anywhere, and as you can see, I'm pretty much out of commission."

She ran her free hand over the gun barrel. "I like holding it. It's like having my very own dick. And this one never gets soft, either." She eyed his sling and clucked her tongue. "Poor baby. I suppose Russ knew who you really were and wanted you out of the way. This is the gun he shot you with, you know. I borrowed it from him before his, uh, unfortunate demise."

"I heard he was broken into a lot of small pieces," Kyle said as if he were impressed. "Did you do that?"

Tammy smiled. "Maybe. Maybe not. Why don't you tell me about Simon's problem?"

"He wants me to bring Matthew up to the Hamilton estate. They've refused to pay the ransom unless they can get a good look at him in person."

"That's ridiculous! They were already convinced that he's their grandchild enough to offer Barbara two million dollars for him."

"But that was different. That money would have bought them legal custody. This way, they'd be paying the money without any guarantee that they'd ever see him once Barbara got him back."

"I don't like it. Too much could go wrong if we move him."

Matt's eyes followed the conversation back and forth while watching closely for any new signal on Kyle's part.

"It's a risk we're going to have to take," Kyle said. "They've refused to pay any other way. Surely between the two of us we can control one boy on a car trip." Kyle walked around behind Matt and pulled on a strap. "There's not much time to spare. How do you undo this?"

"No. Something's not right here. You go back and tell Simon I want to hear this from him personally."

Kyle came back around in front of him and put his hands out as if he were giving in to what

Tammy wanted, but he wiggled his fingers like he was scratching something. What was he saying? Matt caught Kyle's eye as he was turning toward the door. *I don't understand*, he thought to himself. As Kyle opened the door, Matt watched him bring his hand up behind him and scratch his own back three times. *Run as fast as you can*. But he couldn't run anywhere tied to a chair.

Suddenly Matt understood that Kyle was trying to tell him to get out of the way. As hard as he could, he shifted his weight to one side, then the other, toppling himself over.

"What do you think you're doing?" Tammy screeched, and pointed the gun at him.

"No-o-o," Kyle cried, and lunged at Tammy.

She raised the gun and fired. Then the front door crashed open, and several more deafening explosions followed. It happened so fast that all Matt could do was stare in horror as both Kyle and Tammy collapsed on the floor in front of him.

Chapter 20

"Hi," Kyle whispered as his eyes focused on Barbara and Matt on one side of his bed, and Dani and Detective Butler on the other. The pain in his side was so excruciating he could hardly feel the ache in his shoulder.

"This is for you," Dani said, showing him a small round tie tack with a target painted on it. She pinned it onto his hospital gown. "It's from everyone at the station. They thought you deserved a special medal for getting shot twice in the same week."

His mouth twitched into a semblance of a grin. "How are you, Matt? That body slam to the floor must have hurt."

Matt gave an embarrassed shrug. "Just a little. It was better than getting shot."

"He told us how you two used signals to communicate," Dani said. "Sort of puts all our high-tech equipment to shame. Listen, Neil and I will be back a little later to go over all the details with you. We just wanted to say hi and show you our appreciation for your bravery."

"What about Tammy?"

Dani shook her head. "She didn't make it."

"I think she killed Russ. She almost admitted it to me in front of Matt."

Butler nodded. "That's the way the file's going to read."

"And she told me he was the one that shot me the other night. Same gun."

"Right. Ballistics will confirm that."

"You know she was working with Decker?"

Dani and Butler glanced at each other. "We guessed as much," Dani said. "But it doesn't matter now. Decker had a massive stroke in his hotel room after he called the station. He lost the use of most of his body."

Butler said aloud what the others were thinking. "Sometimes the punishment does fit the crime."

"Come on, Matt. Neil and I are going to check out the cafeteria. You've got to be hungry by now."

He took his mom's hand and squeezed.

She smiled and nodded. "Go ahead. I'll keep Kyle company for a while."

After they were out of the room, Kyle patted the bed and she carefully sat down next to him.

"Matt says you saved his life. You can't imagine what all was going through my head while I was trapped in my room and couldn't see what was going on." Leftover tears welled up in her eyes, and she wiped them away. "Sorry, I guess I'm not quite over the shock yet."

"I'm sure it'll take a while."

"I just don't know how to thank you enough for what you did. She was insane. Matt could have been killed. *You* could have been killed."

He held her eyes with his. "I'd do it again . . . if it was the only way I could get you to talk to me." She lowered her eyes, and he brushed her hip with the back of his hand. "I need another chance, Barbara. I know I don't deserve it, but if you'd let me start over with you, I'd . . . well, I'd . . . you name it, and I'd do it."

She sighed. "So much has happened . . ."

He was encouraged by her hesitation. "You're right. I'd go very, very slowly this time. No rushing you into . . . anything."

She narrowed her eyes at him.

"Unless you wanted me to," he amended with a hopeful look.

She bit her cheek to keep from smiling. "Okay, we can start over." She stood up and took his hand in hers. "How do you do? I'm Barbara Mancuso Johnson."

He quit trying to keep a straight face. "Hello. I'm Hamilton Kyle Treadwell."

She wrinkled her nose up. "I don't like the name Hamilton. I think I'll call you Kyle."

His expression became serious again. "Will you ever be able to forgive me?"

She bent forward and pressed her mouth to his, instantly reigniting the passion that had burned between them from the start. "Any other questions?"

Epilogue

"How's she doing today?" Dani asked as she walked in the door of her parents' house.

Her mother smiled softly. "She's been having a lovely time with her Barbie dolls—dressing and undressing them, over and over, in all those beautiful outfits you bought her."

Dani gave her mom a hug and kiss on the cheek. "Good. I'll have to buy her some more."

Mom wagged a finger at her. "What did I tell you about spoiling that child?"

Dani went on to her sister's room and waited for her to notice that she was standing there before moving too close. Her mother had referred to Janine as a child for as long as she could remember, and mentally, her sister was a child—a ten-year-old, preadolescent girl . . . in a forty-year-old woman's body. The doctors all said there was no biological reason for it. Janine simply chose to go back to that age and stay there after her trauma.

"Hi, Dani. Do you have time to play with me today?"

"Sure," she said, sitting down on the floor and picking up one of the dolls. They were all Barbies, not a Ken in the bunch. "I'm off for the rest of the day."

"Why didn't you bring your new friend to play, too? Do you think she'd let me call her Barbie instead of Barbara?"

"I'm sure she'd be flattered," Dani said with a chuckle. "And I promise to bring her by the next time. She's just had a lot of trouble in her life lately."

Janine frowned. "But you're a policewoman. Can't you make her trouble go away?"

The memory those words triggered caused a quick surge of powerful energy to race through Dani's petite frame. With a reassuring smile, she stroked her sister's hair. "Don't worry, sweetie. I already took care of it . . . just like I did for you."

OFFICIAL RULES

1. NO PURCHASE NECESSARY TO ENTER OR WIN A PRIZE. To enter the SEE HOW FAR A GOOD BOOK CAN TAKE YOU SWEEPSTAKES, complete this official entry form (original or photocopy), or, on a 3" x 5" piece of paper, print your name and complete address. Mail your entry to: SEE HOW FAR A GOOD BOOK CAN TAKE YOU SWEEPSTAKES, P.O. Box 8012, Grand Rapids, MN, 55745-8012. Enter as often as you wish, but mail each entry in a separate envelope. All entries must be received by November 29, 1996, to be eligible. Not responsible for illegible entries, lost or misdirected mail.

2. Winners will be selected from all valid entries in a random drawing on or about December 31, 1996, by Marden-Kane, Inc., an independent judging organization whose decisions are final and binding. Odds of winning are dependent upon the number of entries received. Winners will be notified by mail and may be required to execute an affidavit of eligibility and release which must be returned within 14 days of notification or an alternate winner will be selected.

3. One (1) Grand Prize winner will receive 25,000 American Airlines AAdvantage miles. Approximate retail value: $500.00. Five (5) First Place winners will receive 10,000 American Airlines AAdvantage miles. Approximate retail value: $200.00. Ten (10) Second Place winners will receive 3,000 American Airlines AAdvantage miles. Approximate retail value: $60.00. Thirty (30) Third place winners will receive 1,000 American Airlines AAdvantage miles. Approximate retail value: $20.00. Approximate retail value of all prizes: $2,700.00.

4. Sweepstakes open to residents of the U.S. and Canada except employees and the immediate families of Penguin USA, American Airlines, its affiliated companies, advertising and promotion agencies. Void in the Province of Quebec and wherever else prohibited by law. All Federal, State, Local, and Provincial laws apply. Taxes, if any, are the sole responsibility of the prize winners. Canadian winners will be required to answer an arithmetical skill testing question administered by mail. Winners consent to the use of their name and/or photos or likenesses for advertising purposes without additional compensation (except where prohibited). No substitution of prizes is permitted. All prizes are nontransferable.

5. American Airlines may find it necessary to change AAdvantage program rules, regulations, travel awards, and special offers at any time, impacting, for example, participant affiliations, rules for earning mileage and blackout dates and limited seating for travel awards. American Airlines reserves the right to end the AAdvantage program with six months notice. AAdvantage travel awards, mileage accrual, and special offers subject to government regulations.

6. Winners agree that the sponsor, its affiliates, and their agencies and employees are not liable for injuries, loss, or damage of any kind resulting from participation or from the acceptance or use of the prize awarded.

7. For the names of the major prize winners, send a self-addressed, stamped envelope after December 31, 1996, to: SEE HOW FAR A GOOD BOOK CAN TAKE YOU SWEEPSTAKES WINNERS, P.O. Box 714, Sayreville, NJ 08871-0714.

Penguin USA • Mass Market
375 Hudson Street, New York, N.Y. 10014

Printed in the USA

American Airlines and AAdvantage are registered trademarks of American Airlines, Inc.